EVERY PIG GOT A SATURDAY

EVERY PIG GOT A SATURDAY

MIKE FARRIS

Cover and design by Lora Gray

First Printed Edition

2 4 6 8 10 9 7 5 3 1

ISBN 978-0-9903714-1-0

John M. Hardy Publishing Co.
Houston, Texas
www.johnhardypublishing.com

To Susan,
who is my world.

CHAPTER ONE

The bus from Bridgetown, Barbados, dropped Sandra Moore off less than a minute ago but, as she trudged through the fields to the dilapidated hovel she called home, it seemed as if she had walked for hours. The sun beat on her back like a cosmic furnace. She glanced upward, squinting her eyes, and wiped the sweat condensed on her brow.

Something about these canefields attracted the fiercest of the sun's rays and reserved them for the common folk who trod their dusty roads each day. The interior of the island didn't have the advantage of the ocean breezes that air-conditioned the coastal areas, even on the hottest of days. There, the sun was a friend, not the enemy it was inland.

Sandra envied the coast dwellers, whose ranks she hoped to join some day. She wanted to be far removed from Clifton, just west of the St. Thomas/St. Joseph Parish line, almost slap dab in the center of the island. Surrounded not by the cooling waters of the nearby oceans, but by these God awful cane-fields. Baked by the God awful sun.

Her shoes turned white from the chalky dust of the road – the same dust that settled on her cheeks and turned into a gooey paste as it mixed with perspiration. Her shoulders ached from the weight of her tote bag on one arm and grocery bag on the other. God, she hated this place. How could life be more miserable?

A sound to her right derailed her complaining train of thought. Startled, she cocked her head to listen. She heard a rustling noise, like something or someone moving through the thick cane. Stalking her? Sandra knew it wasn't the wind, because there was no wind.

Glancing about, she quickened her step, but the rustling in the cane kept pace. While the first sound merely startled Sandra, its continuation frightened her. It was stalking her! Why else would it adjust its pace to hers?

Sandra turned her footspeed up another notch. As she half-ran down the dusty road, she tried to tell herself it was her imagination. Or maybe kids playing in the cane. But her powers of persuasion remained impotent on her mind. Something or someone was definitely out there – definitely following her.

Panic set in. Her heart raced, keeping time with her feet. She threw her groceries aside, like an airman jettisoning ballast, and sprinted down the canefield road. No longer looking from side to side – the wasted motion only slowed her down – she ducked her head, kicked off her shoes in mid-stride, and poured all her energy into moving her legs. Her tote bag flapped wildly beside her, still gripped in her hand.

Up ahead, the road turned ninety degrees, the first crook in a dog leg that straightened out into a stretch run to the cluster of small houses where she lived with her mother. Safety wasn't yet in sight, but it was around two corners.

As she neared the first bend, the sound faded. Had she out-distanced the unseen in the cane? That didn't seem likely.

Maybe it had lost interest. Maybe all it wanted to do, in the first place, was to frighten her and now, satisfied by obvious success, pursued other amusements.

Still, Sandra kept running. After all, she could be wrong.

As she hit the first turn in the road, Sandra took a wide swing, like a baseball player rounding second, so as not to lose speed. She completed the turn and saw the next turn ahead – third base before the home stretch. She bore down, so intent on her goal that she didn't hear the rustling resume to her right.

Just before the last turn, a dreadlocked man burst out of the canefield and swooped down on Sandra before she could react. In one smooth motion, he lifted his arm like a shepherd's crook and clotheslined her around the neck. Her head came to a dead stop, her surprised shriek stillborn in her throat. Her trunk and legs continued forward, swinging upward from the man's rigid black arm. Her hand reflexively loosened its grip on her tote bag, which flew forward. She landed flat on her back, hard. Her head bounced off the dusty road, stunning her.

Gasping for breath, she looked up. The black face of her assailant stared down, his teeth bared. A wicked scar traversed his right cheek.

"Now you 'ent runnin' no mo'," he said. "Now you is wi' me."

Sandra moaned in protest. She couldn't find her breath, much less her voice. She watched in stunned horror as the man bent over and grabbed her under her armpits. He dragged her off the road and into the canefield. Once out of sight of the road, he hoisted her to her feet and forced her to stand. She swayed unsteadily for a moment, still trying to get her bearings. The man clasped a hand over her mouth then roughly marched her through the thick cane.

Sandra's fear intensified when she felt the hand over her mouth. Something was odd about it. Something missing.

Fingers! At least two, maybe more.

She had heard about a man with missing fingers. A man who had escaped from Dodds Prison. She couldn't remember his name, but she remembered talk of an escaped murderer. An escaped murderer with missing fingers. And a scar on his face.

In minutes, they emerged from the canefield at the base of a low hill. An opening to a cave yawned behind a thick tree just in front of the hill, almost unseen. In all the years she had lived here, Sandra never knew it existed. By now, she knew that he had more in store for her than simple robbery. If he wanted only her money and cheap jewelry, he would have taken that long ago and left her, if not dead, at least stunned in the canefield. He wouldn't have marched her to this cave. No, he had more in mind than her meager material possessions.

As they neared the entrance to the cave, Sandra regained what little strength remained in her frail body. Planting her feet, she jerked away, trying to break his grasp.

He spun her around then brought his fist up hard into her midsection, just below her breastbone. The sharp blow knocked her breath out. Bile rose in her throat and she fought the urge to vomit.

"Be still, bitch," the man said.

He dragged her through the dark opening into the cave. Shallow, with a low ceiling, it was barely deep enough to hide them from outside view. Sandra saw a makeshift grass bed along the side wall, padded with leaves and stalks of sugar cane. The last vestiges of hope drained away. Tears formed in her eyes.

"You 'ent runnin' no mo'. Now, you is mine," the man said. His voice bounced eerily off the low ceiling and reverberated around the small cave.

With a violent jerk of his deformed hand, he ripped Sandra's blouse open. Buttons popped off and scattered on the dirt floor. Like a magician, he produced a knife in his right hand and severed the thin strap connecting the cups of her bra, releasing her small breasts. She shrank back and ducked her head as a flush of shame crept into her face.

The man laughed. He flicked the blade of the knife lightly across her left breast. A single drop of blood appeared below the nipple.

Sandra shuddered, trying to keep from vomiting or passing out. She made only feeble efforts to resist.

With another violent jerk, the man ripped her skirt down and gave it a tug. She sprawled backward, her fall cushioned by the makeshift bed. The reality of what was happening began to sink in. Tears flowed and she choked on her sobs.

"Wha' is you cryin' fo'?" he said, standing over her. "Is you a cut pumpkin? Cut pumpkin can' keep."

He stripped off his shorts and stepped forward. Sandra refused to look at his member, surging obscenely above her eyes. She lay back on the grass, hugging herself and crying. She knew the strange words as a Bajan proverb meaning that, once virginity has been lost, it is almost impossible to abstain from sex thereafter. The man didn't know it, but Sandra was a virgin. This man was about to cut her pumpkin.

He stood over Sandra, totally naked now. His penis, rigid as iron, loomed over her. He looked at the weeping girl. Her tears obviously didn't bother him. She knew that he had no conscience for them to sway. Wielding the knife like a butcher, he sliced through her ragged cotton underwear. She tried to cross her legs, but the man jabbed his knife at her crotch and forced them apart.

Seizing the opportunity, he moved the knife to her throat. He dropped roughly on top of her and forced himself between her legs.

He savagely entered, tearing her apart like a wishbone as he drove himself deep inside. She screamed in pain.

His face leered over her, teeth bared. He thrust harder and deeper. The pain was excruciating as he drove his hot iron into her very soul.

After her initial scream, Sandra bit her lip and refused to make a sound. She thought of distant places, as if she could transport herself there – far away from this cave in the middle of Barbados. Far away from the evil little man cutting her pumpkin. Her mind went numb. She remained only vaguely aware of a pounding weight on top of her and of a dull pain between her legs.

Nothing more.

CHAPTER TWO

An American Airlines jetliner droned over the Caribbean, heading from San Juan, Puerto Rico, to Bridgetown, Barbados. The sun had been down for hours and, to inhabitants of the islands, the plane probably seemed no more than a flashing light coursing across the black sky like a shooting star. The flight was nearly full, most of its passengers having connected in San Juan from a dozen different starting points. Now, on the last leg of their respective journeys, many of them catnapped during the final hour's flight to Grantley Adams Airport on the south side of Barbados.

Karla Reavis sat in an aisle seat on row sixteen and lovingly watched her husband Bobby as he dozed next to her, his head leaned against the window. It had been scarcely twenty-four hours since they stood at the front of the small chapel in Dallas and exchanged marriage vows. Then the preacher pronounced them husband and wife, closing the books on their one-year courtship, but opening the page to a new life ahead.

Karla studied Bobby's peaceful face while he dozed against the window. Images flickered through her memory of the wedding – standing face-to-face in front of the dearly beloved who gathered together. His face wore the same look of contentment and peacefulness then as it wore now. She couldn't fight back the tears that welled in her eyes.

Despite the ten years' difference in their ages, and even though they had known each other for only two years, Karla was certain from the moment they first met that Bobby was the one. The one little girls dream romantically about, the one who rides in on a white horse and sweeps her off her feet and takes her away to live happily ever after. She knew it long before Bobby did.

About a year before, in fact. From the first day she walked into that law firm's conference room as a court reporter and transcribed depositions for Bobby, she knew in her heart that she would someday marry him. She saw it in his face, with its gentle smile that warmed the room, and in his soft-spoken voice and his kind heart that filtered through even a lawsuit's adversarial setting. It was storybook, fairy tale, love-at-first-sight.

Now, as he slept, she studied those same features that first stole her heart. The ones that gave him his boyish look. Thick, sandy brown hair that couldn't stay parted, but which set off his burning brown eyes. Eyes so dark they were almost black. Eyes that looked right through her, but, at the same time, sparkled and shined. She loved his eyes, and his broad mouth, which seemed perpetually curled into a smile.

Nobody ever guessed he was only three years shy of forty. Not with his wrinkle-free face and athletic, six-foot three-inch frame. Their age difference didn't concern Karla. Her only fear was that, when they were both old and gray, they might be cheated out of time together because of his ten-year head start. But she wouldn't worry about that now. They still had a lifetime to go.

A voice came through the overhead speakers. "Ladies and gentlemen, please stow your tray tables and return your seats to their upright and locked positions."

Karla smiled and gently stroked a rogue lock of hair that trespassed on Bobby's forehead. He stretched, slowly opened his eyes, and looked at her. The plane's interior lights coming from behind cast a bright halo around her dark hair. Her blue eyes sparkled beside her perfectly formed nose. Her olive-skinned face, which reflected her Mediterranean heritage, shone with anticipation.

He smiled at his angel. "Are we there?"

"We should be on the ground in about ten minutes."

Bobby looked out the window at the darkness. Their flight had left Dallas shortly after one o'clock in the afternoon. With a two-and-a-half hour layover in San Juan, and a two-hour time change heading east, it would be after eleven when they landed on Barbados.

"Mighty dark out there," Bobby said.

"Paradise at night. Who wouldn't love it?"

Bobby turned back to Karla. "How long was I asleep?"

"Only about twenty minutes or so."

He smiled and yawned, then gently patted her knee. She took his hand in hers and squeezed it.

A few minutes later, the plane landed and they disembarked with the other passengers, stepping off to greet the warm tropical breezes. Another fifteen minutes and they passed the first customs stop then they were herded, along with the rest of the passengers, to the baggage claim area.

At exactly midnight, a Barbadian cab driver deposited them at the front steps of their hotel, Sam Lord's Castle. The bell captain loaded their bags into a golf cart and drove them to their room on the north side of the grounds. As they rode in the small cart, they heard the sound of waves pounding on a beach in the darkness. They stared futilely, straining their eyes, unable to see anything except on the screens of their imaginations. They would have to wait until sunrise to see the source of the sound – the Atlantic Ocean.

*****

Sandra Moore's head hurt and she could scarcely think straight after the beating her assailant had given her. It was only after she passed out that he stopped. When she finally regained consciousness, he was gone. Her clothes were gone with him. That was over an hour ago and she had been wandering around the canefields since.

Now, naked, bleeding, and scared, she stumbled out of the canefield onto the ABC Highway. Never saw the truck bearing down. She died almost instantly on impact.

*****

Bobby awoke early the next morning. Even though the previous day had been spent in airports and on airplanes, and even though he was exhausted, when the six-thirty sunrise lit the room at Sam Lord's Castle, yesterday's exhaustion faded into today's excitement.

He felt the bed beside him, but it was empty. Across the room, he saw Karla's open suitcase and knew immediately where she was. He smiled. Even on her honeymoon, she stuck to her regimen. He had never known anyone so disciplined.

Bobby got out of bed and walked unsteadily to the sliding glass doors. He wiped the sleep from his eyes and pulled back the thin curtains that unsuccessfully screened the sun's morning light. He unlocked the door and, wearing just his shorts, stepped onto the patio and gazed seaward.

The hotel room was perched about thirty yards from a wooden fence along a low cliff that dropped to the beach. Between the room and the cliff lay a thick carpet of grass that aproned around a garden of colorful tropical flowers. Beyond the fence, the sun, still low in its morning ascent, threw its rays on the blue-green waters of the Atlantic. A firm breeze caressed his face, as if to say "welcome." Waves crashed, out of sight, on the beach below.

He stood rooted to the spot for another minute or two, breathing in the sea air and luxuriating in the wind on his face, before going back inside to dress. After brushing his teeth and hair, he threw on a pair of khaki shorts and a T-shirt, slipped into a pair of flip-flops, and left the room, locking the door behind him.

He found Karla exactly where he knew she would be.

She didn't see him at first as she swam laps in the big swimming pool by the Oceanus Grill. Bobby stood at the edge and watched her methodically swim back and forth, face down, breathing only every few strokes. He was amazed at the speed with which her slender frame covered the meters on each lap. Easy to see why she had been a school record-holder in several different events in her competitive swimming days at Texas Tech.

On a flip turn, she saw him looking down at her. Smiling, she spun over and backstroked.

"Hey, Sleepyhead," she said.

"Morning, Sunshine. How long you been at it?"

"What time is it?"

Bobby checked his watch. "Quarter to seven."

"About forty-five minutes."

Bobby settled into a lounge chair where she had piled her towel and clothes. "You about ready for breakfast?"

"Fifteen more minutes."

"You're on your honeymoon, not back at the Olympic trials. It won't kill you to lose fifteen minutes."

"Aye, aye, Sir," she said.

She rolled back over, turned ninety degrees, and cut to the side of the pool. Bobby opened up a towel and greeted her with a kiss as she pulled herself out of the water. He admired her lean body, just two inches shy of six feet, as she dried herself off. Dark skin stretched over muscular arms and legs made strong by years of exercise, with curves in all the right places. A real head-turner.

She put on a T-shirt and shorts, crammed the towel in a container the hotel had set out, then faced Bobby. "Am I presentable for breakfast?"

He grabbed a handful of her wet hair, shining darkly in the morning sun, and squeezed. Water flowed over his hand.

"What do you think?" he asked.

"Maybe we should walk a while first, let that dry," she said.

"I can live with that."

She took his hand in hers, interlocking their fingers. "Let's go."

*****

The hotel included the Castle itself, on a low cliff over-looking Long Bay, which housed a few large suites on the second floor, and the front desk and administrative offices on the first. Several two story wings of rooms lined the edge of the bluff to the north, situated so that virtually every room owned an ocean view.

Beautifully landscaped, a rainbow of color highlighted the hotel's green lawn, bursting from the hibiscus, oleanders, bougainvilleas, and other flowering shrubs scattered about. The brightness and colors of the flowers – pinks, whites, reds, oranges – immediately grabbed their attention as they meandered. These not only complemented the richly-colored Atlantic to the east, but also provided the names for the guest room buildings.

They strolled through a series of ninety-degree turns, past another swimming pool, by The Wanderer restaurant – where they would later return for breakfast – until they came to a terraced lawn between the castle and a low cliff overlooking Long Beach. At the far edge of the lawn, an archway with an open gate invited guests to an elevated walk that fingered out to the water. Sugar white beaches lined either side.

Karla and Bobby accepted the invitation and slowly strolled the pathway to the lookout point at the end. It offered an unobstructed view of the Atlantic, straight ahead, and the palm tree-lined beaches it bordered. Waves crashed on the rocks below. Only a worn wooden fence separated them from disaster.

"Look at the reef," Bobby said. He pointed to a dark area in the water about a quarter mile off. Its darkness contrasted sharply with the greens and blues in between. "I read that Sam Lord used to hang lanterns on coconut trees and on his castle, even on the horns of cows, to try to make the merchant ships think this was Bridgetown at night. When the ships headed this way looking for the harbor, they crashed on that reef."

"Why'd he do that?"

"He was sort of a pirate. He'd row out the next day, kill any survivors, and plunder the ships."

"Nice guy. Like a plaintiffs' lawyer."

Bobby laughed. He shared Karla's notion that many a lawyer he faced in court was nothing more than a modern-day pirate, keelhauling ethics, sending truth off the gangplank, and plundering deep pockets.

"He also swindled his brothers and sisters out of their inheritance. That's what he used to build the castle in the first place," Bobby said.

"See, now I know he was a lawyer."

Bobby put his arms around her and pulled her close. "He also brought a bride over from England."

"So, deep down at heart, he was a romantic."

"Then she must have pissed him off or something, because he locked her up in a dungeon."

Karla broke his grip and pulled away. "Now don't you get any ideas."

"Never had an idea in my life."

She turned and looked back at the reef. Bobby moved beside her, leaning on the wooden fence.

After a few moments, Bobby spoke. "What are you thinking?"

"About how beautiful this place is. And about how horrible it must have been for those sailors."

"What sailors?"

"The ones who crashed on the reef out there. What a bastard that Sam Lord was."

"Yeah, but if it weren't for him, we wouldn't have this great place for our honeymoon."

"Gee, I never took you for a 'the glass is half full' kinda guy."

He laughed. "I guess it's just the hunger talking."

Karla joined his laughter. They clasped hands and strolled back to The Wanderer restaurant. Native craftsmen were setting up their wares on the patio outside the restaurant's entryway. A portly woman sat in a folding chair under the shade of the overhang and proudly arranged shirts, dresses, and cloth tote bags. Fanning herself, she flashed a gap-toothed smile as an invitation to buyers.

Farther down, a thin black man sat at a table, industriously working on pencil sketches of island scenes. He displayed his impressive drawings, all of which captured the Bajan lifestyle. Bobby and Karla paused a minute to study the pictures, but hurried on to The Wanderer before the artist could start his sales-pitch.

They walked down the narrow passageway leading to the hostess stand, where a table held neatly arranged stacks of letter-sized pages and newspapers. Bobby picked up one of the Barbados newspapers, *The Nation,* and they proceeded inside.

The restaurant was fairly large, furnished with rows of two- and four-top tables and rattan chairs, arranged strategically around a square buffet table boasting a variety of fruits and breakfast foods. Next to the buffet, a line formed of shorts and T-shirt clad guests holding plates, hungrily awaiting omelets, which an obese woman made.

The hostess escorted them to a table for two by the paneless windows. Although they couldn't see the ocean from their seats, an ocean breeze cut through, blowing Karla's dark hair, reminding them of the Atlantic's nearby presence. Just outside, another garden of tropical plants painted the grounds with bright hues.

A large, jolly-looking native approached holding menus in one hand and a steaming pot of coffee in the other. "Will you be havin' coffee?" he asked, an ivory-toothed smile punctuating his question.

They both nodded and slid their cups towards the edge of the table. He poured the steaming liquid with a flourish.

"And will you be havin' de buffet?" He pronounced it "boo fay," with heavy emphasis on the "boo." "Or will you be orderin' from de menu?"

Bobby noticed that Karla already had her eye on the omelet woman behind the counter, so he answered, with her tacit approval, "Two buffets."

"Very good. Help yourselves." Then he set the coffee pot on their table and vanished.

"Cool accent," Bobby said. He stood then pulled Karla's chair out. "Let's go get it."

"Remember, this is not your last meal," Karla said. "Go easy."

"But it's all you can eat."

"Just don't eat all you can eat."

"Yes, Dear."

"And stop with the 'Yes, Dear' bit."

"Yes, Dear."

Karla rolled her eyes in mock disgust. "Oh, yeah. This marriage thing is gonna be fun."

The honeymooners headed for the food line and followed it clockwise around the buffet table, filling their plates as they went. Omelets, hash browns, bacon, sausage, French toast, and fresh fruit, including pineapple, strawberries, and watermelon, all beckoned with their aromas and scrumptious appearance. It seemed impossible to walk past a single tray without the urge to add something to their plates, even if only to fill a blank space. Finally, they returned to their table and ate, overindulging themselves.

As they ate, Bobby studied the face of his bride. She looked around the restaurant, making note of all the different body shapes and styles of dress represented. Her eyes ranged with emotions, from amusement to disapproval, depending upon what body was dressed how. Fat women in skimpy shorts and halter tops, skinny men in big shorts, young people in loud clothes – they all evoked a response as the camera of her mind recorded the images.

Bobby loved that about her. She was curious by nature and, wherever she went, her senses drank in information. Bobby was amazed at her powers of observation, not to mention her powers of recall. On more than one occasion, she stunned him with some minute detail she had seen or heard some-where. It was one of the traits that made her an excellent court reporter. No doubt years from now she would remem-ber someone she saw today and describe them down to the color of their socks.

When they finished their meal, which corresponded to being stuffed, Bobby poured them each one last cup of coffee and they sat contentedly in the ocean breeze, savoring the morning. As Karla doctored her coffee with cream and sugar, Bobby reached in his pocket and produced a small, gift-wrapped box. He looked at her for a second then slid it across the table.

"What's this?" she asked.

"I wanted you to have some kind of surprise while we were here."

Karla studied the package and then looked at Bobby.

"Well, open it," Bobby said. "Just because I know what it is doesn't mean I don't want you to."

Karla smiled as she cautiously peeled off the wrapping, saving the bow. She opened the tiny box, gingerly brushed aside the cotton padding, and extracted a glittering gold necklace, adorned with a small, fourteen carat gold letter "K." In its center, a diamond sparkled blue in the morning sun.

Fingers trembling, Karla unhooked the clasp and placed it around her neck. It took her a few tries to close the clasp, but at last she let the gold "K" drop to the middle of her chest.

"It's beautiful," she whispered. "I love it."

"I love you."

Bobby leaned over and gently kissed her on the lips.

"Let's go back to the room," she said.

*****

Bobby left the Barbados newspaper behind as they vacated their table. "CLARKE AT LARGE," the headline screamed in two-inch letters.

Just beneath the headline were two photographs, one picture of a dusty road through a non-descript canefield. A bag of groceries lay scattered in the dirt. The caption beneath the picture read:

This is where a young St. Thomas woman is believed to have been abducted yesterday afternoon. Her body was later found near the ABC Highway. Police suspect prison escapee Oliver Clarke in the abduction.

The second picture was of a dreadlocked black man, his face disfigured by a thick scar that ran horizontally across his right cheek. The caption beneath the picture read:

Police believe Oliver Clarke's attacks on rural Barbadians may be motivated by the fact that since he is already condemned to die, and has exhausted all of his appeals, he will hardly be brought to trial for any offenses he commits while on the run, no matter how violent.

CHAPTER THREE

Fifty-seven year old Miriam Sandiford hummed lightly as she returned the broom and dustpan to the small broom closet. Then she turned to survey the kitchen. Spotless, as it always was when she finished with her work. She took great pride in her housecleaning, especially this house. It belonged to a government minister, and she always wanted to do an extra-special good job for him.

Miriam had been a maid for thirty years, working for the Minister of Education for the past two. The pay wasn't much, but she worked hard, scraping out a meager living for herself and the grandchildren she raised. Working for the Minister helped. She cleaned his house twice weekly, but there was never much work involved. The Minister and his wife were, by nature, tidy people. The house was usually clean when she got there, yet he paid her well. And he often gave her a little extra for the kids.

Miriam made one last pass through the rooms, checking to make sure everything was in order. The Minister and his wife were in Jamaica attending a conference on education, but would return tomorrow. She wanted a clean house to welcome them. She knew they would be tired and she wanted everything to be just right. Besides, she knew from past experience that there might be a bonus in her paycheck if they were pleased.

Finished with her tour of inspection, and satisfied that everything was perfect, Miriam took off her apron, folded it, and placed it in a drawer in the kitchen. She gathered her tote bag and keys from the kitchen table then headed to the back door, glancing at the clock on the wall. Shortly after noon. Good. She had time to make the 12:15 bus. She could eat a quick lunch before her next job.

She came out of the house, locked the door behind her, descended two steps, and walked around the side toward the road in front. With her head down, fumbling with something inside her tote bag, she was oblivious to the presence of a man who emerged from a gully less than twenty feet away. Wearing a dark green shirt and black pants, he stood camouflaged against the tropical lushness, watching. A white scar on his right cheek highlighted his ebony face.

*****

After lunch, Bobby changed into his swimsuit while Karla loaded the beach bag with their essentials – towels, books, and sunscreen. Then they left the room, passed The Wanderer, and turned off to a narrow set of stairs that accessed the sand. On a landing halfway down, a Bajan, or native Barbadian, craftsman worked diligently in a small shed that resembled an outhouse. With precision and patience, he strung beads onto an almost invisible thread, soon to be a Technicolor necklace. He spread samples of his handiwork beside him and hung others in the shed's open doorway.

With his dreadlocked hair tucked into a knit cap that hung behind his head like Santa Claus's bag of goodies, his dark, almost black, complexion, beady eyes and thick goatee,

Bobby thought he more resembled a crack dealer than a craftsman. At their approach, the Bajan looked up from his work and flashed a toothy smile that belied his fierce appearance.

"You likin' a bargain today?" he asked in a raspy voice.

"Not right now," Bobby said. "We may check back with you later."

"When you're ready for a bargain, I'll be here."

"Good to know," Bobby said.

Karla smiled and they walked past him, down the rest of the stairs, and out towards the beach.

"Do you want a bargain?" Bobby mocked. "No, we want to get screwed."

"Lighten up." Karla laughed and slapped at Bobby's shoulder. "He had some nice stuff. I want to look a little closer on our way back."

"Whatever you say."

"I'm glad we got that straight at the beginning of the marriage."

Bobby raised an eyebrow. "Just remember what happened to Sam Lord's bride."

She laughed again. "Yeah. I'm shaking in my boots."

He joined her laughter. "I guess I've lost control already."

The wide beach sloped sharply to the water's edge. Rough waves had beaten against it for eternity, creating a ridge line that separated the slope from the rest of the beach, which leveled out as it worked its way back to the low cliffs that supported the hotel. The sugar-white sand swarmed through and around a stand of palm trees midway between the water and the cliffs. The trees shaded more than half the beach.

Directly ahead, under a large palm tree, stood a stack of lounge chairs that had dwindled to half its original height, as the rest of the chairs had already been strategically placed and occupied. Just to the left of the stack, two ebony-complected men leaned against a tree and jabbered in a language that sounded vaguely like English, but with its own particular slant.

The larger of the two men – the one without dreadlocks – jumped to his feet. He quickly grabbed two chairs off the stack and wiped them with a towel.

"Where would you be likin' dese?" he asked Bobby.

"Follow her," Bobby said, nodding toward Karla.

She found an isolated spot where she stopped, turned around, and waited expectantly. Bobby quickly joined her while the Bajan brought up the rear, dragging both chairs. He positioned them to face the sun, then again wiped the plastic straps with a towel.

Bobby stood next to Karla and watched as he worked. "Do I tip him?" he whispered.

"I think you should."

"With what?"

Karla looked at Bobby and sighed. She opened her beach bag and dug around for her wallet. "Am I going to spend the rest of my life paying your way?" she said.

"I hope so."

"Sorry to disappoint you."

She pulled a couple of dollars from her wallet and gave it to the Bajan. "Is American money okay?"

The man nodded, took the bills, and left.

"You know, Sam Lord would lock you up for smarting off like that," Bobby said.

"Yeah, and Sam Lord would sleep on the couch, too."

Karla stepped out of her beach cover-up. Bobby looked at her trim, athletic figure. Her slim hips filled out her bikini bottom, while firm breasts pressed against the fabric of the top. His own body started to react.

"Okay," he said. "No dungeon for you tonight."

"Shut up and put this on my back," she said, handing him a bottle of sunscreen.

He took it, squeezed a dollop onto his palm, and began rubbing it in. When he finished, he stripped off his shirt and applied lotion to himself. Though not as trim as Karla, his body still testified to his athletic prowess as a four-sport letterman in high school before moving on to a successful career as a two-time All-Big Twelve Conference third baseman at Baylor University. At the same time, the beginnings of a spare tire around his middle betrayed more than a decade at a desk job, coupled with his weakness for cookies 'n cream ice cream.

Soon he situated himself next to Karla, their chairs facing the Atlantic. The sun's heat was plenty hot, but a steady breeze gently air-conditioned them.

Yes sir, Bobby thought, *I could get used to this. I surely could. No worries here.*

*****

As Miriam passed by, the man pulled a handgun from the waistband of his pants. He stepped away from the bushes and came face-to-face with her. She dropped her tote bag as her eyes zoomed in on the gun. He held his other hand out as if reaching for something, displaying two missing fingers. Miriam instantly knew the gun-toting devil's identity.

"You 'ent goin' home, yet," he said, motioning towards the house with the gun. "We is goin' back inside."

"I has no key," Miriam said. "I just pulls de locked do' behin' me."

"Is no problem."

He led her to the back of the house and ordered her to stop. She came to an uncertain halt by the locked door and waited for his next command. Her initial fear intensified as she recalled the stories about this man. Stories of rape, of mayhem, of murder. She wondered if she would join the cast of victims.

The man picked up a large rock that bordered a garden. He held it in his deformed hand for a few seconds, as if testing its weight. All the while he leveled the revolver in her direction.

Baring his teeth in a humorless grin, he raised the rock to shoulder level. It rested there for a moment. Then he stepped forward, grunted, and hurled it through a window. The crash could surely be heard next door, but Miriam knew no one was home to hear it. She cringed as the rock penetrated the pane, showering slivers of glass both inside and outside the house. All over her clean kitchen floor.

Still grinning, he dragged the barrel of his gun along the window's edge and knocked off shards of glass that extended like teeth in a shark's gaping jaw. With his other hand, he reached inside and unlocked a latch then raised what was left of the window.

He stepped back, pointed the gun at Miriam, and nodded toward the window. "Inside!"

Miriam stood rooted to the spot. She believed that as long as she remained outside, in open view, she might be saved. Somebody might pass by and see what was happening. But once inside the house, she could only guess what would happen. She was over fifty, and was quite portly, and knew she surely was not sexually attractive. But as she faced the man's dark look, she knew that didn't matter.

He slapped her with an open hand. "Inside!" he said again.

The sting of the slap brought Miriam back to her senses. Though her fate was inevitable, she knew it could worsen if she antagonized him.

She nodded and moved slowly toward the window. Gripping the base of the opening, she jumped up and forward then threw her upper body over the ledge. She balanced on her waist and teetered precariously, upper body inside, lower body outside. Because she wore a dress, she felt embarrassingly exposed.

She struggled for a few seconds to maintain her balance before working her way in. Without warning, the man grabbed her feet and pushed upward with a nonchalant flip.

Her face crashed into the floor. Hundreds of glass slivers pierced her skin like so many acupuncture needles.

The man leaned in the window to look at his handiwork. Miriam sprawled on the floor, face down, her dress hiked up around her waist and her undergarments shamelessly displayed. She put her hand to her head to massage the beginnings of a bruise. She felt small slivers of glass on her hands and her face. Blood trickled down her skin.

She began to cry.

Oliver "Ocee" Clarke agilely hopped through the window, gun in hand. He stood over the maid and straddled her sprawled body. For a moment he contemplated whether to take her where she lay.

The descendant of a slave brought in from Africa's Gold Coast who had been raped by a Carib tribesman, Ocee's heritage was as tainted as his life. With lusty Carib blood flowing through his veins, Ocee made it a point to inseminate as many women as he possibly could. Whether his partner was willing was, to his way of thinking, beside the point.

Also irrelevant were her age, health, marital status, height, weight, and looks. All that mattered was that she had a vagina, the sole symbol, in his estimation, of her worth. As he once explained his ideas on the subject, relying on a Bajan proverb, "Dirty water does cool hot iron." Translated, it means that when a man is sexually aroused, any woman, good or bad, can satisfy his lust.

But when he realized what the broken glass on the floor might do to him, he decided against it. What it might do to her was of no consequence. Besides, that thick white girdle she wore might as well be a chastity belt. With her looks and weight, he didn't figure it worth the effort to peel everything off and work his way down to her magic spot. Even though "dirty water does cool hot iron," he was a man of some discretion. If it took too much effort to get to the dirty water, he would pass. Of course, he could always change his mind. Besides, there was still plenty more dirty water out there on the island that he didn't have to work as hard for.

That decision made, at least for the moment, he kicked her sharply. "Up!"

The maid whimpered and slowly scrambled to her feet. Her hands and face bled from dozens of cuts. Tiny rivulets of blood left her face looking like a roadmap.

"De owner is havin' a safe?" Ocee raised an eyebrow in inquiry.

She glared sullenly at him, but said nothing.

"A safe?" Ocee punctuated the question by slashing the barrel of the gun across her right cheek.

The maid drew back in pain and surprise as the gun tore her flesh. She quickly put her hand to her face. Blood flowed more heavily from the new gash than from the old wounds, blotting out the tiny roads.

"Yes," she said, sobbing softly and nodding her head. "In de bedroom."

"Show me!" Ocee grabbed her roughly by the shoulder and spun her around. He jabbed her in the small of the back with the gun. "Show me de bedroom."

She led Ocee through the house, down a long hallway, and into the master bedroom, which was richly furnished with a king-size bed, triple dresser, and armoire, with a flat screen in a corner next to a window. The maid stood at the foot of the bed, her back still to Ocee. He swiveled his head slowly, taking in every detail of the room.

"De safe?" He jabbed her in the back with the gun barrel.

"In de closet."

Ocee saw the doorway to a closet on the wall across from a dressing counter. Satisfied that this was the closet she referred to, he walked to the side of the bed and motioned for her to lie down.

She hesitated at first, but he whipped her again across the

cheek with the weapon, tearing still more flesh. She fell forward on the bed, hands covering her face.

"Hands behind de back," he commanded.

She removed her bloodied hands from her face and did as she was told. Ocee rummaged through the triple dresser until he found what he was looking for. Armed with a pair of silk stockings, he leaped on the bed, straddled her, and quickly tied her hands behind her back, like a rodeo cowboy tying a calf. He put one ankle across the other then tied her feet together with a second stocking.

He went back to the dresser for a pair of silk panties, which he wadded into a ball and forced into her mouth. He tied the gag in place with another stocking. With that fat cow out of the way, he thought, there was now time to get into the safe.

Ocee loudly banged the closet door open. Sure enough, in the back corner sat a small safe. It was cheaply made and looked easy to get into. The homeowner obviously had tried to save money when he made the purchase. He would pay today for his frugality.

Ocee left the bedroom and ran back to the kitchen, where he rummaged wildly through the cabinets. With broad sweeps of his arms, he brushed the contents off their shelves. Crystal and porcelain shattered as it fell to the tile floor, joining the shards from the broken window. But when the cabinets were all emptied, Ocee still had not found the toolbox he sought. Of course, he really hadn't expected to find one in the kitchen cabinets, but it was fun looking.

Smiling at the mess he created, he walked from the kitchen and stepped into the garage. He rummaged through cabinets and shelves, leaving the same disaster in his wake as in the kitchen. At last he found a toolbox. Opening the metal container and studying its contents carefully, he selected a hammer and the largest screwdriver then hustled back to the safe.

With a few well-placed blows of the hammer to the handle of the screwdriver, the safe door flew open. Inside, Ocee found jewelry, some negotiable papers, and a small amount of cash. He scooped them all up and stuffed them into the pockets of his baggy trousers.

Next, he began a slow, methodical search of the house, painstakingly tearing apart each room looking for valuables. His search turned up more jewelry and a fine set of silver. Soon, his pockets bulged to overflowing. He stripped a pillowcase from a bed in one of the smaller bedrooms, emptied his pockets, and put his goodies inside the pillow case, like a good trick-or-treater.

He went back to the master bedroom to decide what to do with his prisoner. Trick or treat? The hot iron of the weapon in his hand or the hot iron between his legs?

He stood at the foot of the bed for a moment and gazed at the plump maid, trussed up like a hog. His resolve weakened. She certainly wasn't attractive, but then again, he wasn't interested in her face. His fascination lay between her legs. If he took her from behind, he wouldn't have to look at her face.

His iron began to heat at the thought. He freed it from his pants, where it stood erect and pulsing. He untied her feet, uncrossed her ankles, and pushed her heavy legs apart. His iron became red hot.

He jumped onto the bed on his knees, between her fat legs, and pulled her dress over her hips in the same motion. One look at the thick, tight girdle reminded him why he hadn't already done this, but his hot iron desperately needed cooling.

He began tugging at the thick undergarment.

CHAPTER FOUR

The next morning, Bobby and Karla set out to tour the island. Neither of them had ever heard of a Moke – the narrow, flat rental vehicle that resembled a cross between a jeep and a go-cart. They debated whether to get in it or to carry it on their backs. Finally, Bobby wedged his over-sized frame behind the steering wheel. With the seat pushed all the way back, his knees brushed the bottom of the steering wheel. To grip the wheel, he bent his elbows at a ninety-degree angle. Even Karla struggled to fold herself into the slightly roomier passenger side. Once inside, they laughed as they realized they must look as if they were wearing the car instead of sitting in it.

As Bobby anticipated, fearfully, the steering wheel was on the right, but at least the car had an automatic transmission. Sitting on the wrong side of a car – at least it seemed wrong to him – and driving on the wrong side of the road was complicated by having to work a stick shift backwards with his left hand. After a few practice turns around the parking lot, they geared themselves to go exploring. Bobby slowly drove the car down the narrow exit to the main road, then cautiously, and awkwardly, turned right and eased into the flow of traffic.

"How far is Bridgetown from here?" Bobby asked.

Karla studied the map that the rental agent provided. "It's hard to tell, because there's not a scale of miles. But here's Sam Lord's," she said, pointing. "And here's the airport, and here's where we are now. In Christ Church."

Although she drew her finger across the page as she spoke, Bobby concentrated on staying on the proper side of the road and ignored her pointing.

"So if that's true," Karla continued, "and if this thing is at least drawn to scale, it couldn't be but ten or fifteen minutes down the road."

Bobby checked the rearview mirror, already bothered by tailgaters who loomed murderously close to his bumper, then sped around him at the slightest opportunity. He glanced at the speedometer and satisfied himself that he wasn't going too slow.

"What's the game plan once we get to Bridgetown?" he asked.

Karla refolded the map and dropped it in her lap. "Well, I think we should shop a little bit at some of the duty-free places. Maybe walk around Trafalgar Square, but we don't need to spend a whole lot of time there. We can always come back. After that I think we ought to drive the Caribbean coast."

Bobby nodded but didn't answer. He focused his full attention on his driving. Karla smiled and faced forward. They could discuss the itinerary later.

As they neared Bridgetown, traffic began to thicken. Houses and small stores gave way to places of business, larger stores, and even small offices. A constant stream of oncoming traffic flooded past in the opposite lane, and a seemingly endless line stretched ahead in their own.

As Bobby checked the mirror for the hundredth time, Karla looked back and saw a long line behind them as well. The car immediately in back almost kissed their bumper. She shifted back in her seat and sat quietly as Bobby kept pace in the parade winding into the city.

Bridgetown was home to various tourist attractions, including its parliament buildings, a statue of Lord Horatio Nelson in Trafalgar Square, one of the oldest Jewish synagogues in the western hemisphere, and a downtown shopping area. In addition, over two hundred thousand people were crammed into its city limits. It appeared to Bobby that all of them were driving cars on the streets leading downtown.

A cold sweat broke out on his brow and ran down the side of his face. His knuckles turned white as he squeezed the steering wheel. The thickening traffic, which included tailgaters who thought nothing of cutting in and out of traffic at the slightest opening, gripped his attention.

Bobby eyed his rearview mirror. "I wish that guy would get off my tail."

Karla glanced over her shoulder to see another small vehicle, different from the tailgater she had seen before, seemingly hitched to their bumper. Suddenly, the driver sounded his horn and swung out at the first opening in oncoming traffic. He zipped around and squeezed into the tiny gap between their car and the one in front. Bobby instinctively hit the brakes, then just as quickly moved his foot back to the accelerator to stay with the flow of traffic.

"I don't like this," he said. "It was bad enough on open road, but this traffic is ridiculous."

Karla wiped sweat from Bobby's forehead. "Just don't get in a big hurry. We've got all day."

Karla's words had their desired soothing effect. Bobby felt his blood pressure drop. The white tautness left his knuckles and he settled into the driving routine.

Oncoming traffic soon disappeared. Bobby never saw where the traffic pattern changed but realized he was driving on a one-way, three-lane street, which suddenly narrowed into one just beyond a bridge over Carlyle Harbor. Up ahead, Lord Nelson's statue oversaw what looked like thousands of cars in a parking lot, but that Bobby knew was actually slow-moving traffic. As quickly as he relaxed, he tensed up again.

"How are we supposed to get through all of that?" he asked.

Karla pointed to a sign with an arrow on the left-hand side of the bridge. "Follow the arrows to 'Parking.'"

The stop-and-go traffic lurched forward. On the far side of the bridge, another "Parking" sign indicated he needed to veer left, but the traffic wouldn't let him merge. Frustrated, Bobby stopped. Angry horns beeped. When a gap appeared behind a taxi, he gunned the small Moke and screeched into the flow of traffic.

"Nice going, A.J.," Karla said, grabbing tight on the door handle. "Show them locals how the white boys do it."

Bobby nodded grimly. Now nestled into the middle of three lanes, he looked anxiously for his next turn, afraid to change lanes until he knew his ultimate direction. The cool cucumber in the courtroom was wilting in the mad jumble of Bridgetown traffic.

"Turn right, there," Karla said quickly, pointing to another "Parking" sign, almost hidden from view.

Bobby saw the sign, nodded, and started to make the move to his right. The blast of a horn from a minivan cut him short.

"Drop dead," Bobby said.

The van eased up beside Bobby. Bobby glanced at its driver, who cursed in some Bajan dialect, then moved past.

"Same to you and the horse you rode in on," Bobby said.

Karla hid a smile by looking over her shoulder. "After this blue car, you can get over," she said.

Bobby slowed almost to a halt, afraid he would pass the turn. More horns sounded behind him. At Karla's command, he flipped on his turn signal and pulled a sharp right-hand turn from the middle lane onto a narrow street that appeared to head through the heart of the shopping district. Then the road bent to the right and a parking lot appeared before their very eyes.

"Eureka, we've done it!" Bobby said.

He glanced at Karla, who stifled a laugh.

"That's the same thing you said on our wedding night," she said. "If I'd only known how low you set the bar."

CHAPTER FIVE

Ocee had been hiding out, with the help of friends, since his escape six months earlier from HMP Dodds Prison where he was waiting to hang for murdering a plantation owner. His penchant for violence had made him a regular in Barbados's criminal justice system. His violent history included multiple rapes, murders, aggravated assaults, and armed robberies. He spent almost two thirds of his adult life in confinement, and his longest single place of residence was Dodds Prison. He served his first term at the age of sixteen, and had been in and out ever since.

This marked the second time Ocee escaped from legal custody in the last ten years. He managed to stay free for almost three months the first time, but had now already doubled that record. Ocee knew intimately the island's gullies and caves, which made perfect hiding places. As small as the island was – fourteen miles at its widest point and twenty-six at its longest – his prolonged escape made the police look silly in their attempts to find him.

But not only did he know the island's nooks and crannies, he was also a man of many disguises. Like a chameleon, he often changed his appearance to blend with his surroundings, and was only recaptured the last time by sheer chance –

a fact not lost on the island police. Rumors abounded as to his whereabouts and activities. Rumors that had him well-housed and well-fed, laughing at the feeble efforts to recapture him. The police responded to those rumors, using helicopters and land vehicles, to reported sightings in Cave Hill, Black Rock, Codrington Hill, the Pine in St. Michael Parish, Jack in the Box Gully in St. Thomas Parish, and Cherry Tree Hill in St. Peter Parish.

According to other rumors, he had already skipped the island. Even now, reported sightings continued to flood the police and Barbados Defense Force offices on a weekly basis. Not only on Barbados, but also on St. Lucia, Trinidad, Jamaica, and even as far north as Freeport on Grand Bahama Island. To date, all law enforcement had to show was a lot of overtime pay and a few scathing editorials in the island newspapers.

*****

In a dingy rum-shop in St. Joseph Parish, Ocee planned his immediate future. With his chair leaned back and feet propped up on a table covered with empty bottles, he downed another rum punch and stared out the open door at the sun. Where some drank coffee to start off their days, Ocee's starter of choice was island rum. He still had on the same shabby clothes he wore at the Minister's house the previous day. A shower and clean clothes were not high on his priority list.

The sun quickly chased the long shadows out of the small, one-room shack as it rose steadily higher. Behind the broken-down counter that served as a bar, a lanky Rasta-farian wiped off the countertop and took another hit of his ganja.

"Is true," the Rastafarian said. "De police is close. I see dem here las' night. Dey wantin' to know if anyone see you. If anyone know where you is."

Ocee belched and waved his hand, as if dismissing the thought. He spoke with the bravado of intoxication, even before ten o'clock in the morning.

"Dey don' know Ocee is near. Dey jes' asks evahbody, but does mean nuttin'. De police does not find Ocee."

The lanky man dropped his rag on the counter and leaned forward on his thin elbows. The dimness of the room obscured the features of his black face, one that knew and loved violence as much as did his non-paying customer. Sweat glistened on his temples in the light's faint glow. His voice projected earnest concern.

"Me frien' tell me de heat is up. He tell me de Min'ster of Ed'cashun is back early from Jamaica. He say his maid is attack by you yestaday and de police is turn up de heat."

Ocee dropped his feet to the floor and thumped his chest with the heel of his hand. "So wha' you tink mon? Is Ocee to run? To be scare?"

"No, no, no," the bartender said, shaking his head vigorously. "Not to be scare. To be smart." He tapped his temple with a bony index finger. "To be smart."

Ocee narrowed his blood-shot eyes and stared at his friend.

The bartender leaned over and locked eyes with Ocee. "Don' be like de las' time. You 'membah las' time, mon?"

Ocee nodded. He remembered it as if it were yesterday.

*****

It was almost eight o'clock that Saturday night three years earlier when Ocee made his way to Outland Plantation in St. Michael Parish. The large plantation house was surrounded on three sides by canefields. A large, grassy yard in front led to the dirt street, which in turn fed into the ABC Highway. The Edgegrow family, descendants of the original owners of the plantation, still lived in the plantation house and had just sat down to dinner.

Ocee stealthily made his way to the clearing surrounding the house by moving through the canefields, which were a second home to him. He studied the house from the edge of the clearing, looking for signs of the occupants. A few lights glimmered downstairs, but most of the lights came from upstairs.

Hugging the perimeter of the clearing, Ocee moved around the house, studying it. From the south side, he saw the Edgegrow family at dinner through the upstairs patio doors. He waited a few more minutes, looking for signs of movement downstairs. Satisfied that the whole family was at dinner, he dashed across twenty feet of open area to the French doors on the side.

The sun had been down for about two hours, so he found himself well-hidden in the shadows as he jimmied the lock. Expertly, he pried it open and slipped inside. Finding himself in a large, dimly-lit living room, he waited a few seconds for his eyes to adjust to the darkness, then carefully made his way through the room looking for valuables.

Finished with his search, which turned up a treasure-chest of valuables, including silverware and an antique clock, he sought the stairs leading to the upstairs rooms. As long as the whole family was gathered in the same place, the time seemed right to immobilize them and search the upstairs for jewelry and cash. He also didn't discount the possibility that the Edgegrow family might well include attractive females. His lust for dirty water never waned.

Venturing down a long hallway running beside the living room, Ocee found his way blocked by a wrought-iron gate. He reached to unlatch it.

A sound came from his right. His hand froze in mid-air.

Movement blurred in the corner of his eye. He turned quickly, then stopped short to face a large, mongrel dog.

The two exchanged stares for the briefest of moments. The dog pulled its lips back, baring teeth in a grotesque grin. A soft, guttural rumble sounded.

Ocee held his breath, afraid to move. He averted his eyes, hoping to appease the dog, but kept sight of him in his peripheral vision. Slowly, he walked backward, one agonizing step at a time. Inching closer to the door.

The dog stayed in place. Still growling; still grinning.

Ocee put his hand on the jimmied door.

And the dog sprang into action.

It sprinted down the hallway, untrimmed nails clicking on the hardwood floor. Its growl grew into a locomotive roar. Ocee moved quickly, twisting the doorknob and pulling, but the door refused to open.

Three feet away, the dog leaped, teeth aimed for Ocee's jugular.

In one smooth motion, Ocee pulled a large switchblade from his pocket, snapped the blade out, and extended it at the last minute. The dog's momentum carried it into the knife. The metal dug deep into its chest. A loud, ear-piercing howl split the night.

The dog's forward movement drove Ocee backward. He bounced off the door under its weight, but managed to keep his balance by rolling his shoulders to the side and letting the animal fall to the floor beside him. He left his knife in the dog's chest, forced the jammed door open, and fled outside. He knew the family upstairs must have been alerted by the dog's howl. He wasn't afraid of confronting them, but he wanted to do so on his own terms. Catching them by surprise at the dinner table was one thing; giving them notice to retrieve weapons yet another.

He bolted into the surrounding canefields. Almost instantly, sirens wailed in the distance.

Impossible, he thought. It had been only moments since he knifed the dog. He knew police and military forces were on standby in St. Michael and St. Joseph Parishes in the last few weeks. Still, they could not have already isolated Outland Plantation as his location and arrived there so quickly. No police dragnet was that effective.

What he didn't know then, but learned later, was that Police Commissioner Thomas Siddons was a dinner guest that evening. His personal car patrolled the area, waiting to pick him up after dinner. Upon hearing the dog's death howl, Siddons radioed the car to proceed immediately to the plantation, and put out a call to all other cars in the area, as well. They responded within seconds, sirens blaring.

Ocee scrambled desperately through the canefields. The thickness of the heavy canestalks and a moonless night that made visibility almost nil slowed him. He stumbled blindly ahead, until he finally broke into a clearing next to a dirt road.

A clearing where three policemen lounged against a jeep.

Ocee's sudden appearance startled the policemen as much as their presence startled him. He pulled up short and dug his heels into the soft dirt to keep from running into them. They stopped talking and stared at the intruder.

"Ocee!" one of them shouted.

Ocee pulled a pistol from the waistband of his pants and fired off two quick rounds. The three policemen dove for cover behind the jeep as bullets whizzed past into the darkness.

Ocee disappeared into the canefields.

The officers scrambled to their feet behind the cover of the jeep and opened fire wildly into the thick canes. The noise alerted, and attracted, nearby members of the dragnet.

Gasping for breath, Ocee forged his way back into the thick canes. He hadn't gone far when rifle-fire erupted behind him. It sounded as if half the Barbadian army had opened fire on the field. He dropped to all fours and, keeping as low to the ground as possible, scrambled forward away from the gunfire.

Within half an hour, police had cordoned off the entire canefield, then kept an all-night vigil around its perimeter. Throughout the night, sporadic bursts of gunfire came from one side or another as policemen fired at real or imagined movement among the stalks. At first light, a gang of officers moved in, closing the net on the center of the field. But when the net was drawn all the way, there was no Oliver Clarke.

Later that morning, a scar-faced, dreadlocked man staggered into Bridgetown's Queen Elizabeth Hospital. A quick examination by doctors revealed at least six gunshot wounds in his back, sides, and abdomen. The physician on duty contacted the police. Before treatment could be administered to the wounded man, Oliver Clarke was identified and arrested.

*****

These memories coursed through Ocee's mind as he sought his friend's counsel in the rum shop. He still felt the pain as the bullets tore into his body that night. It was not an experience he cared to relive. His friend was right. This time, the police might not stop shooting.

"Mon, how you tink I is getting' off de island?" Ocee asked. After all, if it were a simple matter, he'd already be long gone.

The bartender joined Ocee at the table. "Wha' you need is a travelin' companion. De police is lookin' for one mon. Dey not lookin' fo' two togedder."

Ocee narrowed his eyes and thought that one through. He didn't know anyone else who wanted off the island as badly as he did. And he certainly didn't know anyone who wanted to get off the island traveling with him.

"Mon, you say to be smart, but who gonna go wit' Ocee?" Ocee tapped the side of his head with his index finger. "Now who is doin' de tinkin'?"

The bartender took a ganja hit and bared his teeth in a grin. "All you has to do is fin' someone de police don' look for. It don' matter if dey don' wanna go. You makes dat one go."

Now that idea made sense to Ocee. Just find somebody who would not arouse suspicion and force that person to travel with him.

Whoever it was would be disposable.

CHAPTER SIX

No more than an hour after parking in Bridgetown, following a hot, sweaty trip on foot through the shopping district, Bobby and Karla were back in their car. Shopping held no real attraction for either of them. The narrow streets, crowded with vendors, workers, and other tourists, quickly wore their nerves thin. Empty-handed, they ventured up the Caribbean coast to see what lay to the north.

Unlike the harsh waves at Sam Lord's Castle, the Caribbean waters lapped mildly at the beaches. The gentle surf had an almost hypnotic effect on them as they gazed at it while driving along the narrow, two-lane road. Bobby noted that these were play-waters. They saw wind-surfers, swimmers, and even water-skiers at various points along the coast. That also contrasted with what they had seen so far of the rough Atlantic, which was barren of water sports other than surfing. Restaurants, hotels, and resorts dotted the white sand beaches, again in contrast to the more native Atlantic side, which was marked by chattel houses, fishing piers, and long stretches of barrenness.

They soon passed through Speightstown in St. Peter Parish, leaving the heavily populated areas behind. The road moved first into an area of sparsely-inhabited villages and then disappeared into the thick canefields of St. Lucy Parish. From there, they bent around to the east before turning southward along the Atlantic. Although they were in awe of the beauty of the Caribbean coast, they found that the northern and eastern coasts offered the most spectacular scenery. While the west was casually laid out with gentle beaches and softly lapping surf, a series of rugged sea cliffs, with pounding Atlantic breakers, broke up these shores less than twenty miles away.

In a matter of a few hours, Bobby and Karla had circumnavigated the entire island along its coastal roads, stopping only periodically to snap photographs of the scenery. That evening, hot and tired, they were finally ready to return to Sam Lord's.

*****

"These people make me nervous," Bobby said.

He eyed the rearview mirror. Still thirty minutes from the hotel, on a dirt road in the midst of a large canefield, he could hardly wait to get out of the car and leave the driving behind.

Karla glanced over her shoulder at a blue car tailgating them. "How long has he been back there?"

"He came out of nowhere a couple of minutes ago. I don't know what his deal is."

Karla looked back again, a hint of nervousness in her glance. "Why don't you slow down and let him go by?"

"I've been slowing down, but he won't pass."

"Pull over."

"Next wide spot on this sorry excuse for a road."

Bobby eased his foot onto the brake and hugged the side of

the road as close as he could. Hanging leaves from canestalks beat against the sideview mirror. The car behind them inched closer until it seemed it must be touching bumpers.

Bobby fidgeted, alternately gripping and releasing the steering wheel. When he checked the mirror again, he saw the native driver behind him flash a toothy smile.

"Why doesn't he just pass?" Bobby muttered, his eye still on the mirror. He tapped the brakes. "Go around, asshole."

Karla looked again. The tailgater's car lurched, but maintained its distance.

For the last fifteen minutes, they had been driving through fields of sugar cane. Other than the tailgater, they saw no one else. There was no oncoming traffic to prevent him from passing. Even for Barbados drivers, this behavior was strange.

Bobby tapped the brakes again. Again, the tailgater's car lurched, but stayed as close as if it were connected by a tow-bar.

"What are you gonna do, jackass?" Bobby said.

He slowly pressed the brake pedal until the Moke was completely stopped, still snug against the rows of sugar cane. The tailgater had dropped back a few feet as Bobby decelerated, then stopped when Bobby stopped.

The two cars sat still in the middle of the canefield. Karla kept a watch over her shoulder. Bobby riveted his attention on the rearview mirror.

"Come on, come on. Go around."

After a few seconds, the second car swung out into the middle of the road.

"There you go. Atta boy."

The car slowly edged up beside the Moke. The driver never looked their way. In profile, his dreadlocks seemed piled up around his shoulders and the back of his head.

Bobby watched him carefully. Perspiration formed at his temples and a drop trickled down his cheek.

The driver kept going, slowly, until his car had just cleared the Moke. Then he suddenly swung to the left, angling sharply in front, cutting off the road.

"What the hell?" Bobby said.

"Get – get – get away from that asshole!" Karla shouted. She clutched at Bobby's arm. "That guy's crazy."

Bobby began to slip the car into reverse, his eyes on the scar-faced, dreadlocked driver. The man stepped out of his car holding his right hand behind him.

"What's he doing?" Bobby asked. "What's he want?"

The man brought his hand around front. Too late, Bobby realized he had a gun.

"Sonuvabitch!"

"Go!" Karla screamed. "Go, go, go, go!"

Bobby settled the transmission into gear and jammed his foot hard on the accelerator. The car lurched.

The highwayman raised the pistol in front of him and sighted down the barrel.

Bobby pressed the pedal to the floor. The tires spun furiously, going nowhere. Then they bit, gripping dirt and gravel. The Moke jumped into motion.

The quick report of a gun sounded three times in rapid succession.

Karla screamed.

A dull pain sprouted in Bobby's chest, followed by a stinging sensation and numbness in his throat. His head jerked backward, bounced off the headrest, and slammed forward onto the steering wheel. Blood leaked from just above his left breast. A spurt of fluid shot out below his chin. The taut whiteness left his knuckles as his hands went limp. The steering wheel spun crazily to the left.

The car whipped wildly in an arc, backwards across the road. Its rear wheels plowed into the sugar cane and settled into the soft dirt with a slight jolt. Bobby's foot slipped off the accelerator and he sprawled awkwardly across the seat.

"Bobby!"

Karla pulled his head back, but he didn't respond. Blood soaked the front of his T-shirt and continued to spill from a hole in his neck. It spurted rhythmically, as if marking musical time. She tried to plug the hole, but the red fluid squirted between her fingers and flowed over her hand.

"Bobby!"

Out of the corner of her eye, she saw movement. Her heart pounded. Her mouth opened in a silent scream.

The man walked to the car and leveled the weapon at her. "Wha' you sayin' now?" he asked nonsensically.

She closed her eyes and pulled Bobby tightly to her, waiting breathlessly for the shot that would send her to join her husband.

But it didn't come.

"Out!" the man said.

She opened her eyes and looked.

He still stood there, grinning, with the gun pointed at her head. With his left hand, he beckoned her to step out of the car. Two of his fingers were missing.

Suddenly, she felt the blood drain from her face, almost as it drained from Bobby's neck onto her blouse. She inhaled, but it seemed as if she took in no air. She opened her mouth and fought for oxygen, taking big exaggerated gulps. Her hands and feet began to tingle. Her head began to spin, and she was helpless to stop it. All she could do was hold tightly to Bobby.

Then everything went black.

CHAPTER SEVEN

Karla blinked her eyes a few times, then opened them, relieved at finally waking from a bad dream. And what a dream it had been! Nightmare better defined it. In the dream, she and Bobby were cornered in a canefield by a scar-faced man – and the bastard shot Bobby!

The last thing she remembered about the dream was holding Bobby's head in her arms as blood pumped from his neck and chest. It seemed so vivid, so real. Even now, she swore it had really happened. She still heard the sound of the gunshots and still saw the bright red of Bobby's free-flowing blood. She also remembered the smiling face of the man who did it, with his white teeth and the ugly scar on his cheek as he motioned to her with his deformed hand. It sent a chill down her spine.

Now she was awake. Her heart pounded and her palms felt clammy. She wanted to wake Bobby, to tell him about the dream. She looked around slowly, trying to get her bearings, but she wasn't sure where she was. She had been in a deep sleep – the kind that sometimes left her head aching – and was still in a fog. She blinked her eyes a few times and shook her head to clear the cobwebs then she looked around again.

She was alone in a tiny room with only one window, barely larger than a porthole, covered with dark paper. Only the faintest of light peeked in from around the edges of the paper, just enough to let her make out the room's furnishings. She was lying on a bed, but not the bed at Sam Lord's Castle. This one was smaller, and the mattress was hard and lumpy. The battered dresser on the far wall and the plastic chair in the corner also were not the furnishings of Sam Lord's.

Karla gasped for breath, and her heart pounded in overdrive. Nothing seemed familiar. Nothing!

Her panicked mind kicked into the same high gear as her desperately-beating heart. Where was she; where was Bobby; was she still asleep; was this all still part of her nightmare? Was it a dream within a dream, or just the next in a succession of bad dreams? As her thoughts collided wildly in her head, Karla willed herself to wake up. But try as she might, she couldn't, nor could she move the dream along. There was no fast-forward. It seemed it had to run its hellish course.

Soon the awful truth began its inevitable descent into her consciousness. This wasn't a dream! It was real! The violent encounter in the canefield hadn't been a dream, either. The unbelievable had happened. Somewhere out there, Bobby was lying alone in the rented Moke, bleeding to death. If he wasn't already dead.

A faint noise came from another room. It sounded like a man's voice, low and guttural, but Karla couldn't make out any words. She sat up and strained to listen. Only then did she realize that her hands were tied together. She swung her legs over the side of the bed and tried to stand, but ropes hobbled her feet as well. The sensation of being unable to freely move her hands and feet was claustrophobic. She ran short of breath again. Her head felt hot and feverish, and she perspired heavily. She sat on the edge of the bed for a few minutes, waiting for the feeling to pass. After it did, she strained at the bonds around her wrists. Almost as quickly as she started, she stopped because all she did was bruise her wrists and abrade the skin on her hands.

She breathed deeply and tried to collect her thoughts. Because her hands were tied in front, she had some freedom. She bent forward and tugged at the thin restraint binding her ankles, but the knot seemed to have melded into the rest of the rope. Even so, she continued to struggle with the knot until she broke two fingernails at the quick.

Finally she gave up and lay back on the bed, fighting tears and a sense of hopelessness. What could she do now?

The door to the tiny room burst open and someone entered.

"Well, now, wha' you say, leddie?"

Karla bolted upright in the bed and twisted around to face her tormentor. Holding her bound hands up to block the light that hurt her eyes, she barely made him out. He grinned wickedly, and his teeth glowed white in the dark. The light from behind him cast a halo around his dreadlocked head. But Karla saw no angel, unless it was Lucifer, cast out of heaven by God, into the the pit of hell.

"What do you want?" she asked. "Where is my husband?"

The man tilted his head back and a high-pitched laugh escaped his mouth. It almost sounded like a witch's cackle.

"Who you tink you is, demandin' from Ocee?" he said. "Ocee have demands to make of you."

He smiled, but there was no mirth in his smile. Only malice.

He stepped toward the bed. Karla struggled awkwardly to her feet.

He moved closer and she just as awkwardly hopped back into a corner where she glowered at him.

"What do you want?" she asked.

He stopped and raised his eyes in mock surprise. "You don' know?" He paused, his eyebrows still raised. "Wha' you tink I wan'? Huh? Wha' you tink?"

Karla shrank farther into the corner, wedging herself into the angle of the two walls. She prayed that he wouldn't come any closer.

But come closer he did, moving with great deliberation around the edge of the bed. He talked rhythmically as he walked.

"Huh? Wha' you tink? Wha' you tink?" He lowered his eyebrows and grabbed his crotch with his right hand. "Wha' you tink I wan', leddie?"

Karla closed her eyes, ducked, and pulled her chin into her chest. She refused to make further eye contact with this obscene bastard.

The man moved closer until he was within arm's length. With his right hand still clutching his groin, he reached toward Karla with his deformed left hand. Her eyes were closed tightly, and she didn't see two fingers straddle her breast, but she felt the nubs of his middle fingers zero in on her nipple.

She flinched and turned sharply away from him.

Ocee leaned his head back and cackled again. "Wha' da matter, pretty leddie? You don' like Ocee?"

Karla shuddered but kept her face turned away, her eyes clenched shut. Her cheeks turned hot. She couldn't be sure if it was tears or merely anger and embarrassment that scalded them.

The man groped at her breasts again, still laughing. With each breath, Karla's chest heaved and his fingerless nubs dug into her nipple. She held her breath and tried to twist farther away. Her necklace – the one Bobby had just given her – became entangled in the man's sparse fingers. He pulled the gold "K" away from her, draped it over his index finger, and studied the diamond center.

"Nice," he murmured. "Nice."

With a sudden yank, he tore the necklace from around her neck. "Now is Ocee's."

Karla cried out softly as he ripped the wedding present from her neck. She glanced at him for the briefest of moments, flashing a killer look his way. She wished him dead.

He met her eyes and laughed.

*****

Thirty minutes later, Karla sat on the passenger seat of the same small car that had run Bobby and her off the road in the canefield. The scar-faced man sat behind her, holding a pistol against her ribs by reaching his hand around the side of the seat and resting it against the door. A lanky Rastafarian drove.

The scar-faced man had undergone a chameleon-like transformation. Shorn of dreadlocks, he had bandaged his left hand with an elastic wrap to hide its deformity. He covered his other identifying characteristic, the scar on his right cheek, with a pair of oversized sunglasses that hid almost half his face. He looked no different than thousands of Bajan men.

Karla sat sullenly in the front seat and listened as her captors jabbered in a strange dialect. Listening carefully, she figured out their immediate plan. The scar-faced man had chartered a sailboat excursion to St. Lucia, one of Barbados's closest neighbors in the Caribbean. He reserved the boat using Karla's credit card, and Karla was to front for him at the marina. No one would suspect an American woman to be traveling with a wanted murderer. No questions would be asked. They were simply friends enjoying a sunset excursion to St. Lucia. Once there, the scar-faced man would make his way from St. Lucia to Jamaica, far from the arm of the Barbados law.

The man had no assurances that Karla wouldn't try to give him away, but he held a threat over her head that he hoped would do the trick. Not the expected threat that he'd kill her if she betrayed him. She expected that to happen anyway. If Bobby was dead, as she already feared him to be, that threat had no hold on her. If he was dead, she was ready to join him. No, the added incentive was his threat to kill the crew of the charter. A threat that he correctly believed would weigh heavily on her conscience. She did not want to be responsible for the deaths of innocent people. And by now, she knew that killing was second nature to this man.

As they drove, Karla silently prayed for her ordeal to be over soon – and that she would be killed quickly.

CHAPTER EIGHT

Sergeant Wallace Walker, of the Barbados National Defense Force, and police constable Glenroy Wood waited as an ambulance lurched to a stop at the emergency entrance to Queen Elizabeth Hospital in Bridgetown. The two men watched hospital personnel unload a stretcher with a wounded white man and rush him into the nearest surgical theater. A team of doctors sprang into action, having already been notified that the man, apparently a tourist, had lost a tremendous amount of blood from at least three gunshot wounds. There might have been more, but he was such a bloody mess, it was hard to tell.

Wallace and Glenroy loitered in the emergency waiting room and waited for preliminary word on the man's condition. Clearly he had been robbed. There was no cell phone and no wallet or jewelry, other than a wedding ring, nor any identification on him when police arrived. What concerned them was the unlikely possibility that an Anglo tourist might have been touring on his own. Until they knew for sure, they were haunted by two unanswered questions: Was the man with the wedding ring traveling with his wife? If so, where was she?

"This sure looks like the work of Oliver Clarke," Walker said, verbalizing the thought that haunted them both since they got the call.

Glenroy took another sip of his coffee. "I was tinkin' de same ting. I jes' dinna wan' say so."

"Sometimes I think if I don't say what I'm thinking, then it won't turn out to be true."

Glenroy smiled, revealing a gap between otherwise perfect teeth; so perfectly straight that they could be used as a straightedge. The brightness of their ivory color virtually glowed in the middle of his ebony complexion. But even his near flawless teeth took second stage to piercing eyes so dark they were almost black. With high cheekbones, a thick, bristly mustache, and coarse hair, he epitomized the Caribbean male.

Wallace Walker, on the other hand, sprang from British descent, his pale skin and fair hair betraying his European heritage. Unlike Glenroy, who was thickly built like an athlete – perfect for the physical aspects of his job as a police officer in the streets – Wallace was thin, almost frail by comparison. He relied on acumen and intelligence, which suited his role as a detective with the National Defense Force. Descended from plantation owners, Wallace had not turned a day's physical labor in his life. That also contrasted with Glenroy, who had been a field-hand in his youth and whose ancestors were slaves on the plantations owned by Wallace's ancestors. But Wallace had always wanted to be in law enforcement and managed to use his brilliant mind to compensate for his less than hardy physique.

Both men had been involved in searching for Oliver Clarke since his most recent escape. Glenroy had been involved before, at the shootout at Outland Plantation three years earlier, but this was Wallace's first involvement. Now, this new evidence of Clarke's handiwork both excited and frightened them.

"Excuse me, Sergeant," a young Defense Force officer said.

"Yes?" Wallace said.

The officer handed him a key with the words Sam Lord's Castle and the number 247 printed on it. "We found this in the rental car."

Walker studied the key as if it contained some hidden meaning. "Have you learned who's registered in this room?"

"Not yet. I thought you should know about the key right away."

Wallace pulled out his cell phone. He looked around the waiting area. "Where's a directory?"

"Nurses' station," Glenroy said. He pointed with his Styrofoam cup.

The two policemen hustled to the nurses' stand. A plump nurse sitting behind the counter looked up at their rapid approach.

"Phone book," Wallace demanded.

The nurse pulled a directory from a drawer and handed it to Glenroy, who flipped through its pages until he found the number. Wallace dialed as Glenroy read it off.

After identifying himself to the desk clerk, Wallace asked, "Who is registered in room 247?"

"I'm not supposed to give out that kind of information, sir," a female clerk answered. A skeptical hint tinged her voice.

"This is a police emergency. We have a patient at Queen Elizabeth who was carrying a key with that room number on it. We are trying to ascertain his identity."

"I understand, sir. But our policy is – "

"Let me speak to your supervisor."

Wallace heard a murmuring of voices on the other end. Then a male voice came over the line. "This is the manager. To whom am I speaking?" he asked officiously.

"Sergeant Wallace Walker, National Defense Force. I need to know who is registered in room 247. There's been a shooting."

"I see." What sounded like genuine concern replaced the officiousness. "One minute please."

A brief pause, then "The registration says Robert and Karla Reavis. From the United States."

"Do you have a home address or phone number for them?"

The manager gave the address of a Dallas, Texas, suburb, then asked, "Are Mr. and Mrs. Reavis all right?"

"Would you know Mr. Reavis by sight?"

"Yes. I was on night duty when they checked in, and they've stopped by the front desk several times. A very nice couple."

"There are two guests?"

"Yes. As I said, their names are Robert and Karla Reavis. Honeymooners."

The words cut Wallace to the quick. A cold chill gripped his spine. As he and Glenroy feared, there was a woman – a bride. And she was nowhere to be found. If this was the aftermath of an encounter with Oliver Clarke, he hated to think what might have become of Karla Reavis.

CHAPTER NINE

Oliver Clarke chartered a monohull sailboat from Bajan Lady Excursions for the one-hundred-fifty mile trip to St. Lucia, "The Helen of the Antilles." For a modest fee of one-hundred-fifty United States dollars each – paid with Karla's MasterCard – Bajan Lady promised dinner, champagne, and a crew of two for a sunset cruise from Bridgetown to St. Lucia's capital, Castries. Everything went smoothly at the marina, with Karla making the payment arrangements with the cashier. Now, as the sun sank on the horizon, they neared their destination.

Karla and Clarke sat at the front of the boat, separated as far as physically possible from the two-man crew. As they neared St. Lucia, Karla noticed that the sea took on a deep blue hue, unlike the green and aquamarine colors closer to land, but was nevertheless crystal clear. She would have loved the excursion had she been taking it with Bobby. Traveling with Oliver Clarke, though, merely took her farther away from her husband and closer to an uncertain fate.

In her heart, she believed Bobby was still alive. But the farther they sailed, the less she harbored what she knew were unrealistic thoughts that he would swoop down, like the cavalry, and rescue her.

Sitting with her back to her tormenter, she began to cry.

*****

Captain Roger Wilson, blonde and tan, thought his passengers a bit odd. He had carried odd passengers before, but something didn't seem right about these two. The beautiful American woman didn't belong with the Bajan man. Something about her bearing, the way she looked and carried herself, clashed with the scruffy man with the bandaged hand. He watched her closely from his vantage point at the rear of the boat. She hadn't spoken a word, either to the crew or to her companion, since boarding the vessel. For that matter, the guy hadn't said much either. But she was too quiet. And now it looked as if she was crying.

Roger watched as Billy, his brother and first mate, also blonde and tan, took sandwiches and drinks to the passengers. The Bajan met him halfway and took the items, as if he wanted to keep Billy away from the woman. When the Bajan offered food to the woman, she refused to eat. She never spoke or made eye contact with him, but merely shook her head and continued to look straight ahead.

The Pitons loomed in the distance, the twin conical peaks that rose twenty-five hundred feet above sea level and majestically landmarked St. Lucia. Soon they would be docked and the passengers gone, leaving the boat and its crew to return empty-handed to Barbados. That, too, was odd. Most fares were round-trip. If all they wanted was passage to the island, why not fly? And why weren't they carrying luggage? It all seemed very strange to Roger.

Billy worked his way back to where his brother stood at the helm. Roger could tell from Billy's furrowed brow that something bothered him, too. Worry lines spread along his tanned forehead, only occasionally obscured by blonde bangs that blew across his face. Billy moved close and stood at Roger's shoulder.

"I've got a funny feeling about those two," Billy whispered.

At six-foot-four, Roger towered over his little brother by at least half-a-foot, and he had to lean a bit to his side to hear what Billy had to say.

"Do what?" Roger asked.

"I said, I've got a funny feeling about those two."

Roger looked at his brother, whose face darkened un-characteristically. Billy had recently turned twenty and, up until now, never seemed overly concerned about anything. Ever since moving from Alabama to join Roger, he had lived the carefree existence of a beach-bum. Worry and concern were foreign companions to him.

Roger kept his eyes on the passengers at the front. The Bajan drank champagne directly from the bottle, but the woman still faced forward, head down. She neither spoke nor ate.

"I don't think she goes with him," Billy continued.

"I hear you. But if we make a big deal out of this, and we're wrong, we'll look pretty stupid." Roger paused, remembering the week before when they ran aground on a reef. "We've got about one more stupid left in us and then we're out of jobs."

"That wasn't our fault. And if we drop them off on Lucia and then find out later something wasn't right with her . . ."

Roger nodded. "Call it in. But make it look natural to our guests."

Billy nodded, then again approached the front of the boat, toward the Bajan. He walked with an easy grace, like an athlete, trying to appear nonchalant. He put his best smile on as he drew near.

The Bajan jumped to his feet and met him halfway.

"You need anything else?" Billy asked.

"Beer," the Bajan monotoned.

Billy looked at the empty champagne bottle in the man's hand and nodded. He glanced over the Bajan's shoulder at the dark-haired woman, but the Bajan sidestepped and blocked his view.

"She want anything?"

"Only beer fo' me."

Billy cast one more long look over the Bajan's shoulder. The Bajan moved again, still blocking his view. Billy smiled at the man, shrugged, and did an about-face.

The Bajan went back to the front, dancing and singing a Jimmy Buffett song on the way.

Billy reached the helm and glanced at Roger, who nodded slightly. Then Billy descended the stairs.

The hold was small, with only the bare essentials for short cruises – a table with charts spread on top, fax, radio, a small refrigerator, and a few cushioned chairs. He reached for the radio microphone and called the office at Bridgetown harbor. When he established contact with the dispatcher, he wasted no time getting to the point.

"Rog and I both got a funny feeling about this charter to St. Lucia. What do you know about them?"

"What do you mean?" a female voice answered, barely intelligible through heavy static.

"They don't seem to go together, these two."

"What do you mean they don't seem to go together?"

Billy sighed in exasperation. "Just tell me what we know about them." His voice took on a touch of agitation. "Why is this ugly son-of-a-bitch traveling with this good-looking lady?"

"I don't understand what you're asking me."

"Goddamnit," Billy said. "Put somebody with a brain on."

A slight pause followed, then the voice of the excursion service's owner came over the air. "Is there a problem, Billy?"

"Eric, I'm just trying to find out about this charter to St. Lucia. It doesn't seem right, this woman traveling with this guy. He's a sleazy-looking Bajan and she's a good-looking white chick. They don't go together."

"She paid for it with her credit card and never said a word about anything being wrong."

"Did she say anything at all?"

"No. He did the talking, then she gave us her MasterCard."

"She signed it?" Billy asked.

"Yeah."

"Check the signature."

"Billy, what's going on?"

"Just do it, okay?"

A few seconds later, Eric said, "Name on the card was Karla Sandone. Name on the signature was Karla Reavis. Huh! I didn't notice that before."

"See, something's not right."

"Probably a maiden name or something."

"I don't think she's married to this guy," Billy said. "I guarantee you he's not her type."

"So what do you want me to do?"

Billy stood silently for a minute, dropping the microphone to his side in exasperation. How could this guy ever run a business? He took a deep breath to hold his temper in check, then slowly raised the microphone back to his mouth.

"Maybe you could call the credit card company and make sure the card's valid. Find out why it's got a different name. Find out if the card has been used anywhere else on the island or if it's been reported stolen. Something like that."

"Goddamnit, Billy! What's going on out there?"

"Eric, please, just do it. Okay?"

Billy heard Eric breathe heavily. "All right. If it'll make you feel better. I'll call back when I know something. But then I want to know what the hell is going on."

After Billy signed off, he stood with his hands on his hips and stared at the radio for a few seconds. He had been down here too long. He was supposed to be getting something. What was it?

Beer. Yeah, that's it. He had better surface with a beer for the Bajan, and fast, if he didn't want to arouse any suspicion. He whirled toward the refrigerator, opened the door, and grabbed a cold bottle. But when he closed the door and turned back to the stairs, he found himself face-to-face with the Bajan.

"Got it," he said.

His phony smile faded as soon as he saw the gun in the Bajan's hand.

"Wha' you sayin' on de radio?" The Bajan's smile told Billy he already knew.

"How long you been standing there?" Billy asked.

"You need drive de boat, mon."

Alarm spread across Billy's face, and he broke out in a cold sweat. Where was Roger? He was supposed to be piloting the boat.

"Come along, now," the Bajan said. He tossed his head to the side and motioned above-deck with the gun. "You frien' is needin' help."

The Bajan stepped aside and cleared a path on the stairs. Billy tried to read clues on the man's black face, but it was a blank.

He ascended the steps as the Bajan fell in behind him and jabbed him in the back with the gun. When he came on deck, he saw the wheel slowly spinning, with Roger sprawled on the deck just behind it. The dark-haired woman sat with him, holding his head in her lap. She looked at Billy as he approached the wheel. Her eyes brimmed with tears.

Billy squatted to check on his big brother. "What happened?"

"He hit him pretty hard," she said.

The Bajan kicked Billy's ribs. Billy winced as he felt a rib crack under the toe of the man's boot.

"No talkin' wit' de pretty leddie. Drive de boat."

Billy slowly stood. He and the Bajan stood less than five feet apart, engaged in a battle of stares. But Billy wasn't stupid. The man had a weapon and he was unarmed.

The Bajan gestured toward the wheel with the gun. "Drive or feel de gun's bite."

Billy didn't move. Hands tightly curled into fists, his knuckles turned white from the tautness.

"He shot my husband," the woman said softly.

Billy looked at her.

"He'll kill you," she added.

The Bajan smiled broadly. He held up his left hand, which he had unbandaged while Billy was below deck. Brandishing his deformity, he said, "Do you know me?"

No dreadlocks, so the man didn't look like his picture in the newspaper, but Billy had read about the man with the hand.

He nodded.

"Den you know to do as I say. Drive de boat!"

Billy grasped the wheel, his knuckles still white. Quickly, he straightened out their course and set the boat on a northwest angle to swing around the northern point of St. Lucia.

"No, no," Clarke said. "Go sout'. You know Sain' Vincen' Passage?"

Billy nodded.

"You know Vieux For' Bay?"

Billy nodded again. He knew that Vieux Fort Bay perched on the southern end of the island, just off Saint Vincent Passage, a channel between the islands of St. Vincent and St. Lucia. It was a sparsely populated area of the island.

"Go dere."

Billy cut the wheel to the left, again adjusting their course. As he did, Clarke came around behind him, to where the woman still sat holding Roger's head in her lap. She glared at him as he came near. Billy cut a glance back over his shoulder.

"You drive!" Clarke said, pointing the gun at him. "I take care of dis."

Billy obeyed, ever mindful of the weapon aimed at his back. Clarke now stood over the woman.

"To de fron'," he said. He pointed to the place where she sat during the first part of the excursion.

She didn't move.

Clarke leaned over and leveled the gun at Roger's head. The cold steel of the barrel pressed to his temple; the skin around it turned red from the pressure.

"Pretty please?" Clarke said.

Karla laid Roger's head gently on the deck and got to her feet. She looked at Clarke, hostility crackling in her eyes.

He winked and smacked his lips in a kissing sound.

Karla ducked her head and hurried to the front of the boat, her cheeks flushed and burning. His cackling laugh rang in her ears.

Billy watched the woman as she awkwardly made her way to the front, then checked back over his shoulder again. His glance was met with the barrel of the gun, which Clarke brought across his face in a sweeping motion. The blow ripped his face and loosed a stream of blood. Billy let out a curse as he spun around to face the front again. He hadn't heard the man sneak up behind him.

Behind Billy, Clarke knelt by the unconscious Roger. He set the gun on the deck by his knee, reached in his pocket, and pulled out a switchblade. He fumbled with the latch for a few seconds before unsheathing the blade.

With his deformed hand, he grabbed Roger's blonde hair and pulled it back roughly. The motion lifted Roger's chin from his chest and exposed his windpipe.

Clarke whipped the knife across Roger's throat, in one move severing the jugular and the thorax.

Blood gushed.

Roger gasped.

Billy heard the choking sound coming from his brother,

followed by a strange gurgling. He swung to look over his shoulder, only to again be met by the barrel of the gun. This time he let out a louder curse, then defiantly turned to face Clarke.

The gun barked twice. Billy felt the sting as bullets tore into his chest.

*****

Sitting at the front of the boat, Karla jumped at the sound of the gunshots. For a moment, she relived the shots that had ripped into Bobby and shed his blood in her lap. She sprang to her feet and spun around, just in time to see the young crewman fall to the deck. Behind him, the captain lay in a pool of bright red blood. Clarke stood over the captain, still holding the pistol at arm's length.

With the grace of an athlete, Karla dove into the crystal waters of the Caribbean.

CHAPTER TEN

As soon as her feet cleared the deck, Karla braced herself for the shock of entering cold water. But even this far from shore, the legendary Caribbean lived up to its reputation for warmth. As Karla's body came to realize it didn't need to expend energy heating up, it began to respond to her efforts to put distance from the boat. She knifed just below the surface, kicking her legs with all her might before finally coming up. Her head broke clear into the evening air, and she stole a quick glance over her shoulder at the hell she had left behind.

The boat sailed in a wide arc away from the direction of her swim. In the few seconds she had been in the water, she had already attained at least a fifty-foot lead. With the boat's crew dead, and a madman at the helm, Karla counted on Clarke's inexperience as a sailor to give her the slim chance she needed.

Turning away, Karla set her sights on St. Lucia. Clearly visible, its mountains and hills cut a dramatic swath across the horizon, but Karla knew it still lay miles off. How many miles, she could only guess. Taking a deep breath, she began to stroke, swimming desperately for land.

"Bitch!"

Ocee watched the woman dive from the boat. He hadn't counted on that. He wasn't used to such boldness from a woman. Up until now she had meekly gone along, too scared – he thought – to take any initiative on her own. Now, as he watched her swim, he realized the boat was sailing away from her, allowing her to put twice as much distance between them with each stroke of her arms.

He wiped the switchblade against his pants-leg to clean off the captain's blood then repocketed the weapon. After tucking the gun in his waistband, he grabbed the blonde with the slit throat under the arms. Backing slowly, he dragged the body to the starboard side of the boat. With a bit of an effort, he hoisted the body over the low protective railing that surrounded the deck. It teetered on the edge for a moment, then dropped.

The body hit with a splash. It dove beneath the surface, then floated back to the top, face down. Once it settled on the surface, it began to drift into the boat's wake.

Ocee repeated the exercise with the other blonde – the gunshot victim. That body, as well, drifted into the boat's wake, just in front of the other.

With both crewmen now disposed of, Ocee positioned himself at the helm and studied the strange instruments on the panel in front of him.

*****

Karla continued to swim as the boat steered southward behind her. Each stroke propelled her ahead. Soon, she opened up a quarter-mile gap between herself and the pirated pleasure craft.

Pleasure craft indeed! The irony of the term was not lost on her as she steadily stroked landward. Her years as a competitive athlete paid dividends now. Throughout her teen years and her adult life, she kept herself in peak physical condition. She never dreamed she would one day be called upon to use her conditioning and athleticism to save her life. Fueled by a combination of fear, rage, and adrenaline, but tempered by a cool head, she settled into a brisk pace of free-style swimming.

Fortunately, the waters remained relatively calm, which allowed her to achieve a high level of efficiency as she swam. Kicking only occasionally with her feet, lest she wear herself out too soon, she stroked steadily with her arms. Each stroke propelled her forward through the Caribbean. Closer to the island before her. Farther from the terror in the boat behind.

*****

Through a process of trial-and-error, Ocee finally got the boat under control and headed toward the eastern shore of St. Lucia. He abandoned his plans to land at Vieux Fort Bay and set his sights somewhere between Savannes Bay and Vierge Point. By his calculations, that was where the woman would be headed. That is, if she was swimming in a straight line for the island. He assumed she was. After all, they were still several miles from shore when she jumped, and the shortest distance between two points is a straight line. If she wasn't looking for the shortest distance, then she was a fool. And he didn't think her a fool. He set the boat to follow that same straight line.

His biggest problem was that he didn't know exactly where the boat had been when she jumped. It had traveled perhaps as much as a quarter-mile to a half-mile before he got it under control, and in a semi-circle at that. If he couldn't figure out the starting point, he knew he might never figure out either where the straight line began or where it ended. His most immediate goal, then, became to find the origin of that straight line.

In short order, he became comfortable with steering the boat. He adjusted the speed to a rate he calculated to be faster than the woman could swim. Then he began to gently weave the boat in a serpentine fashion. His idea was to weave just wide enough so as to intersect the straight line, wherever it might be, on each pass. He tried to keep a rate of speed sufficient to compensate for the time lost weaving, yet fast enough to gain ground on the swimming woman. He had to catch her.

A car and a plane ticket awaited him in Vieux Fort. The ticket would take him from Castries, St. Lucia, to Kingston, Jamaica, where he could blend in and be lost among fellow Rastafarians.

But reaching that plane ticket and making that flight were now in jeopardy because of the woman. If she got ashore and sounded an alarm, it would shut down the airport before he boarded his plane, leaving him back where he started on Barbados, facing the same dilemma: How to get off an island. After all this time, this close, he refused to let her jeopardize his freedom.

*****

Karla pared back her speed slightly and glanced over her shoulder. She had lost sight of the boat some time ago. She wasn't sure how much of a lead she held, or whether Clarke had control over the boat. She assumed he did. And she also assumed that he was looking for her. If that was true, then no lead was enough as long as she remained in the water. She also believed he would assume she was swimming in a direct line.

That, after all, was the logical assumption. So she turned off slightly to the north and headed for shore at an oblique angle. She knew the change in direction added distance to her swim, but she figured to hit shore about a half-mile north of where a direct line would put her.

She had been in the water for close to an hour now. Her arms ached and her lungs burned. Even though adrenaline still pumped, her finely-tuned body was flagging. Will power was her last resource. She had to reach shore, get back to Barbados, and find Bobby. She prayed that he was still alive. If he was, he needed her.

She knew she could make it. She had to, for Bobby.

She stroked harder.

*****

The bodies of the two blonde crew members bobbed limply in the water as Ocee motored by in the monohull. Both floated face down, the water around them stained a faint pinkish hue by their still-flowing blood. Ocee smiled. Pride swelled in his breast. He thought himself a mighty warrior. The two crewmen paid silent tribute to his prowess by their face-down presence.

Ocee looked hard toward shore. He felt confident that he was at least in the general vicinity of where the boat had been when the woman jumped. The Caribbean current was gentle. He was sure that the two corpses could not have floated far since they entered the water. Easing back on the throttle, he simultaneously lessened the spin of the helm, cutting down on the width of his serpentine weave toward St. Lucia. After one last glance at his victims, he turned his eyes landward and squinted toward the horizon, looking for movement in the water.

The first shark's fin breached the surface about twenty yards behind the boat. The shark nudged Roger's body with his nose, then circled around.

Two other fins appeared and joined the circle.

CHAPTER ELEVEN

"Come in Bajan Lady. Over."

Eric Baldwin had repeated that phrase over and over for the past thirty minutes, but the crew of the Bajan Lady failed to respond. He slammed the microphone back into its holder and turned to his wife.

"The radio was just fine yesterday. I don't know why they aren't answering."

"Did you try to call his cell?"

"There's no reception out there," he said.

"They probably just stopped to swim or maybe to do some snorkeling. They like to do that from time to time."

"Someone should still be with the boat. I've told them that a million times. If those pinheads just jumped in the water and left the boat and equipment alone, I'll fry their asses."

"If they're anchored, there's no reason why they couldn't both be in the water."

"The reason is because I've told them not to. That's the god-damned reason," Eric said. "Besides, something's going on out there. Billy was all hot and bothered about something."

"If there had been a real problem, we'd have heard something by now."

"Yeah, I guess so. But if I don't hear from them in the next hour or so . . ."

"If it'll make you feel any better, radio Castries to call you as soon as they dock," she said.

"I'll give 'em one more hour."

*****

Ocee steadily ignored the radio with the staticky voice chirping for the Bajan Lady's crew to answer. "Dey not home," he said out loud.

He debated what to do with the radio. For now, it probably wasn't a problem. There were any number of explanations for why it wasn't being answered. But if the caller thought the radio was out of commission, it might be a different story. Especially with the blonde man's call earlier. He hoped the harbor hadn't given that any credence, though they might if the radio was out. Unfortunately, he didn't know enough about short-wave radios or if the base station could tell if the set had been destroyed. Electronics was not his strong suit. He decided not to take the chance, so he just ignored the calls.

The sun started to sink low in the west, settling below the silhouette of St. Lucia on the horizon. The island lay probably no more than a mile off. Judging from the sun's position, Ocee knew he had only about fifteen minutes of daylight left to find the woman. Tightly gripping the helm, he scanned the water as the boat continued its slight weave. He should be able to cover all the water in between before dark and be on her soon. If he hadn't already passed her, that is. He knew he very well could have.

By the same token, she may well have drowned already. That was a very distinct possibility. After all, they were at least three miles or so from St. Lucia when she jumped. Three miles was a long way to swim.

His first instinct was to sail hell-bent for Vieux Fort, find the car that awaited him, and get to the Castries airport. The last plane for Jamaica left in about two hours and he didn't want to miss it. Especially if the woman was already dead. And surely she was. Surely she couldn't swim this far or stay afloat this long, or make it to shore yet. No way!

Still, he could spare fifteen more minutes. This close to total freedom, no point in taking any chances. If the woman understood anything in the car, or back at the house, she might know that a flight to Jamaica awaited. If she reached shore and got to a phone, or to a policeman, he could kiss that flight good-bye. No, he better keep looking. He might still get lucky. And a little luck would be nice about now.

A sudden movement in the water, just off the starboard bow, grabbed his attention. He squinted and stared hard at the water, trying to pick it up again. Nothing.

He kept his eyes glued to the surface. If it was the woman, and if she saw the boat, she might be under water holding her breath. If that was the case, he wagered he could wait her out.

He cut back on the throttle and idled the boat's engines. Waiting. Patient.

After about a minute, his perseverance paid off. Something broke the surface, directly off starboard. Dorsal fins, swimming hard toward shore. Three of them.

*****

When her arms began to cramp and her shoulders felt as if they could go no more, Karla paused in her swimming to tread

79

water and catch her breath. That had been her pattern from the start. She used her arms to swim, only periodically kicking with her legs, so as to conserve her energy. Then, when her arms and shoulders tired, she rested them by treading water, using her strong and rested legs to stay afloat. When her arms stopped aching, she set off again for shore.

It was starting to get dark, a process Karla tried to will into speeding up. She knew the moon wouldn't make its appearance for an hour or two after sunset. She stared hard at the sun sinking behind St. Lucia, as if she could accelerate its descent with a look. After it set, she would be invisible.

The island seemed so close. She felt as if she could almost touch it if she merely extended her arm, though she knew it was still at least a half-mile away. But that was a mere sprint compared to the distance she had already traveled. Just a closing kick to the finish line. Her emotions chastised her for wasting time treading water with the island that close. Going nowhere. Swim, they screamed.

Swim!

But as loudly as her emotions screamed, her good judgment screamed back louder, urging caution, patience, and pace. Her body needed the rest. She'd cover the distance more quickly with a brief rest, followed by a steady swim, than with a quick spurt that only sapped her precious strength and would probably leave her coming up short. Doubly tragic if she drowned this close to shore. This close to safety. Just rest for a few minutes, her judgment counseled, then go. That's all. Just a few minutes.

Karla's mind swam back to earlier that afternoon. Miles away from her current hell in the Caribbean. Back to an earlier hell. Back to the canefield. Back to the last time she saw Bobby alive. She'd never forget that experience as long as she lived, even assuming she lived for more than another few hours. The whole thing was so unbelievable. Being almost run off the road by the scar-faced man. The horrible look on his face as he pulled the gun from behind him and aimed at their car. Then he fired. Even now, the sound of the gunshots rang in her ears, followed by the sound of breaking glass as bullets shattered the windshield.

She still heard the gasps from her husband as those bullets slammed into his chest and throat. Bobby seemed to move in slow motion as he lurched first backward, then bounced off the headrest. His head rebounded into the steering wheel. Then there was blood – lots of blood. Everywhere, spurting from Bobby's throat, pouring from his chest, painting his lap and torso a bright red.

Karla couldn't remember if she screamed, but she remembered taking Bobby's head in her arms and pulling him to her, cradling his upper body and trying desperately to fill the hole in his throat with her hand. Trying to stop the flow of blood. But there was too much. No way to hold it all inside. He lost what seemed like gallons in just a few short seconds. It continued to flow as she tried to stem the tide.

Now, treading water, she remembered how much he had lost. She remembered the awful gurgling sounds as he gasped for breath. Her heart told her yes, of course he's still alive. But her brain told her no. There was just too much blood. And now Karla wondered if her own life was about to end. If Bobby was already dead, she didn't care. She welcomed death. Since she had met him and especially since they were married just a few short days ago, he had become her reason to live. Together they had hopes for the future. Hopes she never dared entertain before. There was so much they wanted to do and see together. So many dreams to strive for. So many goals to achieve.

Together.

And so many chances. Chances she would have only because of Bobby. A chance to go back to school and finish her degree. To be the first one in her family with a college education, something she had longed for since the day her father died and she dropped out to help support her family. Bobby mentioned it just last night. Did she want to go to college? Did she want to quit her job?

"God, yes!" she said. Did he really mean it? Anything she wanted, he said, was okay with him. Anything.

Yeah, there were so many chances with Bobby. But without him, they were not only gone, they were meaningless even if they weren't gone. So if he was already dead, then she wanted to be dead too. To be with him again. She just didn't want to die at the hands of his murderer. She'd rather drown.

She slowed the kicking of her feet, slowed the paddling of her hands. After a few seconds, all her limbs stilled. She started to sink lower in the water. Lower and lower, until her chin dipped beneath the surface. Going down, she closed her eyes.

But when water flowed over her head, it was as if the warm liquid swept away the morbid melancholy that overtook her. A thought suddenly emblazoned itself on her consciousness: Bobby was still alive! He had to be. And if he was alive, he would be waiting for her to return. She had to get back to him. She at least owed it to him to try.

Low on breath, but with renewed vigor, she kicked with her feet. At the same time, she stroked her arms downward, and propelled herself upward. The pressure of the water weighed her down, pressing against her. It seemed as if she were caught in quicksand, unable to free herself. She stroked harder with her arms, kicked more fiercely with her feet.

Her head spun. A viselike grip tightened around her chest, squeezing what little oxygen was left in her. Looking up, all she saw was darkness. How deep had she sunk? How much farther? A burning pain struck at the center of her chest. Even the darkness of the water grew fuzzy. Her head ached and spun, and her fingers tingled. It felt like pins pricked at her feet and legs. Still she kicked and stroked.

Finally she broke clear, lurching into the night air. She gasped for breath. Slowly her senses returned, her limbs regained their feeling.

Without another wasted second, she struck out again for shore. To safety.

To Bobby.

But she had traveled only a few feet before something hard and rough – and big – hit her legs. Solid, but at the same time giving way. It wasn't like she hit something, but more like something hit her and then moved away.

Not a violent hit. The contact was soft, but firm. More like a nudge than a hit.

Something broke the surface in front of her. Dark and triangular. It seemed as if her heart stopped beating. Her blood froze as recognition set in.

A fin!

She stopped swimming and stilled herself in the water. The fin began to circle.

In a few seconds, it was joined by two more.

CHAPTER TWELVE

Frozen with fear, Karla stopped swimming and began gently treading water. She lightly paddled with her arms and legs to stay afloat. Three fins now circled her, evenly spaced, their circle separated by a diameter of about twenty-five feet. That meant that, at any given point, the sharks were no more than twelve feet from her as they circumnavigated her position. She watched, horrified, as they continued to circle, then gradually began to tighten their circle. Within a matter of minutes, the diameter had squeezed to about fifteen feet, at which point the sharks leveled off and again maintained their distance.

Karla's gentle treading was barely enough to keep her afloat. She sank low in the water, her chin touching liquid. She determined not to do anything to either aggravate or attract the sharks. That included agitating the water by kicking her feet and arms.

The sharks continued to circle.

Periodically, a fin disappeared beneath the surface. Within a few seconds, Karla felt a nudge or bump as the creature scoped her out. Then the fin surfaced again, in its original position in the circle, and the pace continued. She wasn't sure if the sharks were merely cautious, unsure whether she was dangerous to them, or if they were just playing with their food.

A cold chill passed through her as she envisioned herself being torn apart by sharks. She had seen *Jaws*, parts one through whatever, and she remembered the horror as Robert Shaw had been devoured by Bruce, the mechanical shark. She only hoped the end would come as quickly for her. At least, she rationalized, it would likely be quicker, and probably more pleasant, than dying at the hands of Oliver Clarke.

*****

On a hunch, Ocee steered the boat in the direction the sharks had been heading. They seemed to be going somewhere with a purpose. Maybe they knew something, he thought. Maybe they knew where there was a swimmer in distress.

Still uncomfortable with steering the monohull, it had taken him a few minutes to adjust its course from the serpentine weave to the straight line headed obliquely toward shore. By the time he had accomplished the adjustment, he had lost sight of the fins. But he had seen the direction they had been heading. They hadn't been weaving serpentine-fashion. They had been swimming in a straight line. He felt confident he was also now heading in that same straight line.

Carefully watching the horizon ahead, he kept an eye out for the white woman in the water.

*****

Karla winced as a fin again dropped from sight. She held her breath and waited for the inevitable nudge.

Suddenly she felt a sharp pain in her foot. Simultaneously, she felt herself being yanked downward. Her head dipped beneath the water as the shark gripped her foot in its jaws and pulled. She swallowed a mouthful of water, surprised at the suddenness of the attack. This was something new. And definitely not welcome.

Quickly regaining her senses, she realized that the shark's grip on her foot wasn't firm. It hadn't sunk its teeth into her, but merely held her with its teeth as it tugged. Karla remembered what she had heard about crocodiles grabbing their prey and pulling them under water, going into a "death roll" before eating. She wondered if sharks attended the same school of etiquette.

She had once read that sharks have particularly sensitive noses. She bent her knee and raised her free foot upward, bringing her knee almost to her chest. Then, as fast and hard as the water would allow, she brought her heel downward on what she hoped was the shark's nose.

Apparently what she had read had been correct, because the shark immediately released her foot from its grip. When it did, Karla kicked downward with both legs and swam for the surface. She had already been under for about thirty seconds and was almost out of breath. Given the surprise of the attack and the water she had swallowed when she first ducked under, surviving even those thirty seconds seemed miraculous. She kicked furiously with her feet. It seemed as if she made no progress at all. Her body screamed for air, a hot vise grip on her chest. Her arms flailed at the water.

She didn't know how far under she had been dragged. Her lungs seemed to be on the verge of bursting when she finally broke the surface, coughing and sputtering. She breathed in huge gulps, trying to take in as much oxygen as she could. She wiped water from her eyes and oriented herself, scanning the water around her.

Two fins still circled. She wondered if they had kept up their pace all the while she was under, or whether they had themselves gone under to see what their friend was doing with dinner.

She also wondered where the third was and whether it was pissed.

She heard a sudden noise to her left – a rippling of water. She snapped her head in that direction, just in time to see the third fin resurface and take its place back in the circle. Tears formed in her eyes. She bowed her head and prayed for deliverance.

While she desperately prayed and treaded water, Karla heard another sound behind her. This sound seemed more distant. She opened her eyes and twisted around. It sounded like a motor, but was still too far away to see clearly.

As she stared into the dark distance, she found herself torn by two competing emotions – pessimism that said it was Oliver Clarke come to recapture her and optimism that said it was a St. Lucian fisherman returning home from a day of fishing. She renewed her prayers, asking God to deliver unto her the latter.

When she opened her eyes again, the source of the sound was just coming into view. A boat with a familiar shape. One she had seen before. A monohull, with a sole sailor at the helm – a black man, barely visible in the dark. In fact, only visible because of his silhouette and the glint of his pearly white teeth, exposed in a wicked grin.

Oliver Clarke.

She wasn't sure whether Clarke had seen her yet, but the boat quickly bore down upon her, sailing hell-bent in a straight line. The circling fins broke off and swam away, leaving her alone for the first time since their appearance. She had no idea how long they had been her companions.

Karla took a deep breath, ducked under water, and swam to the north at a ninety degree angle away from the path of the oncoming boat. She hoped that when she surfaced, the boat would still be moving in its original path toward shore. Then she would again make for shore at an oblique angle back to the south, following the sharks.

When she surfaced thirty seconds later, the boat was nowhere to be seen.

CHAPTER THIRTEEN

Brit Reavis, Bobby's fraternal twin, sat in a window seat and stared out at the ocean. Beside him in the American Airlines airliner sat Mary Sandone, Karla's mother. Across the aisle from Mary sat Andy Fletcher, one of Bobby's law partners and his best friend. They were soon to arrive in San Juan, Puerto Rico. From there, they would connect to Barbados where Constable Glenroy Wood was to meet them.

Brit had been speechless when he got the call from Andy yesterday afternoon telling him Bobby had been shot. Mary Sandone, on the other hand, went into hysterics when Brit told her Karla was missing. Tall, dark-complected, with long graying hair, Mary was very much her daughter's mother, sharing the same quiet grace and beauty that was so attractive in Karla. But that quiet grace went out the window at the news that her oldest daughter – the one who married the successful lawyer, the one who gave up college to work and help raise the younger kids, the one who was always so bright and cheerful – was missing, possibly kidnapped.

Brit was glad he told her in person. At least he could hug her and tell her that everything was going to be all right – something they both knew was probably a lie. But it helped to get her through the first rough moments.

Then came the waiting. They weren't able to get a plane until today and, cliché though it was, Brit couldn't remember a night so dark and so long. Not even the night when he and Bobby got the call telling them that their mother's cancer had finally won the battle. At least they had each other that night, and shared the peace that her painful struggle was finally over. They took comfort in that, even though they would both miss her terribly.

But now Brit faced uncertainty. Andy told him he thought the Barbadian police were holding something back, but he wasn't sure what. He wasn't sure if it had to do with Bobby or Karla. All he knew for sure was that Bobby was in critical condition with at least three bullet holes in him. Karla was gone, God knows where! Bobby came through surgery all right, but there was no definite prognosis. His condition was still critical and he was still unconscious.

And Karla was still missing.

Brit cast a glance at Mary. She was sleeping. That was good. Brit had stayed with her and the kids last night, and she never once shut her eyes. She spent the whole night pacing and praying, praying and pacing. And crying. Brit was glad that sleep had finally caught up with her. Even though it might not be a peaceful sleep, it was still sleep. He knew her body needed the rest.

Across the aisle, Andy sat rigidly in his seat and held a news magazine in front of him. But Brit knew that Andy wasn't reading. Either that or he was the world's slowest reader, because he was still on the same page as the last time Brit glanced his way. And the time before that, and the time before that.

Brit knew that Andy was probably hurting as much as

anyone. The three of them grew up together in east Dallas, before the Reavis brothers went off to Baylor on baseball scholarships, while Andy took a football scholarship to TCU. But they got back together when Bobby and Andy started law school together at SMU, and Brit entered Southwestern Medical School in Dallas. They rented a house together in the University Park area during those years, and renewed a fast and lasting friendship.

Even though Brit and Bobby were brothers, Brit always thought he and Andy looked more like brothers than did the two Reavis boys. While Bobby was well over six feet tall, both Brit and Andy cleared a six-foot doorway with ease. Bobby was lean yet muscled, but Brit and Andy were both stocky and muscle-bound, their frames befitting their athletic positions – Brit had been a catcher on the baseball team, while Andy was a nose guard on the football team.

The similarities between the two didn't end there. Both Andy and Brit had thick black hair, prominent chins and broad noses. The only real distinguishing features were Brit's glasses, round wire-frames, and Andy's badly chipped front tooth. Most people who saw the three together assumed that Bobby was the non-sibling. But in truth, all three were close as brothers. Now, as they winged their way toward the Caribbean, Brit and Andy felt a bond they had never felt before. Their other brother was slipping away from them, and they felt helpless to stop it.

*****

Word of the shooting and possible abduction spread throughout Barbados to every level of government. Police officials were put on alert and provided descriptions of Karla Reavis. National Defense Force troops were dispatched to the site of the shooting with instructions to fan out from there and to leave no stone unturned in St. Joseph and St. Thomas Parishes.

An official edict was issued by the Prime Minister dedicating all efforts and available resources to find the missing American woman. The past manhunts for Oliver Clarke started to look like nothing more than minor search parties, by comparison, as law enforcement and military personnel instantly mobilized throughout the island nation.

The media was also notified and joined the massive effort. Already, special editions of both island newspapers were being typeset for immediate publication and imminent delivery, while special bulletins were broadcast on Barbadian television and radio. Flyers with Karla's physical description were printed for distribution in stores and public buildings across the island, with plans to update as soon as photographs were available.

Sergeant Walker returned to Queen Elizabeth Hospital long before noon, and only minutes after he received the call from the surgeon who had spent hours yesterday evening trying to stop Reavis's internal bleeding. The doctor told him Reavis was a lucky man. The bullet that entered his throat missed the carotid artery by only the smallest of margins. As it was, it nicked the outer edge, just enough to allow a flow of blood to escape. Fortunately the car in the canefield was found no more than fifteen minutes after the shooting, judging by the loss of Reavis's blood.

And Reavis had lost a lot of blood, no doubt about it. Coupled with the bullet that entered directly into his chest, its path diverted and its speed slowed by a thick slab of pectoral muscle, and the third bullet that passed into

Reavis's side and entered his lung, the three wounds drained a substantial amount of blood from the man's body. None of the three, individually, were life-threatening, except maybe the one that punctured his lung. But taken in combination, the victim was lucky to be alive, with no promise that he would still be this lucky twelve or twenty-four hours from now.

The sound of his cell phone ringing distracted Wallace. He snatched it to his ear. "This is Sergeant Walker."

"Sergeant, dis is Glenroy. I tryin' to reach you all de time since getting' dis report. De report is call in dis mornin', but is only now to me."

"Yes, Glenroy, what is it?" Wallace asked. His voice rose with anticipation.

"De Bajan Lady have a boat missin'. She missin' all night. De owner say one of de boatmen call yesteday, late. De boatman say Bajan man and white woman travel togedder. Say when hog dance, look fuh rain."

Wallace had heard that Bajan proverb before, and he knew it meant that unusual signs were omens of unusual events. And the boatman thought there was something unusual about the couple on board the Bajan Lady's boat.

"A Bajan was traveling with a white woman on the boat?" Wallace asked.

"He also read de paper today. He say de white woman on Bajan Lady is de one we lookin' fo'."

"Where was the boat going?"

"Castries."

"Call St. Lucia. Tell them Oliver Clarke is probably already there. Tell them to watch all boats and planes. And give me the number for Bajan Lady."

*****

Wallace dialed the number for Bajan Lady Excursions and soon had Eric Baldwin on the line, who told him about the call from his crew.

"Did he say anything else, other than that he didn't think they went together?" Wallace asked.

"He just said she was too classy to go with the Bajan. When I tried to radio him later, I couldn't reach anyone. I assumed they were snorkeling or something. But it's been all night now and still no contact."

"Uh huh."

"Then I heard the report on the radio about the missing American, and the girl on the boat sure fit the description. I looked her charge record up – her credit card reserved the excursion. In the corner, in tiny letters, it says 's.o.s.'"

"You didn't notice that before?" Wallace said, sick at heart that she had tried to call for help hours ago and it went unheeded.

"My wife handled the payment, but she said she didn't check the signature. Had no reason to." Baldwin failed to mention that he had looked at the charge slip after Billy's call yesterday, but didn't see the letters then, either.

"Did you get a good look at the Bajan?"

"Not really. No dreadlocks, though. And one of his hands was all bandaged up. I remember that. He had a scar on his face that showed beneath his sunglasses."

"Which hand was bandaged?" Wallace asked.

"I don't remember."

"Which side of his face was the scar on?"

"I don't know. My wife saw it, not me. She just remembers that it ran horizontally across his cheek, under his eye. She could barely see it under the sunglasses."

Wallace was sure the man was Oliver Clarke. Maybe the wife would recognize a photograph. And if it was Clarke, they needed to amend the description they sent across the island. They also needed to send a description to St. Lucia and hope they weren't too late.

*****

Ocee had missed his plane the night before, so he had been forced to hide in the jungle overnight. Driving a stolen car, he now pulled into Vieux Fort less than an hour before the next plane was set to leave. The car he had been promised was where it was supposed to be, so he dumped the stolen vehicle in favor of the one that waited for him. An open plane ticket was in the glove compartment and the keys were under the front seat, just as planned. He jumped in and started the motor, which turned over on the first twist of the key. It was going to be close, and he didn't want to miss a second plane.

*****

The St. Lucia police officer in charge listened carefully as Glenroy described Oliver Clarke and Karla Reavis over the phone. He promised to call the harbor and the airport and to put out the description. He also asked for pictures, if Glenroy had them, and promised to circulate them on the island as well.

When he hung up, he turned back to the pulp novel he was reading. One more chapter before he finished the book. He would make the calls then.

*****

Ocee turned into the parking lot of the small airport. The turbo-prop plane waited on the tarmac with its door open and a jetway pulled up beside it.

Ocee checked his watch – five minutes 'til take-off. He screeched the car to a stop in a space close to the terminal. He tucked his knife and gun under the front seat, grabbed a small suitcase from the back seat, and raced to the gate. With just seconds to spare, he sprinted through the metal detector, down the long hallway, and to the gate. Just before the ground crew pulled the jetway back, he bolted up the stairs, two at a time, and boarded the airplane.

The plane's engines roared to life. The props went into their rapid-spin routine and the pilot taxied to the runway. Within five minutes of Ocee's boarding, the plane left the runway, banked northwest, and headed for Kingston, Jamaica.

As the plane cleared land and began crossing water, the policeman in Castries dialed the director of security at the airport. The director took down the description of a non-dreadlocked Oliver Clarke and promised to post it at all security checks and gates.

CHAPTER FOURTEEN

A tiny gray-haired man approached Wallace Walker and extended his hand. Befitting its owner, it, too, was tiny, with stubby fingers. Hardly what Wallace expected for a surgeon. He shook the hand.

"Sergeant Walker, I hope you got some rest last night," Doctor Rodney Simpson said good-naturedly.

"Enough," Wallace lied. In fact, he hadn't slept a wink because he was overseeing a night search for Oliver Clarke. "How is Mr. Reavis?"

Dr. Simpson folded his arms across his frail chest and sat on the arm of a chair. "Well, his condition stabilized somewhat overnight, and he actually gives indications of regaining consciousness."

"How can you tell that?"

"It's quite simple, really. He moves, he twitches, he even tries to grit his teeth. Of course, he can't because of the oxygen tube, but he tries. That's all consistent with deep sleep, as opposed to unconsciousness. His vital signs are good. All in all, his condition appears to be remarkably good for a man who's been through what he's been through."

Walker nodded. "If he regains consciousness, will I be able to talk to him?"

"Hard to say. If he wakes up and is alert, then I'd say yes. I don't see any reason why he couldn't talk. But he's had quite a jolt, and I can't be sure he won't go into shock when he hears of his wife. So, I caution you, do not simply unload the bad news on him. Let's wait until we see how well he regains his strength, both physical and mental, before burdening him with bad news."

"He's going to want to know."

"Yes, I'm sure he will. I'm just saying be tactful. Diplomatic. Go easy with the news."

Wallace nodded. The doctor made sense. Sooner or later Reavis would have to know, and Wallace dreaded breaking the news to him.

"Mr. Reavis's brother is on his way here from Texas, even as we speak," Wallace said. "Do you think there is any merit to having him deliver the news?"

"That's an excellent idea," Simpson said. "He's going to be upset and disoriented, and it will make him more comfortable, and more receptive to reality, to have familiar faces around."

"Dr. Reavis should be here in a few hours."

"Dr. Reavis?" Simpson asked.

"Yes. Dr. Brit Reavis, the victim's brother. He's a medical doctor in Texas."

"What specialty?" Simpson's tone suggested to Wallace that he feared an American doctor would second-guess his every move.

"I don't know."

"I see," Simpson said, obviously unhappy. "Well, please let me know when he arrives. I should like to speak to him, doctor to doctor."

Bobby had still not awakened by the time Constable Wood ushered Brit Reavis, Andy Fletcher, and Mary Sandone into the waiting room at Queen Elizabeth Hospital. Wallace Walker was still there, talking on his cell as he tried to mix supervising the hunt with waiting to talk to Bobby. When he saw Glenroy leading the three Americans, he terminated his conversation and presented himself. After appropriate introductions were made, Andy got right to the point.

"What the hell happened?"

Wallace briefly related the history of Oliver Clarke, followed by a summary of the events of the past eighteen hours. Andy and Brit listened grimly, their faces devoid of emotion. Mrs. Sandone, in contrast, wept openly as she heard the story of the violent man the police suspected of holding her daughter. It was more than she could bear, and she excused herself to find the ladies' room.

The men stood silently as she made her exit. She rebuffed Brit's pantomimed efforts to comfort her and hurried to cry alone in the restroom. They watched her disappear behind the door, then resumed their discussion. When Walker finished his narrative, the men fell silent for a few minutes before Andy spoke again.

"How can a man stay at large for so long on such a small island?"

Wallace flashed an embarrassed smile. "It's not that simple, Mr. Fletcher. Though the island is small, it is full of hiding places. And Clarke knows them well. We also suspect he's been helped by islanders who are either his friends or who are afraid of him."

"What are the odds of catching him now?"

Wallace smiled again. His face flushed with embarrassment as the conversation led up to something he was reluctant to tell these people – that Oliver Clarke was, in all likelihood, already off the island. If that was the case, they might well never catch him.

"It's hard to speculate on something like that."

"Do you think he's still got Karla?" Brit asked.

"We don't know," Wallace said.

"Well, I assume you've got men crawling all over every hill, cave, and valley on this island," Andy said. An agitated tone invaded his voice. "Like I said, it's a small island. He's got to be here somewhere."

Glenroy, who had been standing silently by, ready to offer any help if asked by Wallace, dropped his head and stared at the floor. Wallace cleared his throat nervously before answering.

"He may have already left the island."

Andy and Brit riveted their eyes on Wallace.

"What do you mean?" Andy asked.

"We received a report from an excursion service that a boat was chartered yesterday for a Bajan man and a white woman. The boat was going to St. Lucia, but apparently never reached its destination. The owner of the service identified Mrs. Reavis as the woman passenger."

"Where is St. Lucia?" Brit asked.

"It's a near island. But if Clarke commandeered the boat, there's no guarantee it went to St. Lucia. There are other islands within easy sailing distance."

"So what you're saying is that he's off this island, and now you don't know what island he's on?"

Wallace nodded. "Yes. Unfortunately that's true."

"So he's going to get away with this." Brit almost spat the words out. "He's going to get away with Karla, and there's not a damn thing anyone can do about it."

"Evah pig got a Saturday," Glenroy said softly.

Andy glared at the native policeman.

"Evah pig got a Saturday," Glenroy repeated.

"What's that mean?" Brit asked. He looked to Wallace for an interpretation.

"That's an old Bajan proverb. On Barbados, farmers take their animals to slaughter on Saturdays. So, every pig has a Saturday when he goes to be slaughtered. It may not be this Saturday, or the next, or the next. But that Saturday will come. The same is true of people. Everybody has to face his day of judgment, sooner or later. Even Oliver Clarke."

"Evah pig got a Saturday," Glenroy said a third time.

"You make damn sure that bastard gets his," Andy said.

CHAPTER FIFTEEN

Glenroy drove the three Americans to a nearby hotel where Wallace had reserved rooms for them. After they checked in, Brit convinced Mary to stay in her room and try to sleep. Exhaustion set in on all three of them, but Mary was reacting the worst, with fits of uncontrollable crying followed by severe depression. Dr. Simpson prescribed a sedative for her, which they filled at the hospital pharmacy before going to the hotel. Now, after seeing that she was comfortable in her room, Brit and Andy returned to the hospital.

Brit convinced Dr. Simpson to allow them to see Bobby, who remained in the intensive care ward. Though he had not yet regained consciousness, his vital signs remained stable. Simpson agreed to break the hospital rules against visitors in intensive care and allowed them in. After all, he rationalized, there were extenuating circumstances and they had traveled a long way.

Simpson ushered Brit and Andy to the ward. He stopped at the door, pointed to Bobby's bed, then left them alone. They paused, as if they feared entering would set some irreversible death march in motion. Finally, with Brit leading the way, they gingerly stepped inside and approached. Andy was afraid to see him, having conjured up visions of Bobby looking like a vegetable, lying limply, hooked up to a vast array of futuristic machines keeping him alive. As he neared his friend, he realized his fears were all in his mind. With the exception of the breathing tube inserted into Bobby's mouth and an i.v. in his muscular left arm, his friend was machine-free. Even the i.v. was innocent enough.

Confident now that Bobby didn't look so terrible, he quickly caught up to Brit, who was already standing beside the bed, softly stroking his brother's hair. But Andy's momentary confidence deserted him as quickly as it had arrived. As he drew abreast of Brit and looked at the still figure in the bed, he was stunned by the pale face in front of him. The bandages swathed around his throat and torso were not nearly as frightening as the lack of color in Bobby's face. Were it not for the steady, yet shallow, breathing aided by the oxygen tube, Andy would have sworn he was looking at a cadaver.

The two men stood together and looked at their brother and friend. Brit continued to stroke the unruly lock of hair that hung over Bobby's forehead. Andy carefully lifted Bobby's limp hand, the one that Bobby used to clamp on him like a vise in their running arm-wrestling competition, and caressed the back of it. Out of the corner of his eye, he saw something drop to the floor beside him. Glancing down, he saw a small pool form on Brit's shoe, added to by a steady rat-tat-tat of tears dropping down. Brit, head down, unashamedly wept for his brother. Andy felt tears well in his own eyes and start their waterfall.

Andy placed his free arm around Brit's shoulder and pulled him close. Brit turned, buried his face in Andy's shoulder, and sobbed uncontrollably. Andy held him tightly, and together they cried for their compadre – for his hurt and pain from the shooting, and for the hurt and pain he didn't yet know about: the loss of his wife.

Karla's loss, in fact, ate at them more than even Bobby's death-like appearance. They knew that Bobby would get over the shooting. He was strong and the doctor said his wounds were not life-threatening. Yeah, he'd recover from that.

But if Karla was gone forever, could he recover from that? And even if the police found her, if something had happened to her, could he recover from that? They both wondered. They knew how much those two loved each other and how much their lives were intertwined. If she was gone for good, Andy and Brit both knew it would leave a hole in Bobby's life that could never be filled. Knowing that, they wept for Bobby.

And for Karla.

*****

Brit sat on a couch in the waiting room while Andy paced, wearing a trail in front of the nurses' station. Neither of them had spoken since leaving Bobby's side an hour ago. They waited, puffy-eyed from crying, and hoped he would regain consciousness soon. But if he did – or when he did, they both preferred to think – another difficult moment was coming.

"How are we gonna tell him?" Andy asked. He stopped his pacing and turned to look at Brit.

Brit returned his gaze and smiled sadly. "What the bullets didn't do, this might. Kill him, I mean."

"I'm not sure I can be the one to tell him."

"It's probably better if he hears it from me."

"It's funny. On the one hand, I want him to wake up

right now. But on the other hand, I keep thinking the police might find her at any minute and she'll be okay, and everything will be all right. And the longer he's out, the better chance it'll happen, so there's no bad news for him when he wakes up."

Brit slipped down in his seat and propped his feet on the coffee table in front of him, accidentally knocking a magazine to the floor. He stared at the magazine for a minute, but at first made no effort to pick it up. Finally, he reached down, picked up the magazine, and replaced it on the table, carefully lining it up with others.

Worn out from his frantic pacing, Andy plopped into a chair across from Brit and watched his friend straighten the magazines. "Bobby would have wanted them that way," Andy said.

Brit frowned.

Andy nodded toward the table. "The magazines. Bobby would have wanted them that way."

Brit smiled. "Yeah. He used to drive me crazy with that. Remember how he always lined 'em up just perfect on his coffee table? Sometimes I'd shuffle 'em like a bunch of dominoes just to get a rise out of him."

Andy chuckled softly and leaned his head back. He closed his eyes and gently massaged his temples. "God, I'm tired."

Brit also leaned his head back and closed his eyes. He had no sooner assumed that position when he heard footsteps behind him. He looked over his shoulder. Andy was already standing as Dr. Simpson walked into the waiting room.

"He's awake," Simpson said.

"Can we talk to him?" Brit asked.

"He's been through a tough time, I guess I don't have to tell you. I've put in a call to Sergeant Walker, who also wants to talk to him, so keep it short if you will. Let's not wear him out right now."

Brit and Andy nodded dumbly as Simpson turned and walked back to the ward. The two friends exchanged glances, then fell in line behind the doctor. Again Simpson stopped at the door, then stepped aside to allow them to enter alone. As before, they both hesitated, each wanting the other to lead the way. It had been hard enough to see Bobby earlier, but it was even harder now. There was bad news to be shared. Unfortunately the "at any minute" they were wishing for just a while ago hadn't materialized. Karla was still missing and, for all they knew, would never be found. There was no silver lining in this dark cloud. At least not as far as they could see.

With a deep breath, Brit took the lead. He tiptoed quietly toward Bobby's bed, then paused a few feet away. Andy pulled even and they both looked at the figure in the bed. He looked no different than he did an hour ago, lying deathly still, his eyes closed and his face painted in a pale death-mask.

"Is he awake?" Andy whispered.

Bobby fluttered his eyes a few times, then opened them. When he saw Brit and Andy, crow's feet spread from his eyes as he crinkled his face into a weak smile. The oxygen-tube had been removed, and he opened his mouth to speak, but only a hoarse growl came out.

"Are you thirsty?" Brit asked.

Bobby nodded slightly, unable to bend his head much because of his heavily bandaged neck.

Brit looked over his shoulder at Simpson, who stood a few

feet behind them. "Doc?" he asked, raising his eyebrows in inquiry.

"On the table by the bed," Simpson said. "His throat is probably sore, so take it easy. But a little water is okay."

Brit picked up the white pitcher and filled a plastic cup, then helped Bobby take a few swallows. His hands shook and a few drops spilled on the bed.

Bobby whispered weakly, too soft to be heard.

"What?" Brit said. He leaned close to listen.

"The steady hands of a surgeon," Bobby said, his voice stronger.

Brit smiled and shook his head. "Sorry, Bubba. Just glad you're still with us. You gave us a pretty good scare, you know."

Bobby nodded again, then looked past Brit to Andy. "Hey, Fletch."

"Good to see you, man," Andy said.

Dr. Simpson stepped between them for a moment. "Remember, gentlemen, not too long. He needs rest."

"Thanks, Doc," Brit said.

Simpson looked at Bobby. "Don't try to talk too much, Mr. Reavis."

Bobby nodded, his new primary form of communication, then lifted his hand and waved. Simpson nodded in return and left the room.

Andy and Brit stood awkwardly beside the bed, shuffling their feet in a moment of uncomfortable silence. It was as if they were strangers who suddenly had been thrown into a room together and found they had nothing in common.

"Where's Karla?"

Neither Brit nor Andy seemed prepared for the question when Bobby asked it. "Her mom is here," Brit said.

Bobby raised his head and tried to look past Brit to the hallway. "Is Karla with her?"

"We checked Mary into a hotel. She was exhausted, so we thought she should rest."

"What happened?" Andy asked.

Bobby laid his head back on the pillow and closed his eyes. He furrowed his brow in a deep frown as he thought back to the canefield. "I saw the gun, then he shot." He paused, then added, "I couldn't go fast enough."

He stopped talking and silence filled the room again.

"You're gonna be okay, Bubba," Brit said. "The doctors say you're gonna make it just fine."

Bobby nodded, then opened his eyes and looked at Brit. "The truth," he whispered. A tear glistened in the corner of his eye. "Karla."

Andy looked at the floor while Brit locked eyes with his brother. "We don't know."

Bobby turned his head away.

The tear leaked and streamed down his left cheek.

CHAPTER SIXTEEN

Wendell Cox met Glenroy at Castries airport on St. Lucia. Wendell had been a member of the Castries Police Department for as long as Glenroy had been with the force in Bridgetown. Glenroy called him as soon as Barbadian authorities learned of the possibility that Oliver Clarke might have commandeered the Bajan Lady to St. Lucia, and Wendell invited him to Castries to join in a coastal search for the boat. After all, if Clarke had actually come to the island, he had to leave the boat somewhere. It would be difficult to hide a boat of the size described by the excursion service's owner. From the airport, the two policemen drove straight to Castries harbor and boarded a police motorboat piloted by yet a third policeman. From there, they set out north around the island.

Wendell knew the island's dimensions by heart. One of the larger of the Windward Islands in the West Indies, St. Lucia was slightly larger than Barbados, but not as large as Martinique, its neighbor twenty-five miles to the north. Somewhat pear-shaped, the island was twenty-seven miles long at its longest point and fourteen miles in breadth at its widest, giving it a circumference of roughly one hundred-fifty miles.

Wendell had seen every mile before. To do justice to their coastal search, particularly given the island's many coves and bays, he knew they might be spending the better part of the day motoring around the island. He wanted a second boat to assist, to start south from Castries, but his superiors had refused. They doubted that Oliver Clarke was on their island and were willing to devote only two officers and one boat as a friendly accommodation to Barbadian authorities.

St. Lucia shared the tropical climate of its neighbor to the east, Barbados, and the temperature was already in the lower eighties, on its way up the thermometer. There had been a slight misting of rain earlier that morning, adding to the island's annual ninety inches, but now the sun burned off the clouds, providing good visibility for the search. Glenroy stood just behind the driver, with Wendell at his side, as they scanned the fringes of the island as the driver hugged the shoreline. Tropical vegetation and a mass of mountains rose steeply from the water. The highest mountains were to the south, but they still presented an imposing backdrop to the island's coast.

The driver kept a constant speed of fifteen miles per hour as he maneuvered through Choc Bay, Gros Islets Bay, between St. Lucia and tiny Pigeon Island, then around Cap Point on the northernmost edge of the island. Just after noon the searchers stopped in Grande Anse on the northeast shore for more fuel, then continued their search.

It quickly became apparent that a second day might be required. Studying a map, they decided to go as far as Vieux Fort on the southern end of the island and then call it a day. There was no point in hurrying just for the sake of finishing in a day and take a chance on missing something.

"You know Ocee is take de woman?" Wendell asked as they

glided toward Bouche Island.

"He is shoot de mon and now she gone. Where else she be?" Glenroy paused a minute to let his friend follow the logic. "She have to be wit' Ocee."

Wendell nodded. Even on St. Lucia, they knew of Oliver Clarke's reputation and his appetites. The real question was whether he had left her alive. History didn't provide an answer – sometimes in the past he left a rape victim alive, sometimes he didn't. But if he was in the process of fleeing from the islands, chances were good that he wouldn't want to leave anyone behind to provide clues as to his whereabouts. Wendell and Glenroy both knew that Karla's only chance was for them to find her before Ocee made his move.

*****

Wallace Walker gingerly tiptoed into the room. Brit Reavis and Andy Fletcher stood beside the bed, nervously shuffling their feet and looking around, while Bobby Reavis wept silently. Wallace knew instantly that the men had told Reavis the bad news. He silently cursed Oliver Clarke for the thousandth time since his involvement in the recapture effort. He had seen this grief before – in other victims of Clarke's vicious attacks and on the faces of their relatives and loved ones. He renewed his vow to bring Oliver Clarke to justice.

Wallace hated to intrude now, but he needed to ask the questions. The excursion service owner had tentatively identified the man who sailed on the Bajan Lady as Oliver Clarke, but he couldn't be positive. The only photographs of Clarke showed him to be dreadlocked, but Eric Baldwin said the scar-faced man who rented the boat wore his hair short. Though it might seem a minor change, the difference in appearance could be dramatic. Wallace needed Reavis's description of his assailant.

Wallace stepped to the foot of the bed. "Mr. Reavis, I'm Sergeant Walker of the Barbados National Defense Force. I'm sorry for what's happened."

No response.

"I'm afraid I have nothing to report at this time," Wallace said, answering Bobby's unspoken question, while at the same time dashing his fondest hopes. "But I'm afraid I have to ask you some questions. Now – "

"Can't this wait?" Andy asked. "I mean, you know, I mean – can't this wait?"

Wallace bit his lip. Although he was sympathetic to their plight, he had been waiting hours for Reavis to awaken so he could question him – before he lapsed back into unconsciousness or, worse yet, repressed or blocked out the entire event. Wallace didn't know what Bobby might know or could tell him, but if there was any chance Clarke said or did something to tip his hand, he wanted to know.

"Mr. Fletcher, I understand how you feel. But I have a job to do. And that job is to capture Oliver Clarke. Anything I can learn that might help me do that will help us find Mrs. Reavis."

"That's all right."

The voice was weak, but it was firm, coming from the figure in the bed. The three men turned to look at the speaker.

"Ask me," Bobby said. "Find Karla."

*****

Just south of Port Praslin, a finger of land known as Trou Gras Point jutted into the Caribbean. The bottom of the finger slid back into St. Lucia, creating a tiny, natural harbor.

Thick vegetation crowded its shoreline. The police boat rounded the point and was heading into the shallow cove when Glenroy noticed an unnatural grouping of vegetation at the deepest point.

"Dere!" he exclaimed, pointing.

The driver cut the motor. The three men moved to the bow of the boat and peered steadily ahead, squinting into the sun that burned high overhead. Just in front of them lay a freshly-cut pile of green brush stacked along the water's edge. The boat slowly floated toward the pile. Someone had been through here recently and apparently tried to hide something. The pile didn't appear big enough to conceal a boat, but it was worth checking out.

As they got closer, the searchers noticed movement in front of the pile. The water flowed in a small channel, coming from the direction of the shoreline. A small river or stream spilled into the bay, its mouth concealed by the brush. Whoever placed the brush wasn't concealing an object; they were concealing a water passage inland.

The nose of the small police boat brushed against the stack of wood and leaves, but the boat had not yet run aground. Wendell tested the bottom and found that the stream cut a channel about five feet deep and about fifteen feet wide. The driver steered the boat ashore to the left of the brush-pile, and the three men got out on dry ground.

Wendell led the way, with Glenroy behind him, while the driver stayed and guarded the boat. After getting past the brush pile, Wendell turned to his right and reached the stream. He saw that its shores had been violently disturbed, as if a large object, too wide for the channel, was forced ashore. Glancing to his left, Wendell's hypothesis was confirmed.

As best he could tell in the shadows, the woman was Anglo, but dark-complected or very tan. Long, slender legs showed signs of belonging to an athlete, given shape by muscles in the calves and thighs. The legs themselves were spread apart, in the trademark position of a rape victim, but she still wore shorts.

Taking a deep breath, Glenroy pushed the brush aside and moved to the body. He took a deep breath before pushing aside the growth that covered the upper torso. He shined the light on the face of a dark-haired woman, her face battered beyond recognition. A deep gash ran horizontally across her throat, from ear to ear.

CHAPTER SEVENTEEN

Brit and Andy both sat in while Sergeant Walker interviewed Bobby. Bobby horrified them as he recounted, in excruciating detail, exactly what happened in the canefield with the scar-faced man. Bobby told how the man cut them off on the dirt road, how he got out of his car, grinning, and then how he leveled the pistol and pulled the trigger.

He recounted the sting of the first shots that pierced his body, slamming him around in the small car. He remembered watching his own blood as it spurted from the wounds and feeling numbness in his chest. Then he remembered Karla pulling him to her, cradling him in her arms, and trying to plug the hole in his throat as his blood spilled.

He was also vaguely aware of the man approaching the car, still holding the pistol, and moving around to the passenger side, where Karla sat, still frantically trying to quell the flow of blood from his throat. He must have blacked out then, because the last he remembered was Karla holding him in her arms, and he remembered thinking that they would both die in the hot, dusty canefield. But he remembered being comforted by the thought that at least they would die together.

After Walker left, Andy drove to the hotel in a car the

police arranged for them, picked up Mary, and brought her to the hospital. Now the three Americans fidgeted in the intensive care waiting room, hoping for word from the police and awaiting Bobby's next awakening.

No one said a word. Andy had already told Mary that Karla was still missing, but that the police were doing everything possible to find her. He didn't tell her that there was a good chance that Karla's captor had escaped the island and might have taken her with him. He wanted her to keep her hopes up, and he knew that if she knew Clarke was off the island, she would find it hard to be optimistic. Still, they held out hopes that the police would arrive any second with good news.

*****

Wallace Walker stepped into the waiting area, reluctant to intrude on their grief, and doubly reluctant to bear bad news. The somber look on his face as he addressed Brit and Andy spoke volumes, and both men felt their hearts sink at his appearance. Mary sat to the side, unable to read Walker's face. Nevertheless, she stiffened in her chair when he addressed Brit.

"Dr. Reavis, may I have a word with you in private?"

Andy and Brit exchanged glances, then Brit looked at Mary. Her face was pale and her lip quivered. Walker looked at Brit and motioned with his head that Brit should follow him out of the waiting area. Andy looked at Brit again and nodded. Brit wordlessly got to his feet, blood draining from his face. He followed Walker down the hall until they were well out of earshot of the others.

"We've found a body," Walker said. "On St. Lucia."

Brit's knees buckled and he sagged against the wall.

"We don't have a positive identification." Walker paused, then added, "Can you assist with the identification?"

"You have her photograph. Isn't that enough?" Brit didn't want to have to look at the dead body of his sister-in-law. Especially if she died a violent death.

"The face has been disfigured a bit," Walker said.

"Define 'disfigured.'"

"She's been beaten about the face a bit." Walker's voice started to quiver. "There is some bruising and swelling. It makes it difficult, particularly since the quality of the photograph is not good."

"Uh huh."

"That's the reason I didn't want to say anything in front of Mrs. Sandone. I don't want to either raise or dash her hopes unnecessarily."

"So what should I tell her?" Brit asked. He tried to bolster his own hopes, but he knew he was only kidding himself.

"Perhaps you can just tell her we need your assistance with some information – descriptions and the like. If it is Mrs. Reavis, you can tell her then. But if it's not, then she won't have had a scare."

Brit looked closely at Walker. His concern seemed to be genuine. "I appreciate your sensitivity, Sergeant."

Walker smiled weakly and shook his head. "It's what I would want for my mother."

*****

Brit filled Andy in, then left Mary in his care and went with Walker. A helicopter waited for them at the Grantley Adams airport when they arrived. At last they reached the morgue in Castries, a small room in the basement of the largest hospital on the island. Glenroy Wood and Wendell Cox waited for them. Brit shook hands with Glenroy, who introduced Wendell. Then they ushered Brit into the small, dimly-lit room that served as the morgue.

Brit stepped inside and surveyed the room. It had very little in the way of furnishings, just a metal autopsy table, a collection of trays, and various medical instruments. Despite the warm Caribbean temperatures outside, the interior was cold and sterile. On the far wall, a lone stretcher held a human body, covered with a sheet. A native doctor – the coroner – stood beside the stretcher.

Brit hesitated before approaching the stretcher. Part of him wanted this to be just a mistake, and for the body beneath the sheet to be someone other than Karla. But at the same time, he wanted it to be Karla so there would at least be some finality to his, and Bobby's, concerns. At this point, based on what knew about Oliver Clarke, if she was still in his hands, she might very well be better off dead.

With a hesitant stride, Brit approached the stretcher, followed closely by Glenroy, Walker, and Wendell. He stopped beside the stretcher and took a deep breath. Walker moved to Brit's side, but Glenroy and Wendell stayed back. They had already seen the body, and neither wanted a second viewing.

Brit glanced at Wallace, then back at the doctor. He took another deep breath. He told himself he was doing this for his brother – sparing Bobby the trauma of having to identify the body. Yet he still hoped that the sheet covered someone else's heartache.

He closed his eyes and said a silent prayer. Then he opened them again and nodded at the coroner, who slowly pulled back the sheet to reveal who lay beneath it. It was a woman's face, battered almost beyond recognition. Almost, but not quite.

One blackened eye seemed swollen shut. Brit knew that even if she tried, the woman couldn't open that eye. The other eye was open, bloodshot, staring vacantly at the ceiling. Both lips were split nearly in two. One cheek was black and blue, the other crushed, leaving loose skin covering a gouge in the cheekbone. What had once been olive-colored skin was now a kaleidoscope of blacks, greens, and blues. Rips and tears in her flesh lay open, with blood dried in streaks down the side of her face.

The last feature of the battering that Brit saw was the mark on the throat, the gash still open across the woman's windpipe. Brit hoped the battering and death had been quick, but he knew better.

"Is that Karla Reavis?" Wallace asked softly.

"Yes," Brit mumbled.

The doctor pulled the sheet back across the body's face.

Brit turned sharply and looked at Wallace. "Was she raped?"

Wallace glanced at the doctor, who was still standing quietly beside the stretcher. He was behind Brit, out of his eyesight. The doctor shook his head.

Wallace looked back at Brit. "No."

Brit sighed heavily. "That's good. At least that's good."

He turned and wearily walked out of the morgue, leaving his sister-in-law behind.

CHAPTER EIGHTEEN

Bobby awoke from a fitful sleep. He blinked his eyes a few times to adjust to the light, then opened them and looked around. The last time he woke, Brit and Andy had been there. Maybe that was a dream, and maybe this time he was waking up for real. And Brit and Andy weren't really here. He couldn't be sure what was real and what wasn't.

The pain in his throat and in his chest were real enough, though. That, and the fact that he was in a hospital, convinced him that the shooting in the canefield really happened. It wasn't a dream, but was real.

He noticed that only two of the other beds in the room were occupied. He deduced that he was in some type of ward, obviously not in a private room. He studied the other patients, looking for Karla. Surely she was close by, but he quickly satisfied himself that she was not one of the patients. Maybe she was in a private room. Or maybe she wasn't even hurt. The thought lifted his spirits momentarily.

But his spirits sagged when he remembered what Brit told him. "He may have her." The words squeezed his heart in a cold vise.

Then he brightened again, his mind riding an emotional roller coaster. If Brit and Andy were only in a dream, if he wasn't awake before, then those words were also a dream. Maybe the convict didn't take her after all.

But the roller coaster continued. He remembered talking with Sergeant Walker. He remembered answering questions about the shooting among the canes. He remembered every detail about Walker, from his fair hair and complexion right down to the buttons on his uniform and his peculiar British accent. His dreams were never that detailed, especially when it came to people he had never met. His conversation with Walker wasn't a dream. Andy and Brit had been there. So that meant that he was awake before, and that meant he talked with Brit.

And that meant that the bastard took Karla.

Bobby tried to sit up. Pain shot through his chest and throbbed in his throat. Ignoring the pain, he wiggled until he slowly maneuvered himself into a fully sitting position. A wave of nausea rolled through, but quickly passed. He forced himself to stay upright.

He wondered how long he had been there. Sergeant Walker talked about things happening "yesterday," but how long ago was that? What were the police doing to find Karla?

An urge to get out of the hospital overwhelmed him. The police will never find her, he thought. He was convinced that only he could find her. He had to. After all, he promised that he would never leave her, and that he would always be there to protect her. But he failed. He had to do something about that.

He had to find her.

Swinging his legs over the side of the bed, Bobby sat on the edge. His head whirled, but the nausea didn't return. He put his hands on the mattress and lowered his head, waiting for the dizziness to pass. When it did, he reached out to the i.v. tube and grasped it tightly. With a grimace, he yanked the needle out of his arm. A sharp pinch of pain ripped at his elbow as the needle pulled loose. Now he felt unchained.

He eased forward until his feet pressed flat on the floor. Pushing off the bed with his hands, he stood. Another dizzy spell passed through him, and his knees turned rubbery. He steadied himself against the side of the bed for a moment. He shook his head to chase away the fog, then tentatively stepped away. Shuffling his feet, rather than lifting them, he began moving toward the door. It was a slow go, but he made painful progress.

Halfway there, he heard voices in the hallway, coming closer. Ignoring them, he kept shuffling forward.

*****

Brit bolted in the door with his head down, barely raising it in time to come face-to-face with his brother before almost bowling him over.

"Good Lord, Bob! Get back in the bed."

Bobby shook his head and pushed away the helping hands reaching out to him. "Gotta go. Gotta find Karla."

Brit quickly overpowered Bobby's feeble efforts to resist. As he led Bobby back to the bed, he called over his shoulder to Walker, "Sergeant, can you get the doctor? He needs to put that i.v. back in."

"Why can't you do it?" Bobby said. "You're a goddamned doctor."

"Right now I'm just your brother."

Brit fought to control his temper. He was angry at what had happened to Karla. He saw how she had been brutalized.

He was also angry at having to be the one to tell Bobby. His nerves worn to a frazzle, he was now angry that Bobby jeopardized his recovery by doing something stupid. But at the same time, he knew what a strain Bobby was under. Worse than that, he knew the shock that was coming.

Dr. Simpson soon arrived and the two of them got Bobby back in the bed and reattached to his i.v. Bobby sulked like a child, glaring angrily at his brother.

Once Simpson and Walker exited, leaving the two brothers alone, Bobby said, "I thought you'd understand. I've got to find Karla."

"Killing yourself won't help."

"I've got to find her."

Brit stared at his brother, searching for the right words. Bobby needed to know, and he needed to know now.

"What are you not telling me?" Bobby asked.

Brit said nothing.

"Brit?"

"Bobby – "

"Just tell me, goddammit."

"Bobby – "

"She's dead, isn't she?"

Brit met his brother's gaze. "Yes."

Bobby stared back. "Bullshit!"

"Why would I lie?"

"No, he's got her and I've got to find her." Bobby shook his head vigorously. "You told me that yourself. You said he's got her."

"They found her."

Bobby stared at his brother, his eyes wide and disbelieving. "Maybe it's somebody else."

Brit wanted desperately to be able to agree with his brother. To say, "Yes, you're right. It's someone else. Karla's still okay, somewhere." But he couldn't.

Brit took his brother's hand. "Bubba, I saw her. It's her."

Bobby continued to stare wide-eyed at Brit. He slowly shook his head from side to side. "How?" He only mouthed the word, no sound coming from his lips.

In that instant, Brit decided that Bobby had suffered enough. It was enough that Karla was dead. That was all he needed to know.

"He hijacked a boat to St. Lucia and she jumped overboard to get away," Brit said. "She drowned."

Brit knew that further explanations would be necessary if Bobby saw her body before it was buried; bruises would have to be explained and how such a strong swimmer could have drowned.

Brit swallowed hard and finished his lie. "They think the boat hit her in the water. Knocked her out."

Bobby studied his brother's face closely. They knew each other well. Brit knew that, as a lawyer, Bobby made a career out of judging other people's credibility. He knew when he was being fed a line. Brit willed his expression to hold up.

"She didn't feel a thing."

CHAPTER NINETEEN

On the day of Karla's funeral, the skies cleared at dawn in a glorious sunrise. A steady breeze blew from the north, complementing the greening of Dallas after the passage of winter. Bobby would have preferred a Hollywood-style, dark, rainy day to match his spirits. The clouds that seemed to have taken permanent residence in his heart clashed with the brightness of this day – the day when his beloved Karla would be forever covered with dirt. Bobby thought he believed in God and heaven, but today he felt only a sense of permanent loss. And a sense that the God he believed in had betrayed him.

He wiped moisture from the bathroom mirror in his brother's house and studied his reflection. His face looked pale and drawn, almost gaunt. In his own eyes, he detected that distant, far-away look that he often saw in the homeless as they wandered the downtown streets and begged for handouts. The look he always associated with the mentally ill. He often wondered what tragedies had occurred in their lives to put them on the streets, ambitionless and aimlessly wandering, simply looking for their next meals and waiting for their meaningless existences to end. Bobby wondered if any of them had lost their wives or husbands to an act of violence. He wondered if the face he now looked at in the mirror would someday join the ranks that pin-striped businessmen would ignore and brush past on the busy streets outside the courthouses and the skyscrapers.

He banished the thought from his mind and began lathering on shaving cream. Though he was haunted on a nightly basis by nightmares of his encounter with Oliver Clarke, he didn't believe he would ever come to that. He was just lonely, that was all. He missed Karla. He wanted her to be with him, and for them to be in their own house, working on their plans for the future. The plans they had been making for the past six months. The plans they talked about that afternoon driving back to Sam Lord's Castle.

After he shaved and completed his grooming, Bobby began to dress. Brit's wife, Angela, had laid out his suit for him and even matched a tie. Moving slowly, as if he were under water, Bobby put on a dark blue suit with a wine-colored stripe, a powder-blue, pinpoint oxford dress shirt, and a conservative blue, polka-dotted tie. Just as if he were going to court. Start buying your blue suits, he was advised when he clerked for a law firm after his second year of law school. They exuded an aura of confidence and a sense of being in control. Juries liked blue suits. Blue suits were perfect for courtrooms.

And funerals.

*****

The law firm of Henderson, Day & O'Neal had virtually shut down for the afternoon, as all but a handful of its lawyers showed up to show their support for one of their most respected partners. Likewise, the majority of the reporters from the court reporting firm Karla worked for had also taken time off to attend the funeral. Like the lawyers, they were honoring one of their most respected co-workers and friends.

When the time came, Bobby entered the sanctuary of the small Baptist church and walked to the front pew following the Sandones. Brit, Angela, and the girls followed. With head held high, but tears already flowing, Bobby reached the front and sat next to Mary, directly in front of the casket. At Bobby's request, the casket was closed. He was the last to see Karla's battered face when he bent over the casket and kissed her just before the lid was sealed.

As the preacher delivered the eulogy, his recitation of the Twenty-third Psalm rang hollow in Bobby's ears:

'The Lord is my Shepherd; I shall not want.

He maketh me to lie down in green pastures.

He leadeth me beside the still waters.

He restoreth my soul.

He leadeth me in the paths of righteousness for his name's sake.

Yea though I walk through the valley of the shadow of death

I will fear no evil,

for thou art with me;

thy rod and thy staff they comfort me.'"

Bobby was definitely walking through that valley. Right here. Right now. And he was finding that it was a deeper and darker valley than he ever dreamed possible. It threatened to over-whelm him. Where was the comfort? Where were the green pastures? Where were the still waters? The words sounded good, but as he grieved, they rang hollow. He listened, still waiting for that word of comfort. Waiting.

Waiting. The promise of pie in the sky, by and by, did not comfort Bobby. He wanted to be together with Karla now, not at some uncertain day in the future. They had a future together. They had made plans together. And Oliver Clarke had taken it all away.

Bobby wondered why God had let it happen.

CHAPTER TWENTY

After the funeral, Bobby went with Brit and his family back to their comfortable North Dallas home. The funeral had been delayed until Bobby regained enough strength to make the flight. Upon returning to Dallas, he had moved in with Brit and his family – at least temporarily. In fact, he had not yet been back to his house.

The day before the wedding, Brit helped move Karla's clothes and furniture to Bobby's house so that the newlyweds could simply return there after the honeymoon. Brit and Angela thought it was still too early for Bobby to deal with the fact that Karla would never live in his house. So, on the pretense of providing medical care, they insisted he stay with them for awhile.

For the first few hours after the funeral, a steady stream of friends and well-wishers paraded through Brit's den, offering their clumsy condolences and sympathies. Those were the most awkward times, when people milled around in hushed silence, never sure what to say or how to act. Bobby appreciated their concern, but he hated the gloomy atmosphere. He already harbored enough gloom in his heart without others bringing theirs along. By early evening, the parade stopped, and Andy Fletcher remained as the only non-family member in the house. The mood was somber. Angela entertained the kids in the back room, leaving the three men alone to talk.

Bobby sat in Brit's favorite chair, a lazy-boy recliner, and slowly sipped coffee – the drink of choice at Baptist funerals. Across the room, Brit sat on a small love seat next to a padded Queen Anne chair that supported Andy. They both grasped coffee cups as well. The only sounds were the hushed slurps of the men sipping their drinks.

Bobby broke the silence. "I want to go home tomorrow."

Andy and Brit exchanged glances. From the time that they arrived at Queen Elizabeth Hospital in Bridgetown, either Brit or Andy, or both, had been Bobby's almost-constant companion. That included grueling, sleepless nights at the hospital. Those long nights were particularly rough as they watched Bobby suffering physically from his gunshot wounds and mentally from the loss of his bride. On more than one occasion, Bobby awakened them with his shouts. They knew he was reliving, in his dreams, the terrible confrontation in the canefield. In their opinions, the mental toll on Bobby might be worse than the physical toll.

"Are you sure you're ready for that?" Brit asked. "It's no problem for you to stay here as long as you want. No problem at all."

Bobby calmly shook his head. "I've got to face up to it sooner or later. There's no point in dragging it out."

"How do you feel physically?" Andy asked.

"I'd be lying if I said I never feel any pain, but the drugs take care of it. I can get around okay. I'll just have to watch myself."

"I don't know," Brit said, quickly. "I'm not talking as your brother, Bob. I'm talking as a doctor."

"What does that mean?"

"I think someone needs to keep an eye on you. If you want my opinion, you checked out of the hospital too soon."

"I don't suppose you think I'm suicidal, do you?" Bobby smiled weakly.

"No, no, no," Brit and Andy both protested, though neither of them totally discounted the possibility.

"But you're not in the best mental state," Andy said. "If you're still having some physical problems on top of that, hell, that's too much for anyone to handle."

"Andy's right," Brit said.

Bobby sat silently for a moment, sipping coffee. Brit and Andy watched him, waiting and wondering. What was he thinking?

"I'm going home, with or without your approval," Bobby said at last.

*****

Shortly after noon the next day, Brit drove Bobby to his house in Sunnyvale, a small community just east of Dallas, wedged between the larger Dallas suburb of Mesquite and the shores of Lake Ray Hubbard. Bobby had lived there for the past four years in a house that was too big for him, but which he felt sure he and Karla could fill together. But now, as he realized that Karla would never live there, it seemed bigger, more cavernous, and emptier than ever.

After removing Bobby's bags from the car, Brit stayed for a while, not anxious to go until reassured that his brother was okay. Only at Bobby's insistence did he finally leave, although he didn't trust Bobby's calm assurances. Bobby was, after all, a lawyer – a trial lawyer at that – and trial lawyers were nothing if not actors. Still, he knew that Bobby was right, that sooner or later he had to face up to the tragedy and get on with his life. And sooner was probably better than later.

After Brit left, Bobby found himself standing just inside the front door of his three thousand square foot house. To the left of the entry-way, a sunken den invited him in. It still contained Bobby's bachelor furniture. He and Karla planned to buy new den furniture upon their return from Barbados. That purchase might never take place now.

The nine-foot ceiling in the den, one of Bobby's favorite features about the room, seemed so distant that he felt insignificant. The paneled walls, which used to create a cheerful, intimate atmosphere, seemed stark, cold, and sterile. Bobby and Karla had spent many an afternoon in here eating popcorn and watching movies, or drinking hot chocolate in front of a roaring fire. But now, as Bobby stared around the room, then focused his eyes on the fireplace, he knew that those moments would never be re-created. He shook his head and quickly left the den, moving into the adjacent kitchen.

He paused for a minute at the kitchen window and stared out at the kidney-shaped swimming pool. The backyard was beautifully landscaped, with red-tipped photinias and periwinkles behind the pool. Yellow jasmine was in fabulous bloom as it clung to the wooden fence. The broad decking around the pool was also fringed with sweet williams, begonias, and other colorful flowers, lending life to the yard. Bobby almost envisioned Karla stretched out in a lounge chair, lemonade in hand, reading a paperback.

Bobby abruptly turned away from the window and continued meandering. He moved down a narrow hallway that stretched a good forty feet from the game room/study at one end, just around the corner from the kitchen, to the master bedroom at the other. When he reached the master bedroom, he paced its perimeter, then moved into the large master bath with walk-in closets. He paused for a second outside the closet assigned to Karla and which already contained some of her clothes. He dared not open the door.

He turned abruptly, walked back through the bedroom, and out the front door. The warmth of the sun, with a hint of a breeze blowing, brushed his face as he stood on the front porch and surveyed the lawn. It was badly in need of mowing. Long grass runners spilled across the once nicely-edged sidewalk. Knowing that he needed to keep his mind occupied, and hoping mild exercise might be therapeutic, he decided to do the yardwork – even though his doctor probably wouldn't have liked it. Bobby thought he knew his own body better than any doctor and, gunshot wounds or not, he knew he could withstand the rigors of steering a self-propelled lawnmower across open grass and negotiating the perimeter of a sidewalk with an edger.

The decision made, he re-entered the house and quickly donned shorts and tennis shoes. Ordinarily he did yardwork shirtless, working on a tan, but the sight of his torso in the bedroom mirror stopped him short. The scars from the gunshots were not visible, but the bandages testified to the damage underneath. Even worse, the bruised, discolored skin surrounding the bandages looked downright nasty. He decided to wear a shirt. No need to make a spectacle of himself in front of the neighbors.

Pacing himself, interspersing work with periodic breaks, Bobby managed to spend the rest of the afternoon in the yard without overly taxing himself. It was not a particularly hot day, though it was sunny. The fresh air, sunshine, and perspiration soothed him, both mentally and physically.

After he finished, he put away his tools, then went inside to shower. Andy promised to come over that evening and take him to dinner. Surprisingly, Bobby had enjoyed himself somewhat that afternoon and wasn't necessarily looking forward to Andy's company. But, at the same time, he dreaded Andy's leaving after dinner, knowing he would have to face the long, dark night alone.

CHAPTER TWENTY ONE

For what seemed like the hundredth time, Bobby checked the clock. The luminous red digits proclaimed almost one in the morning. He had been in bed for at least two hours, but still hadn't slept. He lay with his eyes open, staring at the ceiling, and listened to the familiar night-time sounds. He heard the gentle rumble of the air conditioner as it kicked on and off. Over its rumble, the ceiling fan gently murmured as it twirled overhead, circulating the cool air.

Before Barbados, those were friendly sounds that lulled him to sleep – the comfortable sounds of home. But now they sounded harsh and grating, evoking painful memories. They kept him awake and left his mind active to contemplate his fate. The loud noise that signaled the air conditioner kicking on exploded the silence like gunshots. The fan reminded him of the hospital in Bridgetown.

The yardwork had exhausted him. He took a prescribed pain-killer, confident that the codeine combined with fatigue would knock him out quickly and help him sleep through the night. Then he climbed into bed and turned on the TV, hoping to keep his mind occupied until sleep came. But as he watched mind-numbing late-night drivel, he finally became convinced that television merely distracted him, so he flipped it off and lay in the dark, awaiting results.

*****

Bobby rolled over and frowned. He didn't know how long he had been sleeping, but he had a splitting headache. He rubbed his temples lightly with his forefingers, but to no avail. The pain survived.

Glancing to his right, he saw the printout on the digital clock that announced the time: half past three. He couldn't remember falling asleep or, for that matter, going to bed. It was as if he were waking up with no history.

He continued to massage his temples, trying to figure out why he was awake. He sensed that something woke him, that he hadn't just awakened on his own. He sensed that something wasn't right, but he couldn't quite put his finger on it. He fought to clear his thoughts. He felt terribly confused and disoriented, just like the first time he regained consciousness at Queen Elizabeth Hospital in Bridgetown.

He put his arms at his sides and listened in the dark. He knew it wasn't the familiar whirring of the ceiling fan that woke him. He slept to its sounds every night of the year, summer and winter. Its absence might have produced a deafening silence to rouse him from sleep but not its presence. No, it was something else.

He closed his eyes, as if that would sharpen his hearing. He listened for unknown sounds in the dark, either outside or in the far reaches of the house.

Nothing.

But then there was something in the room with him. He held

his breath, shutting off the in-and-out rush of air from his nostrils, and listened again.

It came from beside him. The deep, even sound of breathing.

He opened his eyes and let his pupils adjust to the dark. After nearly a minute, he raised his head and looked beside him in the bed. He was surprised to see the silhouetted form of a person, clearly female. He knew he was alone when he went to bed. He also knew that no person belonged in the bed with him.

Except Karla.

He slid out of bed and tip-toed to the far side to face the sleeping person. Darkness obscured her features and even Bobby's dilated pupils couldn't make out an identity.

He grasped the wand on the mini-blinds and slowly twisted it, opening the tiny strips of vinyl. As he did, the full moon outside spilled its light in through the window and sent it rushing to the face of a woman.

Karla!

Bobby caught his breath and stood frozen to the spot. It couldn't be. He knew this was all wrong. Confused and disoriented, he tried to make sense of what he saw – but nothing made sense.

Karla moaned softly and rolled onto her back. Now the moonlight fell full on her face. There was no mistaking it. It was Karla.

Bobby slowly sank to his knees beside the bed. He closed his eyes and shook his head, trying to wake up. He must be dreaming. He must be.

But when he opened his eyes again, she still lay there. Sleeping peacefully in his bed.

The sound of breaking glass suddenly snatched his attention. It came from the direction of the kitchen. More sound followed – the rattle of mini-blinds, more tinkling of glass, then a thud of footsteps landing on the kitchen floor. Someone was breaking in!

Bobby sprang to his feet and looked desperately for an escape route. Hopefully he had time to grab Karla and get around the corner and out the front door before the burglar made his way to the bedroom.

He darted to the door and looked, but saw nothing. He slipped into the hall and over to the front entryway, carefully turned the key in the front door deadbolt, then grasped the door handle. Carefully, but quickly, he squeezed the handle until he heard the faint click of the latch clearing the door jamb. He pulled the door open and unlocked the storm door. He pushed it open and propped it with a brick he kept on the front porch for that very purpose. Then he hurried back to Karla's bedside. He'd heard nothing else from the kitchen, but there was no time to waste.

Kneeling beside the bed, he put his hand on Karla's shoulder and gave her a brisk shake.

She didn't awaken.

He tried again, but her head just rolled lifelessly on the pillow.

He yanked the covers back and bent to scoop his arms around her. That's when he noticed the dark stripe across her throat. It looked like a necklace – a dark shadow in a dark room. But something about it didn't look right.

He scrutinized her closely. He realized for the first time that she was nude, her slender body exposed in the moonlight. Not wanting to carry her outside naked, Bobby jerked the sheet loose from the mattress and tenderly wrapped it around her.

She still didn't move.

Confident now that he protected her from voyeuristic eyes, he bent and again scooped her up in his arms. Then he turned to head to the front door. He stopped short when he heard a sound coming from the hall. A shadow appeared at the far end. Bobby stood rooted, watching. The shadow drew nearer, seeming to float down the hallway until it reached the bedroom door.

Bobby saw that it was a man, but couldn't make out any of his features. He plainly saw, though, the outline of thick, dreadlocked hair. He stood facing the man, not daring to move. The man also stood still. It was as if each waited for the other to make the first move.

After at least a minute, but what seemed like forever, Bobby demanded, "Who's there?"

The figure remained silent.

"Who's there? Answer me!"

The figure slowly raised his left arm and extended it toward Bobby. Then he stepped to the side, his arm still extended, and raised his hand as if he were staring at his own palm. Bobby saw the silhouette of the man's fingers – all three of them, the pinkie, index finger, and a thumb.

Bobby sucked in a breath of air and clutched Karla tightly to his breast.

The man flipped the light switch on the wall by his head, flooding the hallway behind him with light. Bobby turned away as light assaulted his dilated pupils. Karla grew heavy in his arms, but he held her tightly, not wanting to let her go. Not this time.

The intruder maintained his position. As Bobby's eyes adjusted, he could now make out the features on the evil face of the intruder. He had seen this man before. The horizontal scar slashing across his cheek was a dead giveaway.

Oliver Clarke smiled. His white teeth contrasted sharply with black skin. He lowered his deformed hand and reached behind his back. He fiddled with something, then he slowly brought his hand back around to the front, holding a long, double-edged knife. He held the knife toward Bobby as if displaying it. Bobby noticed dark red liquid coating the blade, running down the blade and across clenched knuckles.

Clarke raised his other hand. With a sudden jerk, he drew it across his throat from right to left. Then he pointed to Karla and repeated the gesture.

Bobby remembered the necklace around Karla's neck. He looked, but the sheet hid her neck. He plopped down on the end of the bed and held her in his lap, cradling her head in his left arm. With his free hand, he tugged the sheet down from her chin until he had a clear view of her neck. In the light from the hallway, he saw it wasn't a necklace at all. A deep gash ran across her throat. Dried, caked blood lined it. It was an old wound, obviously a fatal wound. Now Bobby understood why Karla hadn't responded to his efforts to rouse her. She was dead.

Bobby slowly raised his head and looked again at the face of his tormentor. Clarke's white-toothed smile stayed in place. He placed his unarmed hand behind his back, then slowly brought it back around to the front. Now he held a gun. A gun Bobby had seen before.

Clarke raised his arm and leveled the gun in Bobby's direction. Bobby sat silently at the foot of the bed and waited.

He welcomed the inevitable. Maybe this time he would die. This time he would join Karla. He stiffened his back, sat up straighter, and locked eyes with Clarke.

The black bastard stared back. His eyes never wavered. His lips peeled back further, transforming from a smile to a snarl.

He squeezed the trigger. The gun barked.

Fire flashed from the muzzle. A bullet spiraled in slow motion and moved toward Bobby, as if it were fired in gelatin.

Bobby watched the bullet float across the space between them. Coming closer. Closer. Until it was only inches from his chest.

And then it disappeared into the skin on his right breast, leaving a small round hole. Blood began to leak. The pain was excruciating.

Bobby closed his eyes and lay back on the bed.

*****

He awoke. He sat up in bed and looked wildly around the room. There was no Oliver Clarke in the doorway.

He glanced at the clock. Half-past three. He glanced to his left. No one in the bed beside him. No Karla. He was alone.

He sat in the darkness for a moment. Soon he began to shake.

CHAPTER TWENTY TWO

Ocee didn't sleep until after one in the morning. He flopped on a pallet in the back room of a small shack in the slums of Kingston, Jamaica. He had been in Jamaica barely a week, shacking up with members of a Jamaican gang, or "posse," called the Gulleymen. The Jamaican police had been cracking down on posse activity in the past month, and the Gulleymen were keeping a low profile. Low profiles didn't suit Ocee's style. He was getting antsy, ready for action. He looked forward to getting out of Jamaica and to the United States.

He knew that major Jamaican posses were already entrenched in Jamaican-immigrant communities on the east coast, most notably New York, Miami, and Washington, D.C. According to what they told Ocee, the Gulleymen and other posses were concentrated in the rest of the U.S., becoming active in Dallas, Houston, Phoenix and, unlikely enough, had established a presence as far away as Anchorage, Alaska. The posses were rooted in the slums around Kingston, where their genesis had been in marijuana-smuggling. The United States crack explosion of the 1980s had first offered them untold potential. They first made their mark in the U.S. crack trade, but were now also actively running guns in addition to pushing drugs.

With Ocee's natural affinity for violence, he saw posse activity in the United States as a dream come true. Kingston was just a stopover for him on his way to achieving his destiny as a drug lord in the Jamaican posses. Being Barbadian, not Jamaican, wouldn't stand in his way. Not with his impressive resume of lawlessness. The Jamaicans welcomed other Caribbean peoples into their ranks if they had the right qualities. In their low-life world, Ocee had the perfect qualities. All he had to do was be patient and they would move him to the mainland.

But Ocee's patience, lacking to start with, quickly wore thin. He was ready for the big time – New York. The locals told him he would probably have to do a stint of duty somewhere else first, maybe Dallas or Houston, to prove himself. But a leadership position in New York City was clearly in the cards. It was his destiny.

With his head spinning from an evening of smoking ganja and drinking rum, Ocee lay in the back room and tried to sleep. He was told that he would soon be taken to Miami and, from there, to his place of service. Like a kid who can't sleep the night before Christmas, Ocee was restless, anxious for tomorrow. Maybe that would be the day. Or maybe the next. Or the next.

Before he knew it, he slept. And he dreamed.

*****

From his perch on the deck of the Bajan Lady, Ocee saw the American woman in the ocean, treading water. Ocee had turned off the boat's lights and motor as he neared shore. It was only by luck that he spotted her on the horizon. She was barely visible through the binoculars but stood out in the beam of the moon's spotlight on the water.

She saw him, turned, and began swimming toward shore. Ocee turned on the boat's spotlight and cast it across her form splashing in the water. Just as he turned the motor back on and steered in her direction, she dove beneath the surface.

He cut back on the motor and waited for her to come up. Her head popped to the surface after less than thirty seconds and only a little farther away from the boat. Ocee raced the engine and narrowed the gap as much as he could before her next dive. It came quickly and he again cut back the motor, waiting for her inevitable return to the water's surface.

This time she came up even quicker than before. Ocee bore down again, and she dove again. He repeated the game a few more times. He was almost on top of her when she went down for the last time. As soon as her head dipped, he grabbed a fishing net lying next to his feet. Harkening back to his fishing days as a youth, Ocee tossed the weighted net overboard in her general area. He watched as it sank beneath the surface.

A few seconds later, he began to draw in the net. It felt heavy and he knew he had caught a big one. A wicked smile crossed his face when the woman broke the surface again, the net draped over her head. With a hand-over-hand motion, he continued to pull upward as the woman thrashed about, splashing and shrieking with fear.

She cleared the water feet first, her head tipped downward. Her body banged roughly against the side of the boat as Ocee strained to pull her aboard. At last he had her on deck, still wrapped in the net. She sprawled at his feet and flopped like a fish out of water. He stood with his hands on his hips and watched her futile efforts to break free. Periodically, he kicked her in the side. Each time his foot connected with her body, she let out a small cry, which evoked howls of amusement from him.

After watching her struggle for a few minutes, Ocee wrapped the excess netting tightly around her, undoing what little success she'd made in gaining freedom. Confident she was secure, he turned back to the helm, cranked up the boat's motor, and aimed for shore.

When he reached shallow water, he turned the craft parallel to the land and began looking for an inlet where he could pull ashore and dock. If he got there soon enough, he still had a bit of time to deal with the woman. That was something he had been looking forward to ever since he first saw her. Her olive skin, long black hair set off by flashing eyes, and shapely form had been stoking the fire in his loins. As the time neared for climax, his iron burned red hot.

Just ahead, a spit of land jutted into the water. Ocee steered the Bajan Lady around it, then followed it back inland. Just where the spit began its extension into the water, he saw a small, natural harbor. He slowed the boat and aimed for its center. He shined a bright light ahead of him and scrutinized the shoreline. At the harbor's deepest point, a narrow channel cut inland. Just wide enough, Ocee guessed, to accommodate the boat – provided it wasn't too shallow.

Steering for the center of the channel, Ocee accelerated, shooting the boat straight ahead. It brushed against the bottom of the channel, slowing somewhat, but the channel wasn't shallow enough to completely stop it. The vessel roared ahead, branches and leaves scraping its sides, until it came to a screeching halt with its bow resting against a tree.

Ocee checked back and saw that the boat was far enough in so as to be out of sight.

After shutting off the motor, Ocee jumped from the back of the boat into the warm water, which was no more than four feet deep. He slogged his way ashore, then moved back to the shoreline. There, he feverishly piled brush across the entrance to the channel.

Satisfied that the entrance was covered and the boat out of sight, he went back to claim his prize. As he clambered on board, he heard something. Squinting in the moonlight, he barely made out the outline of the American woman, who had somehow gotten loose, as she leaped off the bow of the boat.

Ocee's feet barely touched the planks on the ship's deck as he sprinted ahead, then fairly flew off the boat. In the darkness of the evening, and the thickness of the vegetation, he couldn't see the woman, but he could still hear her. He nimbly picked his way through the trees, following the sound. Then the sound abruptly came to a stop with a crash. Ocee nearly tripped over the fallen woman as he tried to hit the brakes. She lay breathless at his feet, sprawled over a thick root. Ocee grabbed her by her ankles and began dragging her to a small clearing they had crossed. She tried to scream, but all that came out was a sob and a whimper, followed by a long, low wail.

Ocee glanced over his shoulder to see where he was going, then looked back at the woman. She clawed desperately at the ground, grabbing at branches, anything to slow down the inevitable. Ocee growled, a snarl emanating from the back of his throat. With one last tug, he broke into the clearing and dropped her feet. Her upper body still lay in the bushes at the edge, but the part that mattered to Ocee had cleared.

She tried to scramble to her feet, but Ocee kicked her legs out from under her. She fell down hard. He jumped on her, straddling her waist. His knees landed on her forearms and pinned them to the ground. Her twisting, writhing trunk brushed against his groin. The sensation only aroused him further. He rose up on his knees, unsnapped his pants, and pushed them down around his hips. His freed erection bobbed obscenely.

Ocee grabbed her blouse with both hands and ripped it open. He pulled his knife from his boot and cut the narrow fabric joining the cups on her bra. Her breasts spilled into the open air. Ocee leaned forward for a closer look. He grabbed them in his hands and squeezed. He flicked his thumbs over the nipples, his teeth glinting in the moonlight as he fondled the struggling woman. She continued to thrash about, violently jerking her head from side to side, trying to free her arms.

With his deformed hand still on a breast, Ocee grasped his hard penis with his other. He closed his eyes, threw his head back, and began to stroke his erection. Slowly at first, then picking up speed. With each movement, he bounced on the woman's midsection, his body moving up and down in rhythm with his self-gratifying hand. Heat welled up in his groin as he neared the bursting point. But just as he brought himself to the verge of ejaculation, he stopped abruptly.

He slid downward on the woman and grasped the snap on her shorts. But when he lifted his knees from her arms, she shot her right hand out, grabbed his penis, and yanked, as if she were tearing it from his groin.

Ocee howled. He reached for her wrist, squeezing to break her grip. She brought her left fist tightly upward into his testicles. The punch drove the swollen organs into his abdomen, shooting pain throughout his body.

Ocee screamed again and grabbed at his groin with both hands. When he did, the woman let go of his penis and delivered a sharp punch to his solar plexus.

Ocee gasped and shifted sideways. He couldn't breathe. Consciousness started to seep away as he threw one hand out to brace himself. It landed on the knife. The woman began crawling out from underneath him. Enraged, he grabbed the knife. With one swift movement, he brought its point down on her throat. The blade plunged deep into her windpipe. A scream died before it escaped her mouth, then transformed into a gurgle and a gasp.

As blood oozed out of the wound, Ocee left the knife embedded in the woman's throat. He lashed furiously at her face with his fists. Blindly, he struck again and again. Bones crunched beneath his knuckles as her cheek caved in. He continued to punch, reacting more from his own pain than from anger. When he finally stopped, her face was a lumpy mass of cuts and bruises. The once-beautiful features were almost indistinguishable. She no longer resembled the dark beauty he had first taken.

Furious, he grabbed the knife with both hands. Like Arthur extracting Excalibur from its granite sheath, he yanked it from the woman's throat. With a left to right movement, he slit her throat with a deep slice, almost to a depth with the initial gash.

He knelt between the woman's knees as if in a trance. He lost track of time as he waited for his erection to return, still wanting desperately to use the woman as he first planned.

He closed his eyes, gingerly took his sore, swollen penis in his good hand, and began tenderly stroking it in hopes that it would respond, but to no avail.

Something nagged at his senses. Something dark. Something threatening.

He opened his eyes and stared at the dead woman. Her face was still battered and bleeding.

Then he saw something he couldn't believe. A mist danced from the gash in her throat, rising to the heavens. Ocee's eyes widened in horror. The mist began to take the shape of a disembodied head. It danced in the air, crystallizing into human features. The features of the American woman.

A duppy! The spirit of the dead!

The duppy looked at Ocee. Ocee shrank back, his eyes wide with fear. He opened his mouth to scream, but no sound came out.

*****

Ocee bolted upright on his pallet in the shack in Kingston. He blinked, adjusting to the darkness. Sweat trickled down his sides, leaving his shirt plastered to his body. He looked around, but the duppy wasn't there. He tried to will himself to relax, to force his pounding heart to ease up. He was safe for now. But he couldn't be sure what would happen if he fell back to sleep.

He reached beneath the pallet then pulled his hand out. In it, he held a driver's license – the license that had belonged to Karla Sandone. He studied her face for a moment – the same face that haunted him in his dreams.

He sprang from his bed and rushed to the part of the shack that passed for a kitchen. With trembling hands, he gathered various herbs from the food-stores and hung them, in a makeshift fashion, at the shack's windows and doorways. He went outside and gathered sand in his hands, which he scattered around the house. Finally, he left his shoes at the door. Satisfied he had done all that custom required to bar the duppy from entering the house, he retreated to his pallet and put the driver's license back beneath it. He sat down and pulled a ragged blanket around his shoulders, keeping a watchful vigil for the duppy of the American woman.

CHAPTER TWENTY THREE

Bobby awoke the next morning, surprised and embarrassed to find himself lying on the floor in the middle of the hall. Surprised, because he didn't remember how he got there, and embarrassed because it made him feel like a passed-out drunk. He struggled to his feet and wiped the sleep from his puffy eyes. He walked back to the bedroom to check the time: eight o'clock.

He went into the bathroom and turned on the shower. As he waited for the water to heat, he stood in front of the sink and splashed cold water on his face. His color still had not returned and his chest ached dully beneath the bandages. He wondered if his heart were breaking.

He had read once that, even when your life is turned upside down, you still needed to keep to a regular routine, showering, dressing, and going about your business. Otherwise, full-scale depression might set in. He knew he was a likely candidate for depression of that sort, so he followed that advice.

After showering, he shaved and dressed. As he retrieved the paper from the front yard, the smell of freshly-cut grass from his previous day's labors raised his spirits. It reminded him of spring and what spring symbolized – new life. But that momentary lifting of his spirits ended as soon as he re-entered the house to be alone.

He started coffee, whipped up a breakfast of eggs, bacon, and toast, then sat at the kitchen table. As he cut into his eggs, he turned to the Metro section of The *Dallas Morning News* to catch up on local news. The paper greeted him with his and Karla's pictures. He guessed that the whole affair in Barbados was prime grist, on a daily basis, for the Dallas media.

He stared at the pictures for a moment. The feelings of emptiness and loneliness that overwhelmed him the night before, and left him lying prone on the hall floor, returned with a vengeance. His mind felt torn in two directions, almost as surely as his heart was being torn apart. He wanted to forget what happened – forget the past – so that he could move on with his life without the pain. At the same time, to forget the past would be to let go of Karla, and he wasn't ready for that.

*****

After two days at home alone, Bobby found himself desperate for company. Even Brit's constant visits and Andy's phone calls didn't fill the hollow in his life. With any time alone, his mind wandered dangerously. To occupy himself, he tried the movies, but everything he saw either reminded him of Karla or of Oliver Clarke. Love stories were out, but action movies seemed too real. He tried reading, but found himself unable to concentrate on the words on the pages in front of him.

He worked in his yard, mowing, trimming, weeding, and planting. But that only reminded him of how much Karla liked to garden. He tried exercising – to the extent his body was able – but he only remembered the jogs, bike rides, and tennis games with Karla.

He had thought he was ready to be alone and to move on with his life, but now he knew better. He might be ready to move on with his life, but he sure wasn't ready to be alone. Now more than ever, he needed to be surrounded by people and things to do. So he decided to go back to work.

On the third morning, he sat in his car heading west on Highway 80, making the twenty-five minute drive downtown. After the loneliness of the past few days, he even welcomed the congestion on the Dallas freeway. The familiarity of being caught in traffic, in a routine, gave him comfort. He marveled that something he once despised had become a security blanket.

Reaching the downtown mix-master, Bobby maneuvered to enter the west end of the central business district. When he pulled into his assigned space in his building's parking garage, he saw that most of the spaces assigned to the firm's partners were still empty, including Andy Fletcher's. He hadn't told Andy he was coming in and didn't even know if Andy would be here today. He felt a twinge of sadness when he saw the empty parking space.

He grabbed his coat from the back seat, locked the doors, and headed for the elevator. In the building's lobby, he went to the bank of elevators that serviced Henderson, Day & O'Neal's offices. He stepped into an empty car that waited on the ground floor and pushed fifty-five. The doors closed before anyone else boarded, then the elevator began its slow ascent.

As it rose, Bobby found himself uncharacteristically nervous. He wanted to see his friends and partners, but he also knew he would have to deal with the inevitable well-wishing that, though uttered with the best of intentions, only evoked the same painful memories he came here to escape. He might be able to occupy his mind catching up on email that surely had accumulated on his computer in the past weeks. Maybe he would even return a few phone calls and get back into his files. Anything to stay busy. Anything to lend a semblance of normalcy to his life.

As the elevator neared the firm's main floor, Bobby took a few deep breaths. His heart raced. His hands trembled. His knees went weak and his stomach knotted. He told himself that if he could just make it from the elevator to his office without throwing up, the day would be a success. He smiled, somewhat cheered that his sense of humor, although buried deep within his grief, still existed.

The elevator stopped and a soft bell announced its arrival on floor fifty-five. Bobby straightened his tie and brushed his hair with his hand as the doors parted at a snail's pace. With more of a sigh than a deep breath, he emerged and turned toward the lobby. He walked with his head high and his eyes straight ahead, hoping and praying that he wouldn't run into anybody on the way to his office. At least not yet. He wanted a few minutes at his desk before venturing out to speak with others.

Out of the corner of his eye, he saw someone standing at the front desk, talking to the receptionist. He heard the sudden silence as he passed by. He felt their eyes on him as he turned left and walked down the hall, away from them. He knew they would talk again when he was out of earshot and that he would be the topic of their renewed conversation. He lengthened his stride as he neared the first corner and turned left again, homing in on his office. He walked past open office doors and secretaries' desks, his eyes still focused ahead, leaving silenced keyboards in his wake.

Finally he reached his office. He quickly ducked inside and closed the door behind him. He leaned his back against the door and shut his eyes. His feet began to slide out in front of him. He gave in to gravity and slumped into a sitting position, his back to the door, his eyes still closed.

After a few minutes, he heard a light tapping on the door – the knock of someone timid, almost as if hoping no one was home. Bobby smiled. It could be only one person.

He got to his feet, took off his coat, and hung it on the hook on the back of the door, then opened it. Andrea Venable, his loyal secretary, stood meekly in the hall. Her brunette hair was pulled back behind her ears, and her wide eyes stared up at him through thick lenses. Though she could scarcely be characterized as physically attractive, her personality and spirit gave her an inner beauty that overrode any physical flaws.

"Hi," he said.

"Hi." She shuffled her feet, then pushed her glasses up on her nose. "Um, are you okay?"

He smiled to reassure her. "Yeah. I'm fine."

"The way you just came right here and shut the door. You know?"

"I'm fine. Really."

She stared at him intently, her eyes wide and caring. She had seen Bobby at the funeral, but they hadn't talked since then.

"I'm glad you're here," she said.

"Me too."

She stood in front of him, awkwardly shifting her weight from leg to leg. It was obvious to Bobby that she wanted to say something else, but that she couldn't find the words. Finally, she said, "That's all. I just wanted to say I'm glad you're back."

"Thanks."

She turned to go back to her desk, but Bobby stopped her. "Andrea?"

She turned and looked at him earnestly.

When he held his arms out, she rushed to him and threw her arms around him. He squeezed her tightly as she cried.

*****

Andrea brought Bobby a fresh cup of coffee, then left him to sort through the stack of mail that covered the center of his desk, most of it faxes or printed emails. As the mail came in each day, she opened or printed it and arranged it in different stacks. One stack was letters on his cases, one was pleadings on those cases, a third was firm memos, and the fourth was advertisements and various other junk. She also typed out a summary to give him a short-cut to what awaited him in the stacks of paper. Anything that required a response in his absence was copied and given to other lawyers to handle. But the copies were in the stacks so he would know what, if anything, had transpired while he was gone.

Bobby decided to go through the junk and firm memos first. Those, he could get rid of quickly. It wasn't necessarily productive, but it reduced the stacks so as to make them seem less daunting. Next, he quickly sorted through the important stuff and segregated it into categories of his own, based on what needed a response or what was just informational. Then he could calendar due-dates for replies and make priorities for handling each piece of mail.

He had just completed his new organization when he heard a knock on his open door. He looked up to see Debbie Grant, an associate who worked with him on several files, standing in the doorway. He stood and motioned for her to enter.

"I heard you were here," she said. She walked inside and stood tentatively beside a chair.

"Sit down," Bobby said.

"I don't want to bother you . . . if you're busy."

"You're not bothering me."

She seemed hesitant but sat in the chair nearest the door. Bobby sat back down. For a few seconds they just looked at each other, the silence loud and awkward. Bobby studied her face. Debbie was exceptionally pretty and had come to the firm after graduating from law school at the University of Texas three years earlier. She was twenty-eight years old, but her auburn hair in a short, loose cut that framed her face, and her big blue eyes and small mouth, combined to give her the look of a teen-ager. At five-foot three, she was more than a foot shorter than Bobby. Just based on her appearance, he found it hard to believe she was a crack lawyer, even after only a few years of practice.

"I'm sorry I wasn't at the funeral," she said. "I didn't know when it would be, and my sister and I had already pre-paid for the cruise and – "

"Nothing to apologize for. Did y'all have fun? Mexico, wasn't it?"

"Yeah. We had a good time." She dropped her eyes and her face turned red.

"What's the matter?" Bobby asked.

"Nothing. It's just that – I mean – I feel like I should have been there."

"You couldn't have known."

Bobby watched as she struggled with her emotions. Whether she ever got the words out or not, Bobby knew what she was thinking. Debbie and Karla had been friendly, often seeking each other's company at firm functions. At the same time, Bobby long suspected that Debbie had a crush on him and that she was a bit jealous of Karla. He knew that Debbie felt a mixture of grief for the loss of a friend, sympathy for Bobby, and maybe a touch of guilt for any bad thoughts she might have harbored for Karla as a rival.

Debbie began to cry. Bobby walked around his desk to where she sat. As he approached, she stood and waited for his embrace. He circled his arms around her and pulled her to his chest, her tears soaked up by his shirt.

*****

"Don't you think you're rushing back in to things?"

Managing Partner Joe O'Neal was getting ready to launch into his pre-planned speech about how Bobby needed to take a little time off before jumping back to law practice. He found himself with mixed concerns. He was Bobby's friend and was genuinely concerned about Bobby's mental health. He wanted Bobby to be ready, emotionally, before he again subjected himself to the pressures of practicing law.

But he was also the firm's managing partner and was concerned about malpractice. A preoccupied lawyer under strain, even a good one like Bobby, was a claim or grievance waiting to happen. As a human being, he cared about Bobby; as a businessman, he cared about the firm's liability. For both reasons, he was prepared to order Bobby to take time off.

"I think you're right," Bobby said, catching O'Neal off guard. "I'd like to take some time off, if that's okay. I'll make whatever arrangements I need on my files."

O'Neal leaned against the door-frame of Bobby's office. "How much time do you need?"

"Enough."

"What are you going to do?"

"I don't know. Maybe go somewhere."

"Where?"

"I haven't thought that far ahead," Bobby said.

O'Neal scrutinized Bobby's face for any signs that could tell him anything. Bobby's face was stone. "You okay?" he asked.

"I will be."

CHAPTER TWENTY FOUR

An excited sixteen-year old Billy James walked across the apartment complex parking lot. No school today. Today he had better things to do. Today he was starting a career as an entrepreneur – a businessman. His brother Rondell waited for him at the apartment on East Ledbetter, just off Interstate 45 on the south side of Dallas. The Jamaicans came by yesterday to meet with Rondell, to deliver the crack, and to show him how to run the operation out of the apartment – the "gate," they called it. And Billy was going to work with him.

For the last few years, Billy had made his spending-money directing customers to similar gates, or crack houses, in South Dallas. His job was simple – flash a few vials of crack, line up the customers, and lead them to the gate where the sale was made. For that, he started out making fifty dollars a week at age thirteen. But the Jamaicans were generous. He got raises over the years. He currently made four-hundred-fifty dollars a week.

Now he would operate a gate with Rondell, with a promise that was much more lucrative. The typical crack house in south and east Dallas took in five to ten thousand dollars a day, and Billy's compensation depended upon the volume of sales. There was the promise of up to a thousand dollars a week if things went well. Not bad for a sixteen-year-old.

The Jamaicans had first moved into Dallas and come to the attention of the police before Billy was born. They started as small-time drug dealers selling marijuana, but soon progressed into powder cocaine and crack. That was how Rondell joined them, delivering drugs. Rondell got Billy his job.

Gun-running was now as big a part of the Jamaicans' operations as were drug sales. Billy had seen a newspaper article that said Texas was battling Florida as the number one center for gun-running by the Jamaicans. Rondell thought that, if they did a good job with the gate, the Jamaicans might let them help with the guns. He and Billy both made it a point to learn how the gun trade worked. They learned that the Jamaicans favored automatic or semi-automatic weapons, and took one of three different methods for obtaining the guns. The first, and easiest, was to find some solid citizen, with no prior record, to make gun buys for them. In Texas, almost anybody, even Billy, could walk in off the street and buy the weapon of his choosing.

The other two approaches were a little more difficult, but, Billy thought, certainly more exciting. Stealing was one. The other was to falsify documents so the Jamaicans could make the purchases directly. Guns ranging in price from two-hundred-fifty to five-hundred dollars could be resold in Chicago, Washington, D.C., or New York for as much as a thousand dollars, or even fifteen-hundred dollars back in Jamaica. Good profit to be made by a budding entrepreneur like Billy.

Billy walked through the depressed complex's playground, with the swings in its swingset hanging limply from broken chains. As he turned the corner of the next building, he pulled up short. Two blue-uniformed Dallas Police officers stood at the end of the sidewalk talking with the apartment manager.

"Got-damn!" Billy muttered under his breath.

He shrank back around the corner, then sprinted around another building and dashed up the stairs, two at a time, to the apartment where Rondell waited. He wheeled into the apartment and slammed the door behind him.

Rondell sat at a small table next to the tiny kitchen. In front of him, on the table, he had lined up a number of two-inch glass vials, each containing their granular treasure – rock cocaine.

Rondell looked at his ashen-faced little brother, out of breath, leaning against the front door.

"What's up?"

"The got-damn cops!" Billy said. "Downstairs."

"Motherfuck!" Rondell quickly scooped the crack off the table and into a brown paper sack. He had just cleared the table when they heard a knock at the door.

"Shit!" Rondell grabbed the sack and raced for the bathroom. "Don't open it! Don't open it!"

Billy waited inside, leaning against the door, holding his breath. Surely the cops hadn't found them already. This couldn't be. This just couldn't be. God-motherfucking-damn! In a few seconds, he heard the sound of the toilet flushing down the hall. His heart was still pounding when Rondell reappeared, empty-handed.

"Okay," Rondell said.

Billy opened the door. Outside stood a ragged-looking black man dressed in jeans and a torn T-shirt. A customer!

"I need something," the man said.

Rondell came up behind Billy and shook his head. "Ain't nothin', man. Not today."

"That's not what I hear."

"Then you hear wrong, motherfucker!" Rondell said. "Now get your raggedy ass on out of here."

Billy slammed the door, then looked at Rondell, who walked over to the couch and plopped down, his head in his hands.

"Motherfuck!" Rondell said. "Gulleyman ain't gonna like this. He ain't gonna like this for shit. What we gonna do?"

Billy knew Gulleyman as the acknowledged leader of the Jamaican Gulleymen posse in Dallas. He didn't know whether Gulleyman had named himself after the posse or the posse after himself. But in either event, Billy felt sure ego was involved. And he shared Rondell's concern. The Jamaicans were not known for leniency and understanding. Tactics they used to punish and intimidate were already legend in the poor, south Dallas communities. Kneecappings, or shooting out the knees or legs, of offenders, were common, as well as other forms of less exotic, but more brutal tortures.

Billy knew that he was on the line as well as his big brother to explain the missing drugs. His young age would not be a factor. Just last week, the police had fished the badly beaten body of a twelve-year-old out of Joe Pool Lake, south of Dallas. A kid from the neighborhood. In addition to being badly beaten, the boy had been shot twelve times in the legs and arms. Nobody believed that the gunshots to the extremities were the cause of death. Those were just for fun.

A sudden inspiration crossed Billy's mind. "What if the police was here?"

Rondell lifted his head and looked at his little brother. "What the fuck you talkin' about?"

"I seen 'em just outside. We could make it look like they was here."

Rondell sat quietly for a minute and let the idea soak in. When the cops raided a gate, they usually tore the place apart looking for drugs and guns. If Rondell and Billy did this just right, it might work.

He sprang to his feet and began scattering the cushions off the cheap sofa. He flipped the sofa over and ripped out the lining underneath. Billy began overturning furniture around the room. He pulled out his pocket knife and cut open cushions, pulling the stuffing out to simulate a search. Room by room, Billy and Rondell moved through the tiny one-bedroom apartment, overturning and trashing furniture, and even tearing out fixtures. In slightly more than fifteen minutes, the two brothers had demolished the apartment. Only then did Rondell dare venture to the phone booth on the corner outside and place the call to Gulleyman to tell him of the "police raid."

*****

Both brothers jumped at the knock on the door. Rondell gathered his wits about him, took a deep breath, then flung the door open to greet two black men. Gulleyman stood no more than six feet tall, but had a thick, muscular frame to support the pounds of gold chains around his neck and wrists. He wore a beige, lightweight suit, vested but no tie, and sported a pencil-thin mustache. He was the epitome of the Caribbean gangster. He smiled, and his white, gold-capped teeth glinted in the sun.

Neither brother had ever seen the second man before. A

vertical scar highlighted his scowling face. He had made a start on dreadlocks, though his hair seemed too short for it, and he constantly ran his hands through his hair as if to make sure the dreadlocks were still in place. In his left ear, he wore a dangling earring, in the shape of the letter "K," with a diamond in the center. The two middle fingers were missing on his left hand.

"Hello, mon," Gulleyman said.

Without waiting for an invitation, he stepped inside. His scar-faced visitor followed just behind. Gulleyman closed the door, then surveyed the wreckage. He paced his way around the apartment, scrutinizing every inch. His face gave no hint of his thoughts. The second man stood in the entryway, still scowling. Rondell and Billy stayed in the room with the man, afraid to move.

In a few seconds, Gulleyman came back into the living area and looked at his companion. "Ocee, wha' you tink, mon?"

Gulleyman's face was impossible to read. Not so his companion's. The man called Ocee had pure malevolence written in his eyes.

Ocee smiled a wicked smile. "Do it."

Gulley looked back at Rondell and spoke earnestly. "Dis does not look like de work of de police."

"But it is!" Rondell protested.

"Not de police."

"Oh, fuck! You gots to believe me!"

As Gulley and Rondell talked, Ocee began to slowly inch his way across the apartment until he stood next to Billy. Intent on the conversation going on in front of him, Billy didn't notice Ocee until he was standing next to him. Turning his head to look at Ocee, he saw Ocee staring back at him. Billy knew instantly what was about to happen.

CHAPTER TWENTY FIVE

Gulleyman lashed out with his fist and struck Rondell squarely in the face. Rondell staggered backward, then tripped over the cheap coffee table lying broken on the floor. Gulleyman roughly turned him over, grabbed the stunned youth's hands, and pulled them behind him. Rondell offered no resistance; he hoped to get out of this alive by remaining passive. Gulleyman produced an electrical extension cord from his coat pocket and tied Rondell's hands together behind his back, like a rodeo cowboy hog-tying a calf.

Things were not going well for Billy, either. Ocee threw his arm around his neck and wrestled him to the ground. Billy lay face down on the floor, his head still twisted beneath Ocee's arm. Ocee grasped the hair on the back of Billy's head, lifted it, then slammed his face into the floor. Billy's nose broke on the first slam and a pool of blood formed on the floor beneath him. Ocee slammed again. And again. And again. Each time, Billy's face splashed into the gooey red fluid that oozed from his nose.

With Rondell secured, Gulleyman crossed the room to where Ocee brutalized the younger boy. Without a word, Gulleyman twisted Billy's arms behind his back and tied them off with a cord. All the while, Ocee continued to pound his face into the floor.

Gulleyman slapped Ocee on the shoulder and said, "Bring to a boil."

Ocee glanced at Gulleyman and nodded. With one last slam, he released his grip on Billy and went to the kitchen.

Billy moaned in pain. He rolled onto his side, afraid to lie on his back lest he strangle on his own blood, but also afraid he would drown in it if he continued to lie face down. Leaning against the wall, he began to cry as blood streamed from his battered nose.

In the kitchen, Ocee located several large containers that he filled with water and placed on the stove. He turned the flame high under each one, then returned to the living area where Gulleyman lectured the James brothers.

"Never try to fool me, mon!" Gulleyman shouted. He gestured to the wreckage of the apartment. "De police don' do dis. You do dis. You do dis, and den you lies to Gulleyman."

"Oh shit, man!" Rondell wailed. "The goddamn po-lice was here, bro'. I'm tellin' ya. It was the motherfuckin' cops."

Rondell sat on the floor with his back to the wall. In two strides, Gulleyman stood next to him. He dramatically raised his foot, tantalizingly slow – drawing it high and back – back – then swung a vicious roundhouse kick to the side of Rondell's head. Rondell's head snapped to the side, sprawling him on the floor. He awkwardly tried to regain his sitting position, but he couldn't move fast enough with his hands tied behind his back. Gulleyman stomped his heel down hard on the side of Rondell's head and pinned him to the floor.

"No!" Gulleyman said. "Don' lie to me."

"I ain't lying, man. Fuck!"

Gulleyman pushed down hard with his foot, squeezing Rondell's head against the floor. His ebony skin turned white. Across the room, Billy lay on his side, propped against the wall. He could only watch helplessly, afraid his brother's head would surely be pushed through the floor.

"Ocee!" Gulleyman barked.

"Yah, mon," Ocee answered. His mouth curved in a jack-o-lantern grin.

Ocee pulled an eight-inch, double-edged knife from his pocket. Dried blood coated the blade. He approached Rondell, still pressed to the ground by Gulleyman's foot, and ripped the shirt off his back. When Gulleyman lifted his foot, Ocee rolled Rondell face down and placed the point of the blade at the base of Rondell's neck. Rondell stiffened when he felt the cold steel on his bare skin.

Ocee shoved the point into the soft skin, barely breaking the surface. Rondell tried to open his mouth to scream, but Gulleyman's foot pressed his head down and mashed his mouth against the hard wood of the floor. Only a muffled moan escaped.

With a surgeon's precision, Ocee drew the knife downward along Rondell's spine. A thin red line trailed behind the blade all the way to Rondell's belt. A few drops of blood began to spill out of the narrow gash by the time Ocee completed his path with the knife, but the cut was so fine and shallow that no major blood vessels were opened. The idea was to inflict pain, not make a mess.

Billy watched in horror as the two torturers seemed preoccupied with his brother. Quietly, slowly, he worked his way upright. Out of the corner of his eye, Gulleyman caught a glimpse of Billy, now sitting against the far wall. He saw Billy making his way up to his haunches, in position to spring to his feet. Without turning his head, Gulleyman quickly surveyed the room. An unused air conditioner window unit sat on the floor in the far corner. Gulleyman released his foot from the back of Rondell's head. He pointed to the air conditioner.

"Move dere," he commanded Billy. He pulled a gun from his pocket, just in case Billy needed more incentive.

Billy slowly straightened until he stood against the wall. Staring at the gun, he slowly walked to the back wall.

"On de floor," Gulleyman said. "Face down."

Billy dropped to his knees, then awkwardly lay forward. With his arms still tied behind him, he banged his already sore and swollen nose on the floor. Gulleyman walked to him, still pointing the weapon at his head.

"You tink you is gettin' away, mon?" Gulleyman taunted. "You tink you is escapin'?"

Gulleyman tucked the gun into his pocket. He straddled the air conditioner and grabbed it with both hands. The unit was heavy, seventy-five pounds, but he lifted it with only the slightest exertion. Once he had it firmly in his hands, he heaved it upward, like a weightlifter cleaning a press, until it rested just above his right shoulder.

He straddled Billy's outstretched body. He pressed the air conditioner upward, over his head. He held it there for a beat. Then he let go and stepped back. The heavy unit dropped quickly, gaining momentum as it fell. It rotated slightly so that the front edge rolled forward. And downward.

Flush onto the back of Billy's head. Billy's whole body jerked at the impact. Blood streamed from a gash that opened in the back of his head. It poured to his neck, where it parted like the Red Sea, streamed down around both sides of his neck, and met in a pool beneath him, joined by the flow from his broken nose.

Meanwhile, Ocee continued to work his artistry on Rondell's back. A series of cuts running left to right now criss-crossed the initial line down Rondell's spine. Rondell buried his face against the floor, which ran as wet with his tears as the floor in front of Billy's face ran wet with blood. Satisfied with his bloody work, Ocee stood and smiled at Gulleyman, who sat on a chair beside the still form of Billy, watching the master sadist at work.

Ocee kicked Rondell sharply in the head. "You don' move, mon," he growled.

Ocee went into the kitchen to check on the boiling water. It bubbled over the edges of the containers on the stove, but he didn't move it yet. He opened the cabinet next to the sink. With a sweep of his hand, he brushed the contents of the cabinet to the floor, just as he had done in the Barbadian Minister of Education's house a few weeks earlier. Methodically, he searched the cabinets until he found a shaker of salt.

He grabbed it and walked back to the bleeding Rondell, who still lay with his face down on the floor.

"Wha' next, mon?" Ocee asked. He leaned close to Rondell's ear. "Wha' next?"

Before Rondell could answer, Ocee extended his arm, the salt shaker in his hand, and slowly turned it over. At first the flow of salt was just a sprinkle. Ocee shook his hand vigorously, forcing the salt out in heavier doses. The white crystals floated downward like snowflakes, covering Rondell's back. They soaked into the open wounds, sending a searing pain deep into the teen's body.

Rondell rolled onto his back, screaming.

Ocee swung his foot viciously, his toe smashing into Rondell's ribs. A brittle crunching sound testified to another fracture.

Another scream from Rondell.

Ocee tried to roll his victim back over with his foot, but Rondell nudged at Ocee's leg with his shoulder and pushed him away. The hard wood of the floor abraded his already torn skin as he fought to keep his back covered. Ocee drew back his foot again and swung. Another direct hit gouged Rondell's side. More crunching of bone. Ocee not only heard, he felt ribs crunch beneath his foot.

Rondell hacked a deep guttural cough. Blood spewed from his mouth. Then he vomited red mush across the floor. Ocee grabbed Rondell and forcibly rolled him onto his stomach. He pushed his face down in the vomit. Rondell's screams choked out into a gurgle. Ocee extended the salt shaker again and emptied the rest of its contents. Rondell tried to scream, but the sound choked off in the bloody mush spewing from his lungs.

Gulleyman casually sauntered into the kitchen where the boiling water bubbled furiously. Using a dish towel as a hot pad, he lifted the first pot of water and carried it to where Rondell lay. Ocee stepped aside. Gulleyman lifted the pot high, then tipped it over. The scalding liquid bubbled out in a waterfall. It made a splattering, sizzling sound when it spilled across Rondell's blood-soaked skin.

Rondell screamed, forcing the sound out from deep inside.

Ocee followed Gulleyman back to the kitchen where they each grabbed a pot and repeated the process, drenching Rondell with more boiling water. Rondell opened his mouth again, but only the blood-vomit mixture from his punctured lungs came out. He slowly sank beneath the waves of unconsciousness, willingly giving himself to them. As the last drops bathed his tortured back, he mercifully blacked out.

174

His face pressed into the pool of fluids that had come from his insides.

Gulleyman and Ocee stood back and looked at their victims. For Gulleyman, it was strictly business that was now almost complete. For Ocee, it was strictly pleasure. With Rondell unconscious, there was nothing more to gain from torture. An unconscious man felt no pain. The same was true for Billy, who had lost consciousness before Ocee could be turned loose on him. All that remained was to send a message.

Ocee pulled his handgun from his pocket. He bent over Rondell and tore off his shoes. He placed the barrel of the gun against the sole of Rondell's right foot, aimed up so that it pointed through the ankle and into the lower leg. When he had it just right, he pulled the trigger.

Rondell's leg jerked as the bullet tore its way upward. It ripped a hole in the bottom of his foot, then exited from the back of the leg, just below the calf, before embedding itself in a wall. Ocee repeated the process on the other foot. This bullet stayed inside.

Ocee rolled Rondell over onto his back and straddled the body. Aiming downward, he fired four more shots, two into each kneecap. As the bullets slammed into Rondell's legs, crippling him, the limbs jumped and jerked like giant snakes. Finally, they lay still. While Ocee kneecapped Rondell, Gulleyman did the same to little brother Billy. Two shots into each leg, and one into each foot. The message? No one rips off the Gulleymen.

After the job was done, the two men repocketed their weapons, then surveyed the damage. Satisfied, they casually strolled to the door, opened it, and left.

CHAPTER TWENTY SIX

Bobby shifted in his seat and stared out the window at the clouds. First-class was almost empty, and he was glad he didn't have to put up with the congestion and noise of coach. He had left Kauai's Lihue airport almost two hours ago, with a brief layover in Honolulu before boarding the American Airlines Luxury Liner for the trip home. He absent-mindedly stroked the beard he had grown in the five weeks he had been there and wondered whether he would keep it once he got back to his law practice. He had grown beards off and on since college, but never kept one for long. But he might this time. He liked the way it looked on his tanned face. It highlighted his dark eyes and gave them an almost piercing look. Maybe he could put that to use in cross-examination. It was at least worth thinking about.

The five weeks in Kauai had been good for him. Of course, he wasn't sure if it was Kauai or just the five weeks. Time was, after all, the great healer. That was not to say that he was over Karla's death, but enough time had passed to help him put her death in perspective. That was good. And since he was alone, now, growing accustomed to that solitude was made easier by being on a beautiful tropical island in the Pacific. Not easy – just easier.

But the first few days, if not the first week, had not been easy at all. After landing at the Lihue airport, Bobby rented a car and headed for the Princeville area on the island's north shore. The condominium he rented sat on a bluff, just behind the Princeville golf course, overlooking the Pacific. From the patio, Bobby enjoyed a perfect view of the sunrise from behind a finger of land that supported the Kilauea lighthouse. Bobby saw every 6:22 a.m. sunrise for the first week. Had the sun risen at 3:00 a.m., he probably would have seen most of those, as well, for all the sleep he was able to get.

But lack of sleep or not, watching the sun rise on the horizon, as the sky turned from gray to orange to baby blue, was a life-affirming experience for him. He began to realize that, even with the horrible devastation of hurricanes in the past, God saw to it that Kauai had a glorious sunrise every morning. It was as if God were reminding him that, even in the face of disaster, he was still God and he was still in control. If that was true for Kauai, Bobby reasoned, it surely must be true for him, as well.

As if the sunrises weren't enough to restore his faith, Bobby made daily trips to Lumahai Beach. The crescent-shaped white sand beach, made famous as the Nurse's Beach in the musical South Pacific, lay protected from the outside world by a heavily wooded cliff that rose behind it and by the strong Pacific in front. Lying on the sand, listening to the pounding surf, Bobby was reminded of the waves of Long Bay Beach at Sam Lord's Castle on Barbados. He remembered being there with Karla, feeling the sun bathe their bodies and souls. He came to realize that he would always have those memories and that, even if they didn't have a future together, nothing and no one could ever take away their past together.

He still hadn't figured out the "why" yet. He wasn't sure he ever would, but he was willing to leave that question unanswered until God was ready to let him know. If there was one thing Bobby believed he truly needed right now, it was hope, because without hope there was nothing. Only one thing gave him that hope – his faith in God. It gave him hope that he could get through this tragedy, hope that there was a better day tomorrow, hope that life was worth living, and hope that he would someday be reunited with, not only Karla, but also his parents and other loved ones he had lost in his life.

As he flew back to Dallas, Bobby knew he still needed to learn to cope without Karla. He knew he would miss her. But he also knew he still had his God and that, somehow, he would get through it. He pressed the button to recline his seat and slid down. He lay his head back and folded his arms across his chest. A faint smile crossed his lips as he closed his eyes and drifted off to sleep.

*****

Lieutenant Derek Larson of the Dallas Police Department left the offices of the Jamaican Drug Task Force in the Earl Cabell Federal Building in downtown Dallas and headed for Parkland Hospital. He was a charter member of the Task Force, formed in response to the growing problem of Jamaican posses in Dallas. The Dallas police had begun linking dozens of killings and maimings – teen-agers showing up at local hospitals with scalds or kneecap gunshot wounds – to drug rings running crack houses in south and west Dallas, with connections to Jamaicans living in New York. The already overworked Dallas police couldn't handle the problem alone. Although they regularly raided crack houses and arrested lower-level crack dealers, they had been unable to capture the leaders, who carefully insulated themselves by hiring teen-agers to run the houses and even to do some of their dirty work.

Because most of the arrests were of juveniles, who were often back on the streets within a matter of hours, Derek and others became increasingly frustrated. It wasn't uncommon for thirteen- and fourteen-year-old kids to strut through the judicial system, openly laughing at law enforcement. One even mockingly offered Derek a job for more money than he made as a police officer. He saw kids with rolls of cash, their necks weighted down by expensive jewelry. And because they were kids, he knew they believed, rightly enough, that they were immune from real prosecution. If you were a kid with nothing, the promise of quick cash made it worth the risk of arrest, which was little more than a nuisance.

The Jamaicans knew this as well. They dispatched teen-agers from New York to places such as Dallas to recruit local help and to set up the drug "gates." The "street worms," as they were called, set up the businesses, arming locals, and then returned to New York. It was the posse equivalent of a Mormon's mission.

Just as the Dallas police seemed to be drowning in the blood being freely let on the streets, local, state, and federal agencies formed the Task Force. Derek was the ranking DPD officer on the Task Force, which consisted of Dallas police officers, Dallas County Sheriff's Department deputies, agents of the U.S. Drug Enforcement Administration, the Bureau of Alcohol, Tobacco and Firearms, and Immigration and Customs Enforcement (ICE). By maintaining a national database on Jamaican criminals, and by having a Task Force member interview every Jamaican citizen arrested and jailed in Dallas County, regardless of the charge, the group kept tabs on Jamaican activity in Dallas.

Still young at the age of thirty-six, Derek had a full head of thick blonde hair, befitting his Scandinavian ancestry. He stood just a shade under six feet, but possessed the broad shoulders, sinewy build, and graceful movements of an athlete. He had, in fact, been an all-metro safety on a district runner-up Couger football team in his senior year at Bryan Adams High School in east Dallas. With blue eyes to complement his blonde hair, and smooth-cheeked good looks, he might have been a model rather than a narcotics officer. But those very features placed him in good stead during his years of undercover work, particularly in the early days when he had been planted in local high schools, posing as a student to sniff out drug dealing among teenagers. Even now, the bad guys tended to underestimate his acumen and resolve, which was carefully disguised beneath his boyish exterior.

Within fifteen minutes, Derek pulled into the parking lot nearest the emergency entrance at Parkland, the county hospital. He jumped out of his car and walked briskly to the sliding doors. As he entered the waiting room, he saw his partner, Ricky Martinez, at the nurse's station talking with a scrub-suited young man. Martinez finished his conversation with the doctor, then turned to face his partner.

"I think we may have caught a break on the Gulleymen."

Derek's attention perked up. "I'm listening."

"We got two kids in here, teenagers, got knee-capped by two Gulleymen. The older one is pissed that his little brother got hurt. He's scared, but he's more pissed than scared. He wants revenge for his brother, and he's willing to finger who did it."

"These guys always get someone else to do their dirty work. We get the street guys all the time. Why – "

"This kid says one of them was Gulleyman. Not a Gulley-man. The Gulleyman."

"He can i.d. him?"

"And if the Task Force gives him protection, he'll testify."

"Seriously?"

"As a heart attack."

*****

Rondell lay face down on a bed in a ward for burn victims. His back was covered with light gauze and both his legs were heavily bandaged from the knees down. As Larson and Martinez entered the room, Rondell turned his head to look at the officers. Tears streaked his face.

Martinez pulled a chair beside the bed and sat down. "Rondell, this is Lieutenant Larson. I want you to tell him what you told me about who did this to you."

Derek stood beside Martinez so that Rondell had to twist his neck to look up at him. Martinez yielded his chair to Derek, who sat down, bringing himself to eye level with the wounded boy.

"I know you," Rondell said through gritted teeth. "I seen you befo'."

"If you've been with these guys very long, or if you've ever been arrested with them, you probably have."

Rondell nodded but didn't respond.

"Tell me who did this," Derek said.

"Gulleyman."

"Describe him."

Rondell grimaced. "Six foot tall. Steroid muscles. Little shit-eatin' mustache. Gold caps on his teeth. Always wear a suit but never wear a tie. Lots of gold aroun' his neck. He hang at the Kool Kool Klub on Second Avenue."

Derek nodded. That fit the description of the leader of the Gulleymen posse. He had even seen him before, but didn't know a name. "What about the second man?"

"Never see him befo'."

"Describe him."

"'Bout my height. Bad lookin' motherfucker. Got this scar on his cheek and got two fingers gone. When he smile, he – he a bad motherfucker."

"Jamaican?"

"Sound like it."

"Ever hear of him before? Just talk around?"

"No."

Derek glanced at Martinez "Check the computer on this guy. That description ought to stand out."

"Done."

While Martinez left to follow up, Derek turned his attention back to Rondell. "How well do you know this Gulleyman?"

Rondell stared at Derek but didn't answer.

"Listen son, I'm your best friend right now. But only if you talk to me."

Rondell shook his head, but didn't say anything.

"I'll get a D.A. down here and make you a deal. The tighter we can tie a noose around Gulleyman's neck, the better it is for you."

"It ain't Gulleyman. It's the other dude. If you don't know nothin' on him, he still gonna be out there. And he still gonna be after me. And after Billy."

"Who's Billy?"

"My brother. They fucked him up bad, man."

"Our best chance to get both of them is if we get full cooperation from you. Then we can put them away good and tight and get you the hell out of here."

"Billy, too?"

"Billy, too."

Rondell considered the offer. At last he said, "What you need from me?"

"We can get him on aggravated assault for you and your brother. But I'd like to get him for murder. Can you help me with that?"

"Yeah."

Derek perked up. "Yeah? What do you know?"

"Some dude in Oak Cliff jes' a couple a weeks ago. In some apartments on Zang. Dude was a addict, tried to cop some crack from one of Gulley's gates. Gulley was gonna set me up with a gate, so he took me with him to see how it worked."

Derek made a few notes, then prodded Rondell when he paused in his narration. "What happened?"

"It was me, Gulley, and two Jamaicans."

"This new guy wasn't one of them?"

"I done tole you, I never see the motherfucker befo'."

"What happened?"

"They all got uzis, man. They jes' knock on the do', pretty as you please. When the dude open the do', they starts shootin'."

"Did Gulley shoot, or just the two with him?"

"Shit, man, Gulley shoot first. When the others stop, Gulley kep' shootin'."

Martinez came back into the room. Derek looked at him and raised his eyebrows in an unspoken question. Martinez shook his head.

"Did Gulleyman call this new guy anything?" Derek asked Rondell.

"He call him O.C., or some shit like that."

Derek made a note. "Is there anything else about this guy you can remember? Jewelry, tattoos, anything?"

Rondell's eyes widened. "He have a earring in his ear. Lef' ear. The letter 'K,' with a stone in the middle. Look like a diamond."

"A 'K'?"

"Yeah, man. A gold 'K.'"

"Are you sure he didn't call him O.K., or K.C.? Something like that?"

Rondell shook his head vigorously. "O.C. That's what he call the motherfucker. O.C."

CHAPTER TWENTY SEVEN

Martinez and Larson piled into Derek's classic Plymouth and left Parkland Hospital, heading for the Kool Kool Klub. Located in the Fair Park area, home to the State Fair of Texas, the club was nothing more than a squat brick storefront in the shadows of downtown Dallas. Reggae was the music of choice. At any given moment, everyone in the club was either native Jamaican or associated with Jamaicans. The Dallas police raided the club on a regular basis. Phone numbers obtained as part of any follow-up investigation invariably included some from the east coast, including New York City.

At just past six in the evening, Derek turned south onto Second Avenue and made his way to the Jamaican night club. He shook his head as he drove through the depressed neighborhood that surrounded Fair Park. He knew the Jamaicans preyed on the hopelessness of the poverty-stricken. They lured them with the flash of fast cash and the temporary escape of a crack-based high, then kept them in line with fear and intimidation. In a conscienceless society, the violent Jamaicans were the lowest of the low as far as Derek was concerned.

He pulled into the parking lot and wheeled to a stop in front of the door, blocking in a run-down, early 2000s Cadillac pimpmobile. The doors to the club were open. The rhythmic pounding of a reggae beat escaped into the Dallas air.

Derek and Martinez got out and walked to the front door. They stepped inside and waited for their eyes to adjust to the darkness, which was in stark contrast to the sun-splashed parking lot outside. A tall, gaunt Rastafarian sat just inside the front door, staring at them.

"Can I help you, Lieutenant?" he asked.

Derek smiled his way. "Cornell, we need to see Peter."

"He in the back. This way."

The tall man led the way, ducking as he stepped through the metal detector just beyond the entryway. When the officers followed, their weapons triggered the device's warning wail. The boom of the music flooded the tiny interior from eight speakers planted strategically around the room, drowning out the high-pitched siren. In the darkness, Derek saw only a handful of customers seated in groups of twos and threes at small round tables. A lone man sat at the bar. The customers suspiciously watched the two white men who were brazen enough to carry weapons into the bar. They resented that their domain had been invaded by the unwelcome. By cops.

At the far side of the bar, a closed door led to the club's office. Cornell paused outside the door, knocked lightly, then opened it.

"Lieutenant Larson," he announced in a loud voice.

A small, well-dressed black man sat behind a large desk, casually smoking a cigarette. He leaned back in his chair and smiled.

"Come in Lieutenant." His spoke in the familiar accent of the Caribbean, but his tone was precise and cultured. It announced, "I am a businessman. I am respectable."

"Peter, I'm looking for somebody," Derek said.

Peter raised his eyebrows questioningly.

"Gulleyman."

Peter threw his head back and laughed. "And you tink I'll tell you where to find him?"

"You will unless you want cops crawling all over this place, twenty-four/seven."

Peter stopped laughing. "You know I can' tell you. He don' tell me where he is. He just come and he go."

"This will be just between us. And I know you know."

"But I don' know."

Derek dragged a chair across from Peter's desk. Martinez stood at attention behind him, keeping an eye on the door, which Cornell closed behind them. Derek leaned forward, elbows on the desk, and peered earnestly at the small man.

"Are you familiar with the forfeiture laws?" Derek asked.

"Wha' you mean?"

"Did you know that we can lawfully seize this bar and flat-ass take it away from you if we find dealing in here?"

Peter stared blankly at Derek, licking his lips nervously.

"I'm talking flat-ass away from you. Then it's no longer yours. Now, what do you think are the odds of us finding drugs on any given day? Fifty-fifty?" Derek smiled and shook his head. "I bet they're even better than that. And besides, if there're enough raids, something will turn up. Sooner or later. You can bet on that."

"Why you doin' dis, mon?"

"You give me Gulleyman and I go away. You don't, I'm your new best customer. Your choice."

Peter shook his head. "You don' know wha' you askin' me to do. You jus' don' know."

"Oh, yeah I do."

"I don' know."

"Peter, if we get Gulleyman, what've you got to worry about?"

"It not he I worry about."

Derek cut a glance at Martinez. "Then who?"

"Ocee."

"Who the hell is O.C.?"

"I don' know he from befo'. I never see he befo'. He show up 'bout two, tree week ago. Evahbody afraid of he. Even Gulleyman afraid of he." He paused and lowered his voice. "I afraid of he."

"Where can we find this O.C.?"

"You find Gulleyman, den you find he."

"Then goddamit, help us find Gulleyman."

Peter stood and paced behind his desk. "I don' know, mon. I jus' don' know."

"Has he ever been in here?"

"Yeah, mon. Two, tree time. Always wit Gulleyman."

"Describe him."

"Scarface and two finger gone. On he lef' hand."

"Anything else?"

"Das enough. You can see he a violent man."

Derek looked back at Martinez. "What do you think, Ricky?

You think we need to check this place out on a regular basis? Get some uniforms down here?"

"Yeah, I think so."

"Wait, wait," Peter protested. "Even dat make Gulleyman angry."

"Well, then it looks like you're in trouble either way. Your best bet is to get him off the streets."

CHAPTER TWENTY EIGHT

It was late evening and the sun was starting to set when Derek and Martinez exited off of U.S. Highway 67 onto Ledbetter Drive in South Oak Cliff. According to Peter, Gulleyman ran a string of crack houses along Ledbetter, between Highway 67 and Interstate 45, and usually made his rounds after eight o'clock to collect the day's take. Derek turned left and cruised the street slowly, looking for Gulleyman's gold Mercedes.

Derek had answered a call along here just last weekend. According to the apartment manager who placed the call, Jamaicans ran close to twenty gates in his two-hundred unit complex. Apparently the different posses that ran the gates were operating under an uneasy truce that had expired violently. The manager said that Jamaicans sprayed machine-gun fire all over the apartment courtyard where children played. One posse member even chased another man down Polk Street in broad daylight before running over him with his car, then knee-capping him. Derek wondered if Gulleyman and his new sidekick, O.C., were involved in that attack.

Ricky's frantic voice snapped Derek's mind back to the present.

"There! There! In that parking lot."

Derek followed Ricky's pointing finger. A gaudy gold Mercedes 450sl was just pulling out of an apartment complex to their right. Derek had already passed the exit before he saw the car. He slammed his foot on the brakes and screeched to a halt. The lone occupant of the Mercedes glanced his way. Derek made eye contact. Gulleyman smiled. Derek nodded in return, the cops-and-robbers equivalent of boxers touching gloves before the bell.

The Mercedes accelerated violently out of the parking lot toward Highway 67. Derek gunned the Fury into a one-hundred-eighty degree turn, then fishtailed off in pursuit.

The Mercedes turned north on Hampton and burst through a red light. Derek turned on his siren, its wail barely audible over the squeal of tires and the roar of racing engines. He took the Hampton turn on two tires. The car threatened to roll for a moment, then settled back on all fours. Martinez grabbed the door handle with one hand, his other on the dash. Derek squeezed the wheel tightly with both hands.

They barely regained their bearings when traffic began spinning out to the right and left. Cars careened recklessly onto curbs and crossed the median. A Jeep just ahead of them turned sharply to the right and ran up a sloping hillside, revealing the cause of the craziness. The gold Mercedes barreled down Hampton toward them in reverse. It bounced off curbs, side-swiped one car, and narrowly missed another.

"Watch out, asshole!" Derek muttered. He glanced quickly at Martinez. "Put a few rounds up his skirt."

Martinez rolled down the passenger window and leaned out, steadying his service revolver in his right hand. The gap between the cars narrowed sharply. Martinez squeezed off four rounds in rapid succession.

Derek twisted the steering wheel to the right. Simultaneously, the Mercedes angled sharply to the left and jumped the center median. The Fury hit the curb, went airborne, then slammed back to earth. Martinez clamped his gun hand against the side of the car to keep from falling out the window.

Derek gritted his teeth as his head bounced off the roof. Determined not to lose control, he swung the car up the shallow incline, then made a sweeping turn to the left and crashed back over the curb. There was a brief moment of smooth ride as the car shot across Hampton's three north-bound lanes. Then it slammed into the center median, hopped it in one leap, and came to earth again with all four tires spinning, headed south.

The Mercedes sped away, still going backward. It backed to the left around Ledbetter, screeched to a halt, then roared forward toward the highway. Derek hit the intersection at fifty miles an hour and skidded around the turn. Just as he lined up behind the Mercedes, Gulleyman began weaving a serpentine path, causing other drivers to spin out of control. Derek tap danced his foot between the brake and the accelerator, weaving his way through the confused drivers. Martinez rode anxiously beside him, gun still in hand, waiting for another clear shot, but there was too much traffic and he dared not fire.

"We need a chopper," Derek said.

Martinez nodded and grabbed the radio microphone. Ahead, the Mercedes turned right and accelerated up the entry ramp to Highway 67.

"He's heading north, toward town," Derek said. He followed and entered the highway traffic. "He's all over the goddamn road."

Gulleyman weaved in and out of traffic, leaving a maze of frightened and confused drivers in his wake. Derek tried to follow the same weave but continually lost speed dodging other cars – a practice not followed by Gulleyman. A few angry drivers deliberately tried to cut Derek off until they realized that the unmarked car was blaring a siren.

As the two cars neared the merger of Highway 67 and Interstate 35, Derek clenched his teeth. He hoped the merging traffic from 35 would yield to the Mercedes, regardless of what the driver's handbook said about right of way. By now, he managed to close the gap somewhat. Most of the innocent traffic that hindered the Jamaican pulled off the road after being passed by him. That left a wide open path for the pursuing police car.

Out of the corner of his eye, Derek saw a small car on his right, heading north on Interstate 35. It moved ahead in the merge lane without apparent regard for what was happening in the almost parallel lanes of Highway 67. Its driver, a teenaged mother, was preoccupied with her infant daughter in the car-seat behind her. The large Mercedes and the small car continued their merging paths unabated. Even though she had a slight lead on the Mercedes, the speed of the Jamaican's car put him on a collision course with her.

When Derek looked back at the car ahead of him, he was horrified at the silhouette he saw through the window. Extending from the Jamaican's shoulder was the unmistakable shape of his arm pointing toward the small car. At the end of his arm was the outline of an automatic weapon, most likely an uzi.

"Hang on," Derek muttered.

He pressed the accelerator to the floor and swerved onto the shoulder to his right, pouring the Fury into the metal barrier separating the two highways.

Ricky dropped the microphone and grabbed the door handle with both hands. Derek saw the outline of Gulleyman's arm shake violently. The small car arced wildly to the right across several lanes of traffic. It shot off the highway and up the side of a hill that bordered the concrete roadway. It continued to forge upward until it smashed into a fence at the top. It went airborne, flipped over onto its top, and began rolling back down the hill.

"Son of a bitch!" Derek exclaimed. He brought his car into the lane behind the Mercedes. "Get an ambulance. Fast!"

Gulleyman shifted the uzi to his left hand. Extending it out the window, he sprayed traffic beside and in front of him. Bewildered drivers spun off in all directions, creating a series of unpredictable roadblocks for the pursuing officers. Like a tank maneuvering its way through the Maginot Line, Derek expertly spun the steering wheel back and forth, dodging the crying, frightened and, occasionally, wounded drivers.

"Where's that goddamn chopper?" Derek asked.

"On its way."

"We need it now. And we need backup."

As if in answer, Derek heard the sounds of a second siren, harmonizing to his right. A Dallas police car rose into view, ascending the entry ramp to the highway from Jefferson Boulevard.

The Mercedes exited onto Interstate 30, going east. It barreled into the maze of overpasses and underpasses just south of downtown Dallas called the "Canyon," and headed toward the suburb of Mesquite. Traffic was light, thanks to the lateness of the day, but the Jamaican still sprayed the cars, continuing to wreak havoc. Without losing speed, Derek hit the I-30 exit less than one hundred feet behind, still weaving in and out of traffic. Two Dallas police cars trailed behind him.

"Let Mesquite P.D. know we're coming."

The microphone was now almost permanently attached to Martinez's hand due to the grip he exerted on it. "The road splits up there, you know," he said. "He can go Highway 80, toward Forney, or stay on I-30 toward Rockwall."

"Either way he goes through Mesquite. Get them on stand-by at the split. Let Rockwall and Forney know, too."

As Martinez alerted neighboring police departments, the parade bolted eastward at speeds exceeding one hundred miles per hour. By the time they reached the Highway 80/Interstate 30 split, the chase vehicles had added two squad cars and one helicopter. The Mercedes hung to the right, toward Highway 80, as the split approached. Waiting Mesquite police officers gunned their engines to life and prepared to join the chase. Another officer, waiting on I-30, started his engine and cut over to Highway 80.

Suddenly, the Mercedes took a hard angle to the left. It shot across three lanes of traffic, barely missing the support beams for the overpass, and flew onto I-30.

Derek hit his brakes and spun the wheel to the left, flinging a bruised Ricky Martinez against the door. The cars behind hit their brakes in rapid succession, narrowly avoiding a chain-reaction collision. By the time the chase parade got back in pursuit, its prey was a quarter of a mile down the road. The chopper kept the car in sight as the pursuers recovered. Not that it would have been difficult to follow the trail of spun-out automobiles scattered in its wake.

Interstate 30 led northeastward out of Dallas through Mesquite, past LBJ Freeway to Garland, across Lake Ray Hubbard to Rockwall, and then on to Greenville, Texarkana, and Arkansas. As part of burgeoning growth in the Rockwall area, traffic congestion had reached its saturation point along the I-30 corridor. To ease traffic worries, highway construction was underway to add additional lanes of traffic along the Ray Hubbard bridge.

Now, as Gulleyman led law enforcement officers on a merry chase along I-30, Texas Department of Public Safety officers and Garland and Rockwall police officers hurriedly positioned heavy construction equipment across the two open, east-bound lanes across the lake. They set up in the center of the lake, to make sure the Mercedes had nowhere else to go. Legitimate traffic was forced to exit just before the highway began its course across the lake. It was all done quickly, because of the speeds of the approaching cars. The cranes were in place, blocking the road, when the Mercedes appeared over the hill and descended toward the lake.

The sun was almost gone when Gulleyman reached Lake Ray Hubbard. He hadn't paid much attention to the line of cars exiting before the lake, nor, in the approaching darkness, did he notice the police officers directing the exodus. He saw two police cars blocking the right lane, but didn't attach any significance to the fact that they left one lane open to the bridge. He swung his Mercedes into that lane and accelerated toward the water, laying down a spray of machine-gun fire at the police vehicles as he screamed past.

*****

Derek slowed a bit as he watched the Mercedes make its way onto the bridge. With the sun sinking in the sky behind him, he could barely see ahead. Ricky got confirmation that the roadblock was in place, but neither of them could see it. Derek figured if he couldn't see it, then neither could Gulleyman, who had not turned on his headlights.

*****

Gulleyman noticed that he was pulling away from his pursuers. He checked his speedometer and saw that he maintained a constant speed. That meant the police were slowing for some reason. Then he remembered the squad cars at the last exit. There was something odd about that. He tried hard to remember what seemed out of place. Only then did he recall the line of cars exiting. None went forward across the lake. None but him.

Why did the police leave one lane open for him? What trap lay ahead?

He pushed the button to turn on his headlights. The lights on the panel came on and confirmed his speed at one-hundred-twenty miles an hour.

He looked up at the road ahead of him.

And saw only massive machinery blocking his way. He knew in an instant that he was hurtling to his death, which would be a violent collision against an immovable object, probably followed by an explosion and fire.

At the last moment, he twisted the steering wheel to the right, losing the game of chicken.

*****

The Mercedes's tail-lights lit up, then disappeared through the guardrail that separated the traffic lanes from Ray Hubbard's waters twenty feet below. Derek wheeled his car to a stop in front of the roadblock. The rest of the parade followed his lead. He and Ricky bolted from the car and raced to the broken guardrail. A handful of officers gathered to watch the Mercedes slowly sink below the surface of the water. Only the trunk was still visible, tilting up toward them.

And then it was gone.

Derek turned back toward his car when he heard a noise behind him. Something out of place. He searched for the source.

To his amazement, a bloodied Gulleyman rose from a pile of sand that lined the bridge's edge. His clothes and skin were peeled from his body after he threw himself from the car, then skittered across the asphalt. He had dropped off a two-foot ledge to the sand in the median, then banged to a crashing halt against the concrete retaining wall dividing the lanes of traffic.

Somehow, Gulleyman maintained his grip on his uzi. The bloody Jamaican raised the weapon and pointed it at the cluster of officers at the edge of the road.

Derek watched, dumbfounded for a second. Then he found his voice.

"Hit it!" He dove for cover and pulled his gun from its holster.

Gulleyman fired a wild burst at the officers but was too weak to hold the weapon steady. Most of the shots slammed into the freshly paved asphalt, ricocheting harmlessly. Policemen scrambled helter-skelter out of the way.

Derek hit the ground and rolled once before coming to a stop on his stomach. He steadied his weapon and squeezed off two quick shots.

Gulleyman went down hard. His back slapped flat against the roadway. His uzi still sprayed wild fire, even from his prone position.

Derek climbed to his knees. In a crouch, he approached the spot where Gulleyman lay. As he neared the man, he stood and gazed at the prone figure.

Gulleyman tried to raise his uzi. Derek emptied his weapon.

Gulleyman dropped his uzi and lay still.

CHAPTER TWENTY NINE

It felt good to Bobby to be back at work, busy again. The other lawyers, as well as the secretaries who worked in his area, paid him a lot of attention. It was as if someone had given a secret command that he was not to be left alone or idle for even one second. But Bobby didn't mind. It filled his days.

His nights were another story. He made it a point to work as late as possible each day so there would be less time to spend at home alone, before going to bed. At the end of the day, he usually walked to the downtown YMCA before heading home. Once home, he either went to the mall or took in a movie, but he generally filled all the daytime hours, and a few of the night, with activity and people.

The problems came when it was time each night to turn off the lights. Some nights, sleep came right away. Other nights, it lagged. Those were the bad hours, when he lay restlessly in bed and tried to clear his mind to induce sleep, only to find himself inexorably drawn back to the Barbadian canefield. But sleep always came, sooner or later, and the nights passed.

By the second week, Bobby was back in full swing. His calendar had filled while he was in Kauai. After the brief respite, he was back on a hectic schedule of depositions, hearings, and briefing deadlines. A few trials even lurked on the horizon on files that were, typically, unprepared. That meant a flurry of last-minute discovery to get them ready for trial.

That also meant coordinating his schedule with the lawyers assisting him on those cases. For the most part, that meant Debbie Grant.

*****

"You got a few minutes?"

Bobby looked into Debbie's smiling face. He smiled back and motioned for her to enter. "Always. Come on in."

She advanced hesitantly, then took a seat across from him. "I don't want to interrupt if you're busy."

"It's nothing that can't wait. Besides, we've got some stuff to talk about, don't we?" He gestured to his calendar. "Lots of stuff that wasn't there before."

"I wasn't sure how long you'd be gone when I scheduled a lot of that. Most of the other lawyers were pretty good about putting things off, but we had scheduling deadlines on some of it."

"I appreciate your handling it."

Debbie dropped her eyes. "I just wanted to do whatever I could."

Bobby smiled kindly at his embarassed associate. "Well, if I haven't already said it yet, thank you."

"You're welcome." She looked back up, blushing, and smiled.

Bobby noticed, for maybe the first time, that she had a nice smile.

"Anyway," she said, "I wanted to talk to you about the Forreston case."

Bobby looked at his calendar again. "Yeah, I see Dr. Forreston's depo is coming up. What do we need to do to get ready?"

"We got some stuff from the hospital on surgery scheduling. I've been putting together a chart summarizing all that."

"Is it ready?"

"Pretty much."

"I'll call Forreston and get him in here to go through it. When are you available in the next week or so?"

"You want me there?"

Bobby knew that some partners were reluctant to let associates have direct contact with their clients. The reasons ranged from lack of confidence in the younger lawyers, to ego, to simply wanting to be in control of every aspect of a client's file. Bobby was not of that mind. He welcomed the opportunity to let young lawyers take on added responsibility, and credit, in representing his clients.

"You did the work," Bobby said. "I think you should help with the depo prep."

She smiled again. "I'm open any day but Friday."

"I'll let you know after I talk to Forreston."

She stood to leave, but stopped when she got to the door. "I'm glad you're back," she said.

"Yeah, me too. Thanks."

Bobby watched her leave. The memory of her smile lingered for a moment, then he went back to work.

CHAPTER THIRTY

With Gulleyman dead, Ocee found himself the natural heir to leadership of the posse. Even though he had been in Dallas for only a short while, his reputation preceded him. He and his exploits were notorious throughout the Caribbean, and his notoriety made him and his "talents" particularly attractive to posse leaders in Kingston and in New York City. In fact, the decision to grant his request to go to Dallas – the home of the white woman who haunted him – for an internship of sorts had been made in New York and directly communicated to Gulleyman by the powers-that-be on the east coast.

Ocee arrived in Dallas intent on living up to his press clippings. He foresaw a rich destiny for himself in the Texas drug and weapons trade. He also saw a future that included power beyond his wildest dreams. He got a head-start on that future by being installed as Gulleyman's right-hand man immediately upon his arrival in Dallas.

What resentment there might have been among Gulleyman's other lieutenants was quickly quelled as Ocee moved to consolidate his position through strong-arm tactics uniquely his own. Of Gulleyman's five chief lieutenants, two mysteriously disappeared less than a week after Ocee's arrival. Their bodies were never recovered. The other three sensed that Ocee was not a man to be trifled with and quickly deferred to him as their superior.

And now, with Gulleyman gone, Ocee was top dog. In the month since Gulleyman's death, Ocee took over his North Dallas apartment and his Jaguar – the new car Gulleyman acquired to complement the gold Mercedes – and even took his wardrobe. It required a bit of tailoring to suit the garments to Ocee's slighter build, but they would do while he built a wardrobe of his own.

He also made regular rounds at his gates, collecting drug money and dropping off new supplies. While Gulleyman often delegated subordinates to handle that chore, Ocee did it himself. He wanted to be visible. He also wanted the word to spread as to what would happen to anyone who bucked his new system. As the rate of knee-cappings and more exotic tortures accelerated, the word had, indeed, spread. Soon, the very mention of his name inspired fear in the listener. Fear and awe, as if he were some kind of god.

The god of violence and death.

*****

Derek Larson and the Jamaican Task Force had no luck making an identification on the mysterious stranger with the scarred face and missing fingers. Repeated searches of the Jamaican database yielded zilch. There was no record anywhere of a Jamaican who answered to the name O.C. and who fit the description. East coast didn't know, nor did Chicago nor Houston. Nor Phoenix. Nor even Kingston, Jamaica.

In the period following Gulleyman's death, the Task Force intensified its efforts to find the man, but no one was talking.

No one, that is, except Rondell James and Peter Cromwell. Billy James wasn't talking. He died in the hospital without regaining consciousness. And Peter Cromwell wasn't saying much.

*****

Rondell was alone at his mother's house when the doorbell rang. He moved slowly on his crutches, dragging his useless legs behind him, to answer the door. The pain in his back and shoulders was still excruciating, but he determined not to be an invalid.

He saw the outline of a person on the porch through the frosted glass window that occupied the upper half of the front door. He clenched his jaw and struggled gamely to make it to the door before the visitor gave up and left. With one last effort, he made it.

"One sec, man," he called. He rested on his crutches, pausing to catch his breath. He put one hand on the deadbolt. "Who is it?"

The glass on the window exploded inward, followed closely by the fat end of a baseball bat. The flying glass stung his face but was nothing compared to the pain of the bat crashing into his nose. Cartilage crunched beneath the blow. Unable to balance on the crutches, and equally unable to put weight on his legs, he fell to the floor, landing hard on his tortured back. The blow to his nose brought tears to his eyes. The pain to the rest of his body was equally blinding.

A hand with two missing fingers reached through the opening, grabbed the deadbolt, and turned it. The door opened.

Rondell watched Ocee enter and close the door behind him. He walked to where Rondell lay sprawled on the floor, still too stunned to move. He stood over Rondell, teeth displayed in an arrogant smile.

Rondell raised his arms, hands out, as if reaching to heaven. "No more. Please. No more."

"Dat's right, mon," Ocee said. "No more."

He tore an electrical cord from a nearby lamp and tied Rondell's hands in front of him. Next, he produced a roll of duct tape from his pocket and wound it round and round Rondell's head, covering his mouth, nose, and eyes, mummifying him.

Rondell moaned, but the tape muffled the sound. He tried to thrash his damaged legs, but Ocee stilled them with a sharp knife. He cut deeply into the bandages and sliced the tendons at the backs of Rondell's knees. Rondell moaned again, an almost inhuman, high-pitched, wail. Ocee tore another cord loose and bound the crippled legs at the ankles. Rondell lay still, a low keening sound barely escaping from the confines of his mummified face.

Ocee surveyed the house, looking for the tools he needed. He found just the item in the garage. Grabbing a length of rope from the corner, he tossed it over a rafter. He went back into the house and man-handled the bound Rondell, dragging him by his feet into the garage, where he dumped the boy in the middle of the floor.

As Rondell continued to wail, Ocee fashioned a make-shift noose from the rope. He pulled Rondell into a sitting position and slipped the noose over his head, positioning it just below the teen-ager's jaw. He didn't want to strangle the boy, just suspend him from the ceiling.

Grabbing the other end of the rope, Ocee hoisted Rondell off the floor, pulling until he hung from the ceiling, his feet dangling just inches off the floor. His body twitched and thrashed in futile efforts at escape. Ocee tied the other end of the rope to a cross-bar on a workbench on the side wall. Then he retrieved his baseball bat from the corner where he found the rope.

Holding the bat in both hands, Ocee circled the hanging boy, like a wolf looking for a weak spot before moving in for the kill.

Circling.

Circling.

Suddenly he planted his feet and swung with all his strength. The fat part of the bat cut a swath through the dark air of the garage and connected just below Rondell's third rib on his left side. A crackling sound punctuated the silence.

Ocee swung again.

And again.

And again and again. The more he swung, the softer the target felt, as the bat tenderized Rondell's muscle and bone.

Confident that all the ribs were broken, Ocee lowered his swing and connected with Rondell's already crippled legs. They swung limply through the air, propelling the body around like a rag doll. For fully five minutes he worked on Rondell's legs, before moving up to his back. It took only a few blows for the two hundred stitches that held the skin together to begin tearing apart. Blood soaked Rondell's shirt and ran down the back of his pants. Ocee continued to deliver blow after blow after blow. At last, his own exhaustion stopped him.

He dropped the bat and pulled a pistol from his waistband. He approached the battered hanging form, extended his arm, and placed the barrel of the weapon against Rondell's taped forehead.

He pulled the trigger.

CHAPTER THIRTY ONE

"I can't believe you've done this." Brit Reavis set the good china on the dining table. "He's not going to like it."

"It's not going to be that bad," Angela called from the kitchen. "Besides, it'll be good for him."

"I don't think it's a good idea. When he's ready, he'll make the move on his own. It's not our place to do it for him."

Angela brought tea glasses and placed them on the table. "We're not doing it for him. We're just giving him a little prod. That's all."

"You mean you're giving him a little prod. I'm gonna make it real clear, if this is a disaster, that I had nothing to do with it."

"Well, if it comes to that, I'll be glad to tell him you didn't even know until this evening that I invited Paula to join us. But I don't think it's going to be a problem. Besides, he might like her and decide it's time to start dating again."

Brit exhaled a puff of air and rolled his eyes. "It's barely been six months. Do you really think that's enough time?"

Angela pulled out a chair and sat down. She placed her elbows on the table, rested her chin on one hand, and thoughtfully stroked her hair with the other. "Look, Babe, I'm not trying to push him into something. But he doesn't need to be alone.

I just think if he got involved in a relationship, it might help him move on with his life."

"He's doing just fine on his own. He's busy at work, already tried one case and got a big one coming up in a couple of months. He's got plenty to keep his mind occupied without us setting him up with your friends."

"Can't you see that he's using work as an escape?"

"What's wrong with that?" Brit stood with his arms akimbo, his arguing stance. "It's his decision. When he's ready to replace work with a relationship, he'll do it."

Angela went back to the kitchen to check the roast. Brit followed her to the door, where he resumed his arguing stance and waited to parry her next point.

"Look," she said, closing the oven, "I can't stand to see him unhappy."

Brit walked over to Angela and grabbed her in a bear hug. "I know you're concerned about him. I just hope you're not pushing him too fast."

"I don't think I am."

"I want to be able to say I had nothing to do with it if the night's a disaster. Plausible deniability is all I need."

Angela laughed and twisted away. She playfully slapped him on the arm. "It'll be fine. Wait and see."

*****

Brit led Bobby into the den, where Angela and a blonde Bobby had never seen before were sitting. Bobby glanced at Brit, who almost imperceptibly shrugged his shoulders and averted his eyes.

Bobby stepped across the room and gave Angela a kiss on the cheek. "Hi."

The blonde stood and faced Bobby. She was strikingly pretty, with dimples that gave her a pert look when she smiled.

"Bobby, this is Paula Little," Angela said.

Paula extended her hand and Bobby gave it a shake. "Nice to meet you."

"Nice to meet you, too," she said. Her voice was high-pitched, bordering on squeaky.

Bobby smiled and relaxed his hand, but she wouldn't let go. As soon as he squeezed again, she let go, only now she couldn't get her hand out of his. Embarrassed, Bobby let go suddenly and allowed her hand to drop.

"Well," Angela said. "The roast got done a little sooner than I planned, so we might as well go to the table."

"Lead the way and tell us where to sit," Brit said. He avoided the dirty looks Bobby sent his way.

The four herded into the dining room and sat boy/girl/boy/ girl, with Bobby facing Paula and Brit facing Angela. Not a good arrangement for Bobby since Paula managed to wedge a sizeable chunk of lettuce between her front teeth on the first bite of salad. Oblivious to that fact, she insisted on smiling at him throughout the meal.

Angela tried her best to draw Bobby into conversation with Paula by dropping little tidbits about how interested Paula was in the fascinating world of law practice. That prompted follow-up questions from Paula to Bobby, as if to confirm Angela's point.

For his part, Bobby tried to be pleasant, smiling and answering questions, but he couldn't force himself to ask Paula about herself. He simply wasn't interested. If this had been a deposition, he could have prepared a list of insightful questions designed to draw out information about her background and interests. But it wasn't a deposition, and he hadn't prepared. And he really didn't care. Instead of a pleasant dinner with his brother and sister-in-law, this was turning into torture. All he wanted was for the evening to end so he could go home.

When Angela and Paula went into the kitchen to get the dessert, Bobby and Brit sat alone in the dining room. Bobby let Brit know the depth of his unhappiness about being set up. And Brit let Bobby know he had nothing to do with it. After the women returned, Paula sat down again across from Bobby and flashed a moonstruck smile. Glad to see the lettuce gone, Bobby smiled in return. But when he saw Angela looking at them, then smile at Brit, he knew Angela had read too much into their exchange of smiles. When he saw Angela's smile quickly disappear, he surmised, correctly, that Brit's expression had disabused her of any misconceptions.

The evening ended with Bobby walking Paula to her car, reluctantly accepting her telephone number, and lying about calling her. He didn't kiss her good-night, but simply put her in the car, closed the door, and waved good-bye. After she drove away, Bobby returned to the house. Brit and Angela sat in the den, like disobedient children. Bobby couldn't help laughing at the expressions on their faces.

"What's so funny?" Brit asked.

"Those hang-dog looks."

Brit and Angela exchanged glances, but didn't see the humor. They looked back at Bobby, awaiting their lecture.

Bobby kept them in suspense for a moment, then said, "Don't ever do this again. You know I love y'all, but don't push it."

"It was Angie's idea," Brit said. "I didn't –"

Bobby stilled him with his uplifted hand. "You're a couple. You're both responsible."

"It really wasn't his fault," Angela said, fulfilling her promise to her husband. "He didn't know until this evening."

"You don't seem too mad," Brit said.

"She's a nice girl and I appreciate the thought. But I'm not ready. When I am, it may or may not be Paula. If I decide I want to see her again, I've got her number and I'll give her a call. But it'll be my decision in my own good time."

"She's nuts about you, you know," Angela said. "She's going to be hurt if you don't call."

"Does she know about Karla?"

Angela nodded.

"Then you can tell her that it's too soon for me. Surely she can understand that."

She nodded again.

"If she asks, tell her I said all the right things. She's bright, pretty, and all that. Whatever you want to say."

Bobby looked from his sister-in-law to Brit, then shook his head. "I'm going to be all right. I really am."

Angela got up and ran across the room where Bobby swooped her off the floor in a hug.

"I'm sorry," she said. "I just want you to be happy."

He squeezed her tightly.

"All in due time," he said. "All in due time."

CHAPTER THIRTY TWO

It had been another lucrative night of collections. After midnight, Ocee finally made his way back to the North Dallas apartment he once shared with Gulleyman, but which he now considered his own. He took off his shoes and left them at the door before walking into the apartment. Sand abraded his stocking feet. Instead of cleaning it up, he went directly to the big jar of sand he kept in the bedroom closet and spread a few more handfuls around. Then he checked to make sure the proper herbs hung at the apartment's windows and doorways. He brought these superstitions from Barbados. Necessary superstitions to vanquish the duppy of the murdered American woman – the reason he asked to go to Texas, her home.

He observed the superstitions faithfully since leaving Jamaica, but they weren't doing their job. Instead of vanquishing the duppy, it seemed as if the duppy moved about at will. Some days, he saw it floating airily in the sky as he made his rounds, as if it were tailing him. So far, it only deprived him of sleep, and perhaps frightened him a bit, but it hadn't actually harmed him. At least not yet.

Before he slipped into the king-sized bed with the silk sheets, Ocee sprinkled a few drops of rum on the floor around the bed. Just one more gift to appease the duppy. The more he did, the more likely he was to be left alone. Then he drifted off to sleep. To dream.

In the dream, it was Saturday on Barbados. The day to slaughter pigs. There was a slaughterhouse, an active slaughterhouse by the sound of it. The squeals of dying animals filled the air. A row of pigs walked single file up a narrow path to the slaughterhouse. The pigs knew what would happen inside, but on they pressed, like lemmings over a cliff. In the middle of the pack, one pig looked out of place. Strange. A mutant, perhaps. Closer examination revealed it to be a creature with the body of a pig but the face of a man. The face of Oliver Clarke.

High over the slaughterhouse, the duppy of the American woman loomed. Her face was beautiful, her skin dark, her hair long and silky. She hovered above the doorway, as if supervising the parade of pigs.

The Ocee-pig balked, halting the whole line. The duppy looked at the Ocee-pig.

"Come, Ocee," it said. "It's your Saturday."

"No," the Ocee-pig said. "Today 'ent my Satuhday."

The pig behind bumped him and began pushing him forward. Toward the slaughterhouse. The Ocee-pig tried to resist. He dug his hooves in, but the other pigs ganged up on him. Pushing him forward. Closer and closer. Right to the lip of the door.

The duppy laughed. "That's right, Ocee. Enter." And it laughed and it laughed.

And then Ocee woke in a cold sweat. He sat up in bed, his body trembling. The silk sheets were drenched with his perspiration. He felt a tightness in his chest, as if his heart were about to burst. He'd had the dream before, often, but this was the closest he had come to entering the slaughter-house.

Ocee threw his legs over the side of the bed and wiped the sweat from his face. Whenever this happened, he knew he had to get out. To go on the prowl. He had business to take care of, anyway. He had been putting it off, but several weeks ago he had learned that the police paid a visit to Peter Cromwell at the Kool Kool Klub. That same evening, Gulleyman was killed. He hadn't minded Gulleyman's death. Sooner or later, he would have killed Gulleyman himself. How else could he advance? But others must not be allowed to do it. Examples had to be set. At first he blamed Gulleyman's death on Rondell James, but now he knew better. It was Peter. Ocee was waiting for the right time to act. Maybe tonight was that time.

Besides, if he was up and about, the duppy would leave him alone. Duppies only took advantage of those who were weak. As the Bajans said, "Duppy know who to frighten." If Ocee showed his power, his strength, the duppy would know he was not weak.

*****

Cornell was still at the club when Ocee arrived, but all the customers were gone. He let Ocee in, then left and locked the door behind him. Cornell was Ocee's source and would take over the club if anything happened to Peter. It was best that he wasn't there. Less to answer to the police for.

Ocee opened the door to Peter's office without knocking. Peter was deep in paperwork, oblivious to Ocee's presence.

Ocee slammed a blood-stained baseball bat on the edge of the desk.

"Shit!" Peter jumped, scattering papers. He looked at Ocee, then smiled nervously. "You scare me, mon."

Ocee fixed his beady eyes on Peter and smiled back. The smile exuded no warmth. He tapped the end of the bat on the desk, but didn't say anything. Just kept tapping.

"Wha' you want, mon?" Peter asked. He shifted in his chair. He harbored no illusions about the dark stains on the end of the bat.

"Many mont' ago, Gulleyman is kill by de police," Ocee said.

"I knows dat, mon."

"De same police dat comes to see Peter at de Kool Kool. De same day."

"Coincidence." Peter's voice lacked conviction.

"I tink no."

Though the room temperature was comfortable, Peter began to perspire. Sweat beaded on his forehead and trickled down his cheek. He licked his lips. "Someone tol' you dat?"

"News don' lack a carrier."

"Look, mon, we work dis out. You an' me."

Peter eyed the bat as he pleaded. He stood and perched on his toes, gauging his chances for making it around the desk and to the door without feeling the bat's sting.

Ocee watched Peter inch his way toward the side of the desk. He laughed. "Manure can' mek ole plant grow." Translation: It is pointless to try to improve a hopeless situation.

Peter made a sudden move, a feint to his left, then dashed to his right. Ocee bit on the fake, but regained in time to deliver a well-aimed swing of the bat at the back of Peter's head as he ran by. The wood smacked hard into the frightened man's

218

skull and knocked him face forward on the floor. He slid headfirst and crashed against the wall. Before he could move, Ocee stood over him and raised the bat high above his head. Peter rolled over to see where the danger would come from. He tried to put his hand up for protection.

The fat end of the bat crashed into Peter's forehead, driving him into the floor. A gaping gash opened up just above his left eye. Blood oozed. Ocee aimed for the gash with his next blow, which tore it wide apart. The ooze turned to a flood.

More blows followed. The speed and ferocity of the swings increased with each. One blow crushed the front of Peter's skull. A thin membrane of skin hung limply over the chasm behind it. Ocee knew that the man must be dead, but he continued the attack. The savagery of the assault would be determined by the condition of the body when found. Ocee wanted to leave no doubt as to how vicious the assault had been. That would help consolidate his power over the posse.

It would also show the duppy that he was not a weak man. Maybe then it would leave him alone. His Saturday had not yet come.

CHAPTER THIRTY THREE

Bobby sat at the defendants' table and waited for the plaintiff's lawyer to finish his closing argument. To his left sat Debbie Grant, who was second-chairing the Forreston trial with him. Beside her sat the lawyers for their co-defendant, the hospital where Dr. Forreston worked on staff. This was Debbie's first full-blown trial in her few years of practice, and she was understandably nervous when it began. Bobby assigned her a number of witnesses to examine or cross-examine, and he spent almost as much time helping her prepare as he did getting himself ready.

Debbie proved invaluable to Bobby in the months preceding trial, handling a lot of the depositions single-handedly while Bobby tried to put out other fires that had started during his sabbatical in Kauai. He decided to reward her by giving her an expanded role when they actually started the trial. He also knew that such a reward carried a high stress factor with it. He remembered his first trial and how lost he had felt from start to finish. He vowed to spare Debbie that same experience, even at the expense of his own preparation time.

Bobby found Debbie to be incredibly bright, picking up on subtle nuances in both the facts and the law. He reviewed the depositions she had taken and was delighted at her thoroughness and insight in asking questions. As they began spending more time together, he also found her to be witty and personable. She possessed a keen sense of humor and a degree of charm and poise that he was unprepared for.

He also found himself becoming attracted to her. He didn't want to be, because it had been only nine months since Karla's death. He didn't believe he was ready to seek another relationship. He still hadn't called Angela's friend, Paula Little, and didn't think he would, even when he was ready. He now found himself thinking that, when the time came, maybe he would call Debbie, instead.

It took the plaintiff two weeks to put on his case, then almost that long for the defendants to put on theirs. Throughout the trial, Bobby and Debbie spent time together almost every evening, going over the day's testimony and getting ready for the next. Bobby had watched Debbie's confidence grow almost tangibly during the past few weeks. He watched with pride as she mastered the courtroom when she questioned witnesses. Now that the trial was coming to an end, he would miss the time they spent together.

The plaintiff's lawyer finished his argument, and Bobby went next, followed by the hospital's lawyer. Afterward, the plaintiff's lawyer took the last few minutes, as was his right, to make a final appeal to the jury. Then the judge read his charge to the jury and sent them to begin their deliberations.

After the jury retired, the lawyers exchanged obligatory compliments and began packing their files. Dr. Forreston thanked Bobby and Debbie, and Bobby promised to call him when the jury came back.

"It's out of our hands now," Bobby said, when he and Debbie were at last alone in the courtroom.

Debbie smiled. "I guess so."

Bobby stuffed the last few files into his briefcase, then faced her. They looked at each other for a few seconds, both shifting nervously on their feet and struggling for something to say.

"I'm not going to know what to do tonight since I don't have anything to get ready for tomorrow," Debbie said. She laughed nervously after she spoke.

"Yeah," Bobby answered. He found himself uncustomarily tongue-tied, as if he were on a first date.

Debbie closed her briefcase. "Are you going back to the office or are you going home?"

Bobby looked at his watch. "It's already after four. I can't imagine the jury'll do anything more than pick a foreman and maybe read through the charge again. They won't need us anymore today."

"So you're going home?"

"Yeah. How about you?"

"I guess so."

"I'll walk you to your car."

Bobby grabbed his briefcase and fell in at Debbie's side as they exited the courtroom. On the way, they spoke only sparingly, mentioning things they might have done differently during the trial – typical second-guessing after it was too late. They reached Debbie's car in the parking garage where they stopped and faced each other again.

"Listen," Debbie said. "How about we meet somewhere tonight for one more dinner and celebrate the end of the trial."

"What if we lose?"

"We'll just celebrate that it's over. And if we lose, we'll have a wake later."

"Okay. I'm up for it. Pick you up at seven o'clock?"

"I'll be ready."

Bobby opened Debbie's door for her after she unlocked it. Debbie tossed her briefcase in the back seat, then slid in behind the steering wheel. Bobby closed the door and she rolled down her window.

"We did good, didn't we?" she asked.

Bobby winked at her and nodded his head. "Let's hope the jury thinks so."

*****

Dinner that night went well. Bobby opted for casual dress, wearing jeans and a blue button-down oxford, but Debbie turned out in a dark skirt and white blouse. She had obviously dressed up for the occasion, like it was a date. Bobby thought she looked particularly attractive and he wondered whether she was sending him a signal.

Their mood was light as they ate. Bobby dined on a ribeye steak while Debbie opted for a more exotic pasta dish. They made only casual conversation, shying away from talking business or about Bobby's continuing emotional recovery. It was a pleasant evening for both of them that seemed to end too soon.

After dinner, Bobby drove Debbie back to her apartment in the Lakewood area of east Dallas, close to White Rock Lake. This was the neighborhood in which Bobby had grown up while attending Woodrow Wilson High School. The conversation waned as they neared the apartment and the air took an awkward turn. Bobby pulled into a parking space and left the motor running. They sat silently for a few beats, neither of them quite knowing how to end the evening.

"You want to come in?" Debbie asked at last.

Bobby hesitated before replying, "Sure."

He turned off the car and they both got out, then walked silently up the stairs to her second floor apartment. The apartment's main room was small, but nicely decorated. There was no overhead light, but a lamp at the end of a heavily-cushioned sofa threw off a nice glow. The room had a homey feel to it with a scattering of pictures and knick-knacks on the walls and shelves. The furniture, a couch and two chairs, formed a conversation pit centered in front of a wood-burning fireplace.

While Debbie went into the kitchen to make coffee, Bobby turned on the stereo and popped in an Eric Clapton CD. He turned the volume low until Clapton's raspy crooning was mere background music, then he sat on the end of the couch. He fidgeted nervously, picking at nonexistent lint on his jeans while he waited for Debbie. She returned in a few minutes carrying a tray with two coffee cups and bowl of sugar. She placed the tray on the coffee table, then sat in the middle of the couch, right next to Bobby.

"I hope you like it strong," she said.

"Strong is good, as long as it's got enough sugar."

He reached for the sugar just as she leaned forward for the far cup. The back of his hand brushed against her breast. He jerked his hand back as if it had been burned and put it in his lap. Embarrassment torched his cheeks. My God, what she must think!

"I'm sorry," he said.

"It's okay."

Debbie straightened up and looked at him. An awkward moment passed.

"It's okay," she repeated.

Bobby couldn't understand what she meant. He was out of practice at this dating thing. Besides, wasn't this just another business dinner?

Debbie took his hand and carefully placed it on her breast.

"I said it's okay."

His fingers curled naturally around her firm breast. It felt good. Feelings stirred within him that had lain dormant since Karla's death.

Karla. She would want him to continue living. Wouldn't she want this for him? He wasn't sure.

Bobby looked at Debbie for a moment. Then she leaned back on the couch and closed her eyes. With his other hand, Bobby brushed the hair back from her face, then ran his fingers across her cheek.

She reached to the lamp on the end table and turned it off.

CHAPTER THIRTY FOUR

Undercover police officer Sergeant Ed Delancy sat in a vintage blue Chevrolet Camaro in an east Dallas convenience store parking lot. Directly across the street, in another parking lot, two more officers sat in another unmarked car. Two others waited in the grocery store parking lot across from the side of the convenience store. The latter four monitored Delancy, who was wired with a microphone.

The officers were employing their most basic method of making drug arrests – a "buy-bust." The idea was to buy the drugs, then immediately arrest the dealers. Since the dealers weren't ordinarily the leaders of the drug organizations, the police often allowed the arrested suspects to escape prosecution if they led officers to bigger drug deals and the higher-ups in the drug organizations. That tactic wasn't as effective with the Jamaicans, though. Their street-level dealers were rarely anything more than hired thugs. And they knew about the Jamaicans' disciplinary tactics. For them, the risk of prison was preferable to the inevitable scalding or knee-capping.

Delancy was supposed to meet his seller at nine-thirty, after dark, so he chose this well-lighted convenience store for the buy. To maintain the charade of being a drug-dealer, he didn't wear a bulletproof vest or carry a gun on his hip. Standard procedure allowed him a partner in the car, if he chose, but he elected, as he always did, to work one-on-one with the seller. He would make the buy alone, then signal the other officers to move in.

Two men, both black and appearing to be in their teens, approached Delancy's car on foot. "Heads up," Delancy said for the benefit of the microphone.

The taller man leaned on the roof of the car, while the other waited behind. His head swiveled as he constantly looked around.

Delancy rolled down his window. "You got it?"

"It's coming. You got the money?"

"When the product gets here."

"How much you got?"

"Don't fuck with me man," Delancy said. "The price is already set. You got a problem if you want to renegotiate now."

The tall man straightened up and held his hands out in front of him. "Hey, no problem, my man. Shee-it! Just making sure. That's all."

"I got what we agreed to."

"Okay, man. Okay. Shit! Ease up, broth-uh. You got too much stress."

"Fuck that shit. Where's the stuff?"

"It'll be here. Don't worry, my man. All in good time."

"I'm not worried," Delancy said. "I'm just not giving you fuckin' nothin' til I get it."

A battered Toyota Camry pulled into the lot, driven by a lone black man.

"Here it comes," the tall man said. He motioned for Delancy to get out of the car. Delancy complied, then the two walked to the Camry. Delancy slid into the passenger seat, leaving the door open. The tall man stood beside the open door. His companion walked away.

"Let's see it," Delancy said, his voice low.

The driver, a thin man with a missing tooth, extracted a small bag from his pocket and handed it to Delancy. "Good shit, bro."

Delancy took the bag and hefted it in his hand briefly. He tossed it back in the driver's lap. "Nope."

"Hey, man," the driver said, a quiver to his voice. "You a fuckin' scale? You can tell just by holdin' it in your fuckin' hand?"

"Just like that. So don't fuck with me. You either deliver what we agreed on or you can shove that up your ass."

"Hey, lighten up, broth-uh. Shit. Everything's cool. Know what I'm saying?"

*****

In the unmarked car directly across the street, officers Buddy Higgins and Roy Garcia hung on every word. Just as Delancy rejected the drugs, a late-model pick-up pulled into the parking lot behind the Camry and stopped, its motor still running.

"What the hell's that?" Higgins asked.

"Beats me," Garcia answered.

"I don't like it. First this dick's fucking with Delancy and now that truck's bird-dogging him."

"Just take it easy. Everything's copasetic."

*****

"You got it or not, motherfucker?" Delancy asked.

"Just chill. Everything's cool, broth-uh. Won't take five minutes."

"Just don't tell me I got too much stress."

"But you do, my man."

"No. What I got is assholes like you fuckin' with me."

Delancy got out of the car and slammed the door. He leaned over the window. "When you're ready to deal, you let me know. Broth-uh!"

Delancy pushed his way past the tall man and went to his Camaro. He looked back at the Camry and saw the tall man get in. Then the car drove off, with the late-model pickup following close behind. Delancy got in his car and closed the door. He gripped the steering wheel with both hands and spoke again for the benefit of the microphone. "I hope y'all saw that truck pull in. He shouldn't have been there."

Delancy hoped his message got through. He could send on his microphone, but not receive. The others couldn't approach the Camaro without blowing his cover and screwing the deal. They had to leave it to Delancy's discretion. If Delancy called it off, it was over. But they couldn't call it off.

Delancy gripped the steering wheel tighter. A few minutes later, the Camry rounded the corner, then turned into the parking lot where Higgins and Garcia monitored from their car. The pick-up truck followed but parked on the street by the convenience store.

The tall man got out of the Camry then casually sauntered across the street. A squat, muscular black man got out of the pick-up truck and approached the passenger side of his Camaro.

"Okay," Delancy whispered. "Here comes dumb and dumber."

The tall man approached the Camaro as Delancy rolled his window down.

"We copasetic?" Delancy asked.

"Everything's cool, my man," the man said. He gestured with his head to the muscular man on the passenger side. "It's coming."

Delancy nodded. He leaned over and rolled down the passenger side window.

*****

Higgins and Garcia watched as the muscular man approached Delancy's car. He wore a brown leather coat, and he reached into his pocket as he drew up beside the car. He pulled something out of his pocket, then tossed it into the car.

A split second later, Garcia noticed the barrel of a gun appear from under the man's coat. "What the fuck –" they heard Delancy say. A volley of shots drowned out the rest.

As the muscular man held his finger down on the trigger, Delancy's body jerked and twisted grotesquely.

When the gunman released the trigger, the tall man who had been standing by the driver's side, but who stepped aside when his partner began firing, grabbed the door handle and yanked it open. He leaned inside and rummaged through Delancy's bloody clothing for the money.

Higgins and Garcia jumped out of their car and ran toward Delancy's Camaro. They both had their guns drawn and at the ready. Higgins fired several rounds at the gunman. A bullet slammed into his shoulder. He dropped his gun and grabbed his wounded arm. The gun skittered across the pavement.

The tall man scrambled back out of the Camaro and faced Garcia. He made a quick move with his hand toward the pocket of his coat. Garcia went to his knees and squeezed off two quick shots. Both struck the man in the stomach. He dropped heavily to the pavement.

Garcia straightened and slowly approached the wounded man.

He heard a sound behind him. Spinning, he saw a puff of smoke coming from the driver's window of the Camry. Instinctively, he fired two shots through the front windshield. Both shots struck the driver in the face, killing him instantly.

The two officers in the grocery store parking lot made their way across the street, with guns drawn. They restrained both of the wounded men, who tried to crawl away. As the officers covered the men, Higgins and Garcia rushed to the Camaro to check on Delancy.

An engine roared to life and the pick-up truck screeched away. Higgins couldn't see through its tinted windows how many were inside, but he knew it was probably already too late. They were gone.

Garcia leaned into the Camaro. Delancy gasped for breath. His torso and lap were covered with blood. Garcia tried to stem the flow with his hands.

"We need an ambulance," he screamed. "Someone get a god-damn ambulance!"

CHAPTER THIRTY FIVE

Bobby woke earlier than usual. He had not slept well, over-whelmed by feelings of guilt. He wished Karla were there to tell him what to do. But, then again, if Karla had been there, last night would never have happened. He saw the hurt in Debbie's eyes as she sat on the couch, her clothes disheveled, watching him leave.

*****

"Did I do something wrong?" she asked.

"No."

"Then what is it?"

"I'm just not ready for this," he said.

"It's a little late for that."

"It was a mistake."

Pain registered on her whole being when he said that. "I need more time," he added, hoping to cushion the blow.

She stood and straightened her clothes. "I don't know how much longer I can wait," she said. Then she left the room.

*****

Bobby shook his head to chase away the images. He dragged

himself out of bed, threw on a robe, and went out front to get the morning paper. The headline screamed:

"POLICE OFFICER KILLED IN DRUG DEAL."

Back in the kitchen for coffee, he tossed the paper on the breakfast bar, then flipped on the small television on the counter. He filled his cup, popped two frozen waffles into the toaster, and sat down. Attracted to the paper's headline, he read the story of the killing of the undercover police officer. At the same time, the TV newscaster began a story on the shooting. Bobby tried to listen with one ear as he read the front page and, at the same time, keep an eye on the waffles.

On the screen, Lieutenant Derek Larson of the Jamaican Drug Task Force grabbed his attention. He dropped the paper to listen.

"So is this gang leader a Jamaican?" the reporter asked.

"We don't know," the striking-looking blonde officer answered. "But we assume he is."

"And he's the man the shooting suspect said ordered him to kill Officer Delancy last night. Is that right?"

"The suspect didn't know Delancy was a policeman. But the Jamaicans threatened to kill his family if he didn't do what he was told."

"Why are you unable to determine if this gang leader is Jamaican?"

"We keep records on Jamaican activity throughout the country, but he doesn't show up in our database."

"Then how can you be sure he's behind the shooting?"

"Because he matches the description we've previously gotten of him."

"Give us that description again, for our viewers."

"He's medium height and slight build, with a vertical scar on his right cheek, just under his eye. He's also got two missing fingers on one of his hands – we're not sure which – has dreadlocks, and is extremely violent."

Bobby set his coffee cup on the counter and stared at the television screen. The bell rang on the toaster, announcing the browning of his waffles, but he didn't hear it. As Larson described the mysterious gang leader, Bobby felt as if his heart had stopped beating. When he reached toward the TV to turn up the volume, he noticed that his hand quivered. He listened as Larson continued talking.

"No," Larson said, in answer to a question Bobby hadn't heard. "He apparently goes by the nickname O.C., but we don't know what that stands for."

"Anything else?" the reporter asked.

"He wears a gold earring, with a diamond in the middle. The earring is in the shape of the letter 'K.' That may have something to do with his real name, but we're not sure."

Bobby remembered sitting across from Karla at The Wanderer restaurant at Sam Lord's Castle. He saw, as vividly as if it were yesterday, the sparkle in her eyes when she opened the small box holding the gold necklace, with the gold "K" and the diamond in the middle. He remembered the look on her face as she clasped it around her neck and smiled at him. She was wearing it the last time he saw her.

On the screen, the anchorman called for public assistance. "If anyone has any information on the man just described, please contact officers with the Jamaican Drug Task Force located in the Earl Cabell Federal Building in downtown Dallas."

*****

Bobby opened the door marked "Task Force" and entered. It was a typical police-type squad room filled with metal desks jammed together, bulletin boards, filing cabinets, and florescent lighting. The room was electric with activity. After all, one of their own had died last night. Nothing sped the rush of adrenaline through law enforcement like a cop-killing. And the people in this room felt responsible because they allowed the man behind the killing to exist, filling the void left by Gulleyman's death.

"Can I help you?" a young officer asked. He was seated at a desk just inside the door.

"I'd like to talk to the officer who was interviewed on TV about the drug shooting last night. I may have some information."

The officer switched into a higher gear. He gestured to a chair across from his desk, then stood. "Have a seat. I'll be right back."

Bobby sat down and watched as the young officer walked to an office at the back. He moved briskly, disappeared inside, then re-emerged a few minutes later. He gestured for Bobby, who followed to the open door. When Bobby entered the office, he immediately recognized the blonde officer behind the desk.

The big blonde stood and extended his hand. "Derek Larson."

Bobby shook his hand and nodded. He sensed an intelligence that comforted him. "Bobby Reavis."

Derek motioned to a chair. "Have a seat."

Bobby sat as Derek returned to his own chair.

"Anything else, Lieutenant?" the young officer asked. When Larson shook his head, the officer left, leaving the door open.

"Boyd tells me you may have information on the shooting."

"I think I know who your gang leader is."

Derek's whole body stiffened. He cocked his head, his eyebrows raised in suspicion. "How would you know that?"

"Just less than a year ago, I was shot and my wife murdered while we were on our honeymoon in Barbados."

A glint of recognition registered in Derek's eyes. It had, after all, been all over the Dallas papers. "I remember that. That was you?"

"Yeah."

"They never got the guy, did they?"

"His name is Oliver Clarke," Bobby said, "but in Barbados he goes by the name 'Ocee.'"

"I don't remember that being in the papers."

"It wasn't. Not here, anyway. He's missing the two middle fingers on his left hand and has a vertical scar on his right cheek."

"Sonuvabitch!" Derek exclaimed. "That's why we can't find him in our database."

"He's not Jamaican. He's Barbadian. And nobody knows where he went. He just disappeared."

"Until now."

Bobby nodded. "Is he following me?"

"If he was following you, he'd have found you by now."

"So why is he in Dallas?"

Derek sighed. "Because we're a garden spot for third world

thugs. Seems they like our gun laws. But, hell, what thug doesn't? More guns end up in this country from Texas than anywhere else, except maybe Florida."

"So it's pure coincidence?"

"Some folks don't believe in 'em, but they do happen." Derek paused, then asked, "Who can I talk to in Barbados?"

"Wallace Walker. He's with the Barbados National Defense Force in Bridgetown."

Derek wrote the information on a notepad. "This may be the break we need."

"I hope so."

Bobby pulled a business card from his wallet, wrote his cell number on the back, and gave it to Derek. "I can ID him. If you catch him, give me a call. That's got my office and cell numbers on it."

Derek took the card and paper-clipped it to his notes. He pulled one of his own cards out of the top drawer of his desk and handed it to Bobby. "Use it anytime."

Bobby pocketed the card and stood to leave.

"Let me ask you one more thing," Derek said. "This guy wears an earring with the letter 'K' on it. You know anything about that?"

Bobby's eyes filled with tears and his voice quivered as he spoke. "The morning it happened, I gave my wife one last wedding gift. A gold chain with an initial on it – a 'K,' with a diamond in the middle. Her name was Karla. When they found her body, she still had all her jewelry except the necklace."

Derek's face grew solemn. "I'm sorry about your wife. I really am."

Bobby just looked at him, unable to speak.

"If there's anything we can do for you, let me know," Derek said.

"I can think of only one thing."

"What's that?"

"Catch the sonuvabitch."

CHAPTER THIRTY SIX

Andy Fletcher leaned against the door of Bobby's office and congratulated him on the favorable jury verdict. "I assume Dr. Forreston is happy about it."

"I told him they'll probably appeal, so not to get too excited."

"How'd Debbie do?" Andy asked. "This was her first trial, wasn't it?"

Bobby scrutinized Andy's face. Why was he asking about Debbie? Did he know about the other night? He quickly dismissed that as impossible. Not that it was any of Andy's business, anyway.

"She did great," Bobby said "She was a little nervous at first, but that went away."

Bobby's phone rang, but he ignored it, figuring his secretary would take a message. She surprised him by interrupting.

"That's Lieutenant Larson with the Drug Task Force," she said. "I thought you'd want to talk to him."

"Thanks." He turned to grab the phone.

"You think they've caught him already?" Andy asked.

"I doubt it."

"Let me know what he says."

After Andy left, Bobby picked up the phone.

"Lieutenant, what can I do for you?"

"I've been in touch with Sergeant Walker in Barbados and now we've got his prior record. Damn, this is one mean bastard."

"I can testify to that." Bobby laughed weakly. "What do you need from me?"

Derek sighed audibly. "We've got pictures of Oliver Clarke, but they're not so great. You said you'd recognize him if you saw him again."

"His face has been permanently etched into my brain. Damn straight I'd recognize him."

"Then I've got a favor to ask and you can feel free to say no."

"You need me to talk to a sketch artist?"

"More than that. Except for the shooter we've got in custody now, no one has ever lived long enough to make an identification for us. We can't very well drive our cop-killer around South Dallas looking for him. We might as well put a sign on our car that says, 'Please blow us away.'"

"So – "

"So – " Derek hesitated. "So we need someone who knows him by sight, but who he won't necessarily recognize, to make the rounds with me."

"And you think that someone is me."

"Well . . . yeah."

"He's seen me before. We weren't more than fifteen feet apart."

"Would he remember your face after all this time?"

Bobby remembered how quickly the whole thing had happened. He looked Oliver Clarke squarely in the eyes, saw the flash from the gun, and then it was all over. He didn't think Clarke looked at him any longer than it took to pull the trigger.

"I was probably no more significant to him, at the time, than any of his other victims."

"But you think there's a chance."

"There's always a chance."

"Look," Derek said, "Here's what I'm asking. I need you to actually go into clubs and apartments with me. If there's any chance he might recognize you, then it could be dangerous."

"You want to know if I'm willing to do that."

"Yes."

Bobby thought again. On the one hand, he wanted the man who killed Karla caught. On the other hand, he felt as if he was on the verge of putting that terrible chapter behind him and moving on with his life. Why risk that by stirring up the past, or by putting himself at risk? If he had been asked six months ago, he would have had nothing to think about. Without Karla, he wouldn't have cared, then, what happened to him. But now, with the passing of the healing months, he wasn't so sure anymore.

At the same time, being on the verge of moving on with his life wasn't the same as actually being ready to move on. He knew he needed something more to push him forward. Maybe, just maybe, what he needed was a sense of finality to what had happened.

"When do we start?"

*****

Debbie was working on a brief when Bobby knocked on her door. She smiled nervously when she looked up. "Come in."

Bobby walked in and sat down. They had not spoken about their night together, not even while waiting out the jury. They were friendly and polite to each other, but all their conversation had been strictly business. Bobby was confused about his feelings, not wanting to lead Debbie on, yet not wanting to make any commitments, either. He wasn't altogether sure why he came to her office now, but for some reason he couldn't quite put his finger on, her opinion mattered to him. He hadn't talked to Andy, nor had he called his brother about Larson's request. He wanted Debbie's opinion first.

"Remember when I went to talk with the Jamaican Task Force guys?"

"Uh huh."

"The guy I talked to called just a while ago. He wants me to ride with him tonight in the drug neighborhoods. To see if I can identify Oliver Clarke."

A cloud crossed her face. "Do you think that's wise?"

"Apparently I'm about the only person in Dallas who can actually identify this guy."

"You mean who's still alive."

"Something like that."

"So they need you."

"Desperately."

"Is it dangerous?"

"Could be."

Debbie leaned her head back and closed her eyes. He couldn't

242

tell what she was thinking, but she looked pained. What was she thinking?

"Do you want to do it?" she asked, eyes still closed.

"It's not a question of want to. I feel like I have to."

Debbie leaned forward and opened her eyes. "Do you feel like you owe this to Karla?"

He nodded.

"If you help the police find him, do you think maybe you'll be able to let go of her and move on?"

"Yes," he said. His quivering lip betrayed his emotion.

Debbie continued to read his mind. "But you're not sure you're ready to let go of her."

"Right."

A tear trickled over her bottom lid and rolled down her cheek. It left a track of mascara in its wake. "If this guy is dangerous, the police need all the help they can get. If you can give it to them, you should. And if you think you owe this to Karla, you should, even if it means letting go of her. But you have to make that decision for yourself."

Bobby locked eyes with her. "You think I should."

"Yes."

He nodded. "I'm scared."

"I know," Debbie said.

They continued to stare at each other for a few minutes. Both looked as if they had more to say, but neither spoke. At last Bobby broke the silence.

"Thanks for the advice." Then he turned and left.

When he was out of earshot, Debbie said, "I'll be here for you."

CHAPTER THIRTY SEVEN

In the next two weeks, Bobby rode with Derek Larson four times, touring the neighborhoods where the Jamaicans had the most influence. Bobby was struck by the poverty of the people who lived within the shadows of the downtown skyscrapers. They worked hard to eke out existences for themselves and their families, while the lawyers and businessmen in those buildings grumbled if their annual incomes dipped below two hundred thousand dollars. The more Bobby saw, the more he understood the lure of illicit money. He almost began to feel ashamed of his relative affluence and the material things he owned while so many went without the bare necessities. Necessities like food for their children.

He listened, fascinated, as Derek told him about the Jamaican posses and the violence their presence, and the presence of the drugs they brought with them, spawned in this depressed part of town. He had seen firsthand the violence of Oliver Clarke. But that was easier to accept because that was something that happened in some uncivilized – at least to a lot of Dallasites' smug, self-important way of thinking – island nation in the Caribbean.

But it was hard to believe it was here, in his own community. In his own backyard. Reading about it in the papers and watching the reports on the news hadn't brought it home. It all seemed so distant and so surreal, far from his protected environment. Listening to Derek, and seeing where the violence he described had happened, dealt Bobby a dose of reality.

Though each ride brought Bobby to a new and different part of town, they always included pass-throughs in the particular neighborhoods where the Jamaicans held their tightest grips. That included a regular visit to the Kool Kool Klub on Second Avenue. Derek explained that the club was a well-known Jamaican hangout and that its former owner previously provided one of the few descriptions that the police had of Oliver Clarke. Derek also mentioned that, sometime later, the owner was found beaten to death. The police suspected Clarke, but had nothing to connect him to the crime.

After finishing their usual route, Derek drove toward Fair Park, turned onto Second Avenue, and headed toward the Kool Kool Klub. Bobby cringed when he realized where they were going. Since hearing about the murder of the club's owner, and since his first experience inside the club, with its pounding, screaming reggae music and its ebony-faced, dreadlocked patrons – each of whom evoked memories of his one encounter with Oliver Clarke – Bobby hated going there. Something inside told him that, of all the places they visited, he was more likely to run into Clarke there than anywhere else. For all of his willingness to help the Task Force, he wasn't totally convinced he wanted to see Clarke again. And he was definitely sure he didn't want Clarke to see him, regardless of whether Clarke remembered him.

It was after dark when Derek turned into the parking lot outside the shabby club. Even as they approached from Second Avenue, the reggae beat pulsated through the night air. By the time they pulled up in front of the open door, the racket was stifling. Derek put the car in park and turned off the engine. He watched Bobby. Muscles bunched in Bobby's jaw.

Derek grinned and tapped him on the arm. "You don't have to go in if you don't want to."

Bobby looked at Derek and smiled grimly. "I don't like this place."

"Hell, Bob, nobody in their right mind does. Everybody in there is crazy."

"You're a great encouragement."

Derek laughed. "Don't worry. Nothing's going to happen as long as you're with me. These drug dealers like to shoot cops, but they don't like to do it in their own house. If they wanted to take us out for some reason, they'd do it somewhere else, not here. They know the police would shut this place down and squeeze everybody until someone talked. That's too risky for them."

"That sounds logical."

"They may seem crazy, but there's a method to their madness."

"If you say so."

"Trust me," Derek said as he opened the door and got out of the car.

Bobby looked at him for a minute, then opened his door and stepped into the parking lot. Derek stood on the other side of the car and waited for Bobby to join him before he approached the front door. That was fine with Bobby, who didn't want too much space to come between him and the cop with the gun.

Derek stepped up on the sidewalk, then entered the open

door. Bobby followed close behind, but Derek had already disappeared ahead of him, swallowed up in the dim light and overwhelming music. Bobby walked cautiously, letting his eyes adjust to the dimness. He finally saw Derek about ten paces ahead, casually patrolling the main lounge. Derek turned. Seeing that Bobby lagged behind, he motioned for him to move closer.

Bobby stepped forward briskly, embarrassed at the look Derek gave him. The look said, "What on earth am I doing with this wimp?" Bobby dropped his head for a moment. When he glanced back up, he saw a black man jostle Derek, whose head was still turned. Something seemed familiar about the man – his face, expression. Bobby stepped aside to let him pass. As the man moved by, he stepped into the splay of light from one of the small spotlights overhead. The beam shone on his face, and he made eye contact with Bobby, a scar across his face.

Disbelieving, not three feet away, Bobby stared at Oliver Clarke.

Clarke stopped in his tracks. He seemed bothered by this white man staring at him. His eyes cold and hard, he stared back at Bobby. Bobby shuddered. He remembered the last time he had seen that scar. He drew back a step, his eyes wide in both recognition and fear. Clarke scrutinized him for a brief second, not blinking. His lips curled into a snarl. He raised his deformed hand in front of him, pulled his little finger into his fist and pointed his index finger, like a gun. A cold shiver cut through Bobby. He wondered whether Clarke recognized him or was simply trying to intimidate him.

"Is that him?"

Derek's voice from across the way snapped Bobby from

his trance. He slowly nodded his head, his eyes still fixed on Clarke. Clarke's eyes suddenly widened at the sound of Derek's voice. He grabbed Bobby by the arm and swung him in the direction of Derek, who fast approached. Bobby stumbled forward into Derek, who caught him just before he fell. Clarke bolted for the door.

"That's him?" Derek asked. He held Bobby up by the arm and looked him in the eye.

"That's him."

"You're positive?"

"That's him."

Derek tightened his grip on Bobby's arm and dragged him toward the door. "Let's go."

Outside the club, a late-model Jaguar screeched out of the parking lot, turned right on Second Avenue, and sped away. Derek pulled a notepad from his pocket and scribbled. He turned to Bobby, who panted breathlessly beside him.

"I just wanted to get a look at what he was driving," Derek said.

Bobby heaved a sigh of relief and nodded his head.

"You're sure that was him?" Derek asked.

"Yeah. Did you get a good look at him?"

"Decent. And now we know what he's driving. I even got a partial on the plate." Derek headed toward his car. "Come on. Let's get the hell out of here."

Bobby followed and got in on the passenger side. As Derek started the engine, Bobby said, "I think he recognized me."

Derek snapped his head around. "Are you serious?"

"I'm pretty sure."

"Does he have any reason to know who you are? I mean, your name?"

Bobby shook his head. "I don't know. I doubt it."

"We can give you some protection. I'll put a car outside your place if you want me to."

"I doubt if he knows who I am. And he doesn't know where I live."

"Just the same, until we catch him – "

"That's not necessary."

But he wondered as they drove away. He wondered, and he worried.

CHAPTER THIRTY EIGHT

Bobby and Debbie spent the day on the law school campus of Texas Tech University in Lubbock, judging the advanced mock trial finals. Their flight home didn't arrive in Dallas until a quarter past nine. Tired from the long day, and from lack of sleep the night before, Bobby could barely keep his eyes open driving home from the airport. At that time of the evening, traffic was light and it took less than twenty-five minutes to make the drive from Love Field to Sunnyvale. It was good that the drive time was short because if it had been much longer, Bobby might have fallen asleep at the wheel. It was also good that traffic was light because he had considerable difficulty keeping his car in his lane. He was fortunate not to run into any police. He might well have been stopped for DWI, the way he was driving.

After what seemed like hours, he finally exited Highway 80 onto Belt Line Road, past the Wal-Mart Super Center, and headed for the home stretch. As he turned right on Tripp Road, moving into the subdivision where he lived, Bobby found himself nodding off. His head bobbed down, then jerked back up, waking him.

One more street, a left turn, then right into the alley leading to his garage. As he pulled into the driveway, he hit the garage door opener on his visor. He paused to wait for the door to make its slow ascent before he cruised inside and turned off the engine. He sat for a moment behind the wheel of the car and leaned his head against the headrest. With his eyes closed, he thought back to Debbie's invitation to her apartment for dinner – a real-live, pre-planned date – and debated how to respond. Last time had been spontaneous, his actions arguably forgivable in the heat of passion. But this time would be different. This time involved rational thought and any actions flowing from it would imply meaning. Was he ready for a meaningful relationship?

He had more than a passing interest in Debbie. Although she was ten years younger than he, Karla had been too, so age wasn't an excuse. She was extraordinarily pretty, particularly for a lawyer. Good looks weren't the most important quality in a woman, but they were a nice bonus. She possessed other qualities that mattered more to him – ones he became closely acquainted with during the Forreston trial. She was bright, witty, sensitive, honest, and full of life. She was fun to be with. In fact, she possessed a lot of the same qualities that caused him to fall head-over-heels for Karla.

And that was the real hang-up. She reminded him too much of Karla. Not that he wanted to forget Karla. Not that he ever could. But he didn't want her memory to put his life forever on hold. As long as Debbie reminded him of Karla, he feared he could never separate his feelings for her from his feelings for Karla. If he was going to have a relationship with Debbie, it needed to be with her and not with the memory of his dead wife. He would tell her "no."

Bobby suddenly sat bolt upright and opened his eyes. Looking around in the darkened garage, he felt disoriented. Where the hell was he?

Then he saw his familiar junk – lawnmower, lawn tools, bicycle. He was home. He was safe. He shook his head to clear the fog. How long had he been there? He checked his watch. Ten-thirty. It had been a quarter till ten when he had pulled into the driveway. He'd been asleep for the past forty-five minutes.

Bobby took the keys out of the ignition, opened the door, and stepped out of the car. He stretched, rising on his toes and extending his arms over his head. He ignored his briefcase in the back seat, shuffled to the back door, and unlocked it. He punched the button to lower the garage door, then entered the house and locked the door. He hung his keys on a hook on the wall, checked the answering machine – no messages – then virtually sleep-walked through the kitchen to the long hallway to the master bedroom.

Lights were on in the den and bedroom, both hooked up to timers that came on automatically at dusk. Other than that, the house lay in darkness.

Bobby took off his coat as he started down the hallway. Next came his tie, then his shirt. He entered the bedroom and tossed his clothes on the floor. But something didn't seem right about the bed. Something out of sorts. What was it? Tired and fuzzy-thinking, he couldn't quite put his finger on it. But he couldn't shake the notion that something was wrong.

He kicked off his shoes and stripped off his pants, which he also tossed on the floor. He stepped over to the bed to pull back the covers.

It would have been easy to overlook in the dimness, especially in his present state of mind. He might have just yanked back the bedspread and covered it up, or knocked it off the bed behind a nightstand. Or kicked it under the bed, and not have discovered it for days, weeks, or maybe months. But he saw it before he grabbed the bedspread, just below the pillow on his side. It hadn't been there when he made up the bed and left that morning. But it was there now.

Bobby picked it up. He sat on the edge of the bed and held it under the lamp. It was a little over three inches long, two inches wide, covered with a laminated plastic. On the right edge was a picture of a dark-complected, dark-haired, very pretty woman. Across the top, the words TEXAS DEPART-MENT OF PUBLIC SAFETY. Toward the bottom, the name of the owner of the driver's license: Karla Sandone.

Bobby dropped the license. He felt short of breath and his legs turned to jelly. He leaned his hands on the bed and sank to his knees. The last time he had seen it, Karla was alive and it was in her wallet. Bobby flashed back to that terrible canefield in Barbados. He had relived that moment hundreds of times, but it had been months since the last time. After the initial awful flashbacks, the first few months, he was finally able to force it from his mind. It was as if his mind had blocked out the moment as being too terrible to remember. Since then, he preferred to think about the good times. The image he preferred to keep in his mind was of the smiling, dark-haired beauty.

But now, in a rush, he again saw the look of stark terror on her face. He again heard her screams echo in his ears. And then he felt the terrible searing pain in his throat and chest.

He clutched his throat and sprawled face-forward onto the bed. A spasm of tears churned out. He grasped Karla's driver's license and pulled it to his chest, clutching tightly. As if he could pull her back from the grave and into his heart.

But he knew he couldn't. That cold reality turned up the pace of his tears. Soon the bedspread was soaked with his grief.

A nagging in his mind began to replace the pain in his heart. A nagging in his rational mind. The part of him that had to brush the emotions aside and go on with his life. The part of him that told him he was overlooking something even now. He bolted upright, still on his knees. His back went rigid, his head high. The implications of finding the license on the bed slowly forced their way to the surface of his consciousness. The Barbadian police never found Karla's fanny pack with her wallet. They concluded that Oliver Clarke took it when he kidnapped Karla. That meant Oliver Clarke last had her driver's license. And that license didn't just materialize in his bedroom tonight.

Oliver Clarke put it there!

Bobby leaped to his feet. He tore through the house, frantically looked for signs of forced entry and checking closets for hidden bogeymen. The idea that Oliver Clarke had broken into his house violated him all over again. The evil that the man brought with him was more than Bobby could take. He sprinted from room to room, violently throwing aside mini-blinds to see if window locks had been tampered with, ripping open doors and thrashing through hanging clothes. Finding nothing only fed his frenzy. He repeated the process a second time.

Then a third.

Then a fourth.

Then it hit him. Not only had Karla's driver's license been in her fanny pack, so were her keys – including a key to his house. The maniac didn't break in. He simply unlocked the door and walked in. As if he owned the place.

The boldness of the move overwhelmed Bobby, but it paled next to the fact that the man had keys to his house. Bobby dashed to the phone and snatched it off the cradle. Extracting Derek Larson's phone number from his wallet, he dialed. Derek answered on the second ring.

"I'm sorry to call you so late but – "

"S'ok. What's up?"

Bobby took a deep breath, then spoke rapidly, spilling his story.

"Slow down a bit," Derek said when Bobby finished. "Is anything missing?"

"Nothing jumps out at me. The only thing out of place is her license."

"You're sure he had it?"

"That bastard's making a point. He knows who I am. He's reminding me of what he did before, and he's telling me he knows where I live and that he can get in my house at his pleasure."

"Get your locks changed first thing in the morning."

Bobby nodded vigorously, even though Derek couldn't see him.

"You got a gun?"

Bobby paused a few seconds before answering. "No."

"Get one."

"I don't want one."

"Doesn't matter what you want. You damn sure better have a gun the next time he pays you a visit."

"I thought cops always told people not to keep guns at home."

"Look, Bobby, if you were just worried about burglars, it'd be one thing. But this is different. Hell, this guy's already shot you once. He'll try to kill you whether you're armed or not. The only chance you've got is to arm yourself."

Derek made sense. The canefield in Barbados might have had a different result if Bobby had been armed.

"I don't know anything about guns," Bobby said.

"Get those locks changed first thing in the morning, then meet me at my office."

"I'm busy tomorrow."

"Goddamnit!" Derek snapped. "This guy's trying to kill you and you're too fuckin' busy?"

"Point taken."

"And one more thing. Stay in a motel tonight."

CHAPTER THIRTY NINE

It was just over a week since Oliver Clarke placed Karla's driver's license on Bobby's bed as a message. And the message hadn't been lost. Though Bobby again rebuffed an offer to put a car outside his house, Derek still promised regular patrols in his neighborhood. And with Derek's assistance, he armed himself with a .38. With Derek's help and at his insistence, Bobby also took daily trips to a shooting range to practice with the weapon. As Derek said, "There's no point in having a gun unless you're prepared to use it. And there's no point in being prepared unless you know how."

So now Bobby knew how.

That didn't make him comfortable with a gun in the house. Owning a weapon wasn't the problem. It was the idea of using it against a human being that bothered him. The fact that Oliver Clarke was who he was still did not make palatable the idea that Bobby had a human target in mind when he bought the weapon and that the bullets he bought were already engraved with Clarke's name on them.

Sleep did not come easily for Bobby during the past week. The loaded weapon in a nightstand drawer, just inches from his head, reminded him of the last weapon he saw face-to-face. The one that spiraled three bullets into his body and separated him from Karla. All of which only served to remind him why he bought the gun in the first place. And the round-robin tug-of-war continued in his conscience.

Bobby used the remote to flip off the TV and settled deep into the covers. He felt drowsy, which was good. That offered at least faint hope that he might drop off to sleep without too much trouble. He had stared at enough dark ceilings in the past year to last him a lifetime.

His hope came true and, within thirty minutes, he nodded off. He didn't sleep restfully, but at least he slept. It wasn't yet two a.m., but that, in itself, was a dramatic improvement over the past few nights when he had stayed awake into the wee hours, fearing Oliver Clarke's return.

Just as the digital clock on the nightstand turned over to three o'clock, Bobby emerged from his shallow sleep. Something had awakened him. A noise that didn't belong. Not the rattle of the ice-maker in the refrigerator down the hall, nor the sound of the air-conditioner kicking on. Something that didn't belong. Something threatening.

Because his sleep had been shallow, he was wide awake now. He listened earnestly to pick up the sound again. He sat up and cocked his head. He closed his eyes, concentrating all his energy on only one of his senses: hearing.

Silence.

He lay back down and pulled the sheets to his chest.

There it was again. A sound like someone trying to open the front door. The clang of a key in a lock. The jiggle of a handle, the press of wooden door against frame. Faintly familiar sounds that were terribly wrong for this time of night.

Afraid to turn on the light, Bobby snatched the phone off

the nightstand beside him. He paused for a minute, his finger poised over the dimly-lit dial. He couldn't swear to the sounds he heard. Could he simply have psyched himself out with the knowledge that Clarke had a key and had been there before? Was he willing himself to hear something that wasn't there? What would Derek or a 9-1-1 operator say if he complained of hearing a key in the lock or a door handle being jiggled? That didn't sound like your run-of-the-mill police emergency.

Bobby waited, listening.

Silence.

He dropped the phone back onto its receiver and replaced it on the nightstand. He slumped back down in the bed again and closed his eyes. Still in the dark, he strained to hear the sounds that went bump in the night. The air conditioner cut off with a thud. Then nothing. Still he lay and he listened. Five minutes passed. Still silence. He smiled, embarrassed at his own imagination.

But then the distinct tinkle of breaking glass bolted him upright. The sound came from the kitchen. That meant the intruder had scaled the six-foot fence surrounding the backyard and was out of sight to any sheriff's patrols that might make their way down the alley.

Bobby slipped out of bed and knelt on the floor. With one hand, he again lifted the phone from its resting place. With the other hand – the trembling one – he opened the nightstand drawer and gripped the handle of the .38. Even with the wooden grip, the gun felt cold and awkward. His hand continued to tremble as he pulled it from the drawer. The barrel banged against the wooden nightstand with a sound he felt sure could be heard halfway across Dallas County.

He froze, listening.

Silence again.

He closed the drawer and sat on the floor with his back against the nightstand. He faced the hallway, a tunnel of darkness that seemed to stretch endlessly to the kitchen. He squinted, waiting for his eyes to adjust, but saw nothing.

And heard nothing.

He set the gun on the floor beside him and punched Derek's number on his phone's speed dial. It went straight to voice mail. He then hit 9-1-1. After what seemed like minutes, but surely was only seconds, a female dispatcher came on the line.

"Nine-one-one. Can I help you?"

"I think there's someone in my house," Bobby whispered. "I just heard a window breaking."

"All right, sir. Stay on the line with me. Where did the sound come from?"

"The kitchen. I'm in the bedroom, around the corner and down the hall."

"Do you hear any sounds now?"

Bobby listened briefly. "No. Not for a few minutes."

"But you're sure you heard glass breaking?"

"I thought I'd heard something earlier, so I was awake and listening. I heard it."

He heard another sound from the kitchen: The rattle of mini-blinds being pushed aside. Bobby surmised that the intruder had been waiting to see if the broken glass would produce any response. Apparently satisfied, he now worked his way inside. Bobby heard the crunch of glass underfoot on the tile floor.

"He's in the kitchen," Bobby said urgently. "Are the police on the way?"

"Yes, I've dispatched the police to the address in Sunnyvale. Are you Mr. Reavis?"

"Please hurry."

Bobby tried to keep his voice low, so he wouldn't be heard by the intruder and so he could, at the same time, hear the intruder.

"Stay on the line with me, Mr. Reavis. I need you to tell me what's going on so I can inform the officers. Do you hear anything else?"

"There's a long hall between me and the kitchen. But if he's gone into the den, there's carpet. I wouldn't hear anything."

"Can you see anything?"

"It's too dark."

"Are any lights on in the house?"

"The front porch light's on, but none in the house."

"Can you get out of the house?"

Legally, Bobby knew he didn't have to abandon his house before resorting to deadly force. Of course, he knew that wasn't why the dispatcher asked the question. She wasn't concerned about legal niceties in case he killed an intruder. She was concerned that he might be killed, and leaving the house was preferable to that alternative.

"Maybe," he answered.

If the intruder had already moved into the den, it would be a no-go. If he was still in the kitchen, or came down the hall, maybe – if Bobby moved before he got into the hall.

Bobby leaned forward and squinted hard at the darkness. Was anybody there? He couldn't tell.

"Where exactly in the house are you?" the dispatcher asked. "Where are you in relation to the front door, for instance, and where is the intruder?"

"When the cops get here, as they face the front door, there are three windows to their right. That's where I am."

"And the intruder?"

"He's —"

Another sound in the kitchen choked off the words in Bobby's throat. It sounded like it came from where the door joined the hall. As soon as the intruder stepped in the hallway, he would be directly ahead of Bobby, about forty feet away.

Just like in Bobby's dream.

Bobby picked up the .38. He leaned forward again, still squinting at the darkness.

"Mr. Reavis, are you there?"

The dispatcher's voice irritated him. He strained to hear over her. From the end of the hallway, he heard a muffled sound. Then a voice, loud and clear. A voice that chilled him to the bone.

"Wha' you say now, mon?"

Bobby never heard Oliver Clarke's voice before, but the Bajan dialect was unmistakable. He put the phone on the floor and grasped the revolver in both hands. He rested his elbows on his bent knees. Sweat materialized at his temples and streaked down the sides of his face. His pajamas were soaking wet, the cotton cloth plastered to his body by his own perspiration. The sound of his heartbeat drummed in his ears, drowning out the squawking of the 9-1-1 dispatcher coming from the telephone receiver on the floor beside him.

"You is lookin' fo' Ocee, eh mon?" The voice accelerated down the hallway and overwhelmed the silence in the darkened bedroom. "You is helpin' de police ketch Ocee, eh? Egg have no right at rockstone dance."

Bobby recognized the last sentence as a Barbadian proverb he had learned last year. It meant that people should not get into situations with which they cannot cope. Like the one Bobby was in right now.

"You is helpin' de police cause you is one-smart mon. But Ocee is two-smart mon. An' one-smart get dead at two-smart door."

Bobby sat silently. Did Clarke really know he was there, or was he just talking? Maybe he was merely testing the waters. Maybe he would leave if he thought no one was home. He hadn't turned on any lights yet, and Bobby gambled that he wouldn't. He assumed Clarke thought himself more menacing and dangerous in the dark.

If that's what Clarke thought, Bobby told himself, he was right. Bobby sat petrified, frozen with fear. The .38 shook in front of him, hopefully pointed down the hall. As badly as his hands trembled, Bobby couldn't be sure where he pointed it at any given moment.

"You dere, mon?"

The voice sounded closer, though still probably not yet halfway down the hall. Bobby squinted. He thought he made out a darkness in the shadows that could well be a man. It wasn't distinct. Just a darker spot in the overall blackness.

He wiped his face on his shoulder, then re-propped his hands on his knees. Dear God, just make him go away, he prayed

263

silently. Deliver me from evil.

"De woman, she pretty, pretty, pretty." Then Clarke laughed, a high-pitched cackle. The sound echoed through the house.

Bobby found his fear overtaken by anger. That black bastard thought it was all a big joke. All of it – shooting Bobby, killing Karla, all just one big laugh. Bobby's hands steadied on the gun. His finger pressed against the trigger, feeling the tension. He squeezed, slowly, steadily.

A crackling explosion, like a firecracker going off, reverberated from down the hallway. Wood and plaster shattered above and behind him as a bullet slammed into the headboard of his bed and pierced the wall behind it. Just above the spot where Clarke had placed Karla's driver's license. Charke even knew which side of the bed Bobby slept on. Had he been there, Bobby knew he surely would be dead now.

He heard that cackling laugh again. Closer still. Just all one big joke!

Bobby squeezed the trigger the rest of the way, firing three shots in rapid succession. His finger moved so instinctively as to give the impression of an automatic weapon being fired. Then he paused, listening. Had any of his shots met their mark? He had not heard any cries of pain. No thumps of bodies hitting the floor. But at least he had stilled that hyena laugh.

Then he heard the sound of footsteps on the hardwood floor. Still in the hallway, but farther away. Headed back to the kitchen, leaving, Bobby hoped.

With a still trembling hand, Bobby squeezed off the final rounds. As the explosion of those shots died away, he heard footsteps on the kitchen floor, then the jangle of mini-blinds, mixed with the tinkling of broken glass being kicked about on the floor.

Bobby turned on a lamp, blinding himself with its sudden brilliance. Checking over his shoulder to see if Clarke was there, like the ever-present bogeyman, he yanked open the top drawer of the nightstand. He pulled out the box of bullets and fished inside for a reload. His hand shook so badly it was all he could do to grasp the shells in his fingers. Dropping them all over the floor, he finally steadied his hand enough to slide in three. Then he rushed down the hall.

At the end, he peered cautiously into the kitchen. Nothing.

He waited a few seconds, then closed his eyes and flipped on the lightswitch.

After a few seconds to allow his eyes to adjust, he looked again. Scattered at the foot of the large window by the kitchen table was the glass he had heard breaking just a few minutes before. Leading to the window, starting at his feet, a trail of blood led across the floor to the windows.

He'd hit him!

Bobby turned on the light in the hall and looked back toward the bedroom. The red stream continued back up the hall to its ultimate starting point – a pizza-sized splotch in the center of the floor. A red brushstroke spanned the side wall for about six feet, as if the wounded man had used the wall for support. Just before the kitchen door was a bloody handprint, perfect right down to the two missing fingers.

Bobby stood rooted to the spot, mouth open, staring at the mess in his house. His knees wobbled. My God! He had shot a man.

He slid to the floor and leaned against the wall. Outside, the wail of a siren screamed, drawing closer.

CHAPTER FORTY

The elevator doors opened on the law firm's main floor and Bobby exited just as Debbie walked by on her way to the library. Things had been tense between them for some time. They still saw each other at the office, still worked together on a few files, but had decided to keep things on a professional level. Bobby hadn't told her about shooting Clarke last month, but she knew. Everybody knew. And, Bobby thought, it confirmed his decision to keep Debbie at arm's length. After all, he told himself, it was for her own protection.

"How'd it go?" she asked.

"Motion denied. He's going to set it for trial."

"Did he say how soon?"

"Said he'd get an order out this week."

"If you need help, I'm available."

Bobby studied her face, trying to read between the lines. Was this an olive branch? But her face betrayed nothing.

"I'll let you know when I get the scheduling order," he said.

She nodded, then walked away. He stood still for a few seconds and watched her walk. Her auburn hair shone in the lights as she crossed in front of the elevators, entered the glass doors to the library, and disappeared into the stacks. He turned away and headed to his office.

He grabbed his message slips off the transaction counter at his secretary's station and awkwardly thumbed through them with one hand, holding his briefcase with the other, as he entered his office. The second slip grabbed his attention. He dropped his briefcase on the floor and went directly to his desk.

He stared at the slip for a full minute, then snatched up the phone and dialed. After what seemed like an eternity, the call went through.

A distinctively British voice answered on the fourth ring. "Sergeant Walker."

Bobby cleared his throat then licked his dry lips. "Sergeant Walker, this is Bobby Reavis in Dallas, Texas."

"Mr. Reavis. It's good to hear your voice again."

Bobby couldn't say the same. The sound of Walker's voice only dredged up memories that he kept trying to bury. But someone or something was always dredging them up, most recently in his own home.

"What can I do for you, Sergeant?"

"We have Oliver Clarke in custody."

Bobby tried to swallow, but his throat went dry. So that's where he had been for the past month, he thought. Back in Barbados. And now they've got him.

They've got him!

THEY'VE GOT HIM!

"How? And when?"

"Just last week. We got lucky, actually. We didn't even know he was on the island, but your Derek Larson has been in touch. When he told us Clarke had been keeping a low profile in Texas lately, we wondered if he might have come back to the Caribbean. So we kept our eyes out. An alert constable spotted him in Bath-sheba, kept him under surveillance until we could get a force there, and we nicked him just this morning."

Bobby listened, his thoughts a jumble. Was it really all over?

"He's not talking much," Walker continued. "He appears to have a fairly recent wound to his side. From what your policeman Larson told us, that might be your handiwork, eh? That's quite lovely."

"Maybe," Bobby said. He had shot him, yes, but now knew he hadn't killed him. That thought had nagged at him during the recent weeks when it seemed as if Clarke had disappeared from the scene in Dallas. He knew he was justified in shooting and he knew this man had forfeited his right to live. But Bobby had difficulty dealing with the possibility that he might have killed somebody. It relieved his conscience to learn he hadn't.

"Anyway," Walker continued, "we've got him now. And he's under close watch. No three-time escape for Mr. Oliver Clarke."

"Thank you for calling me, Sergeant Walker. It's a huge weight off my mind."

"Yes, well, I also have a request."

"Whatever you want."

"We want to prosecute Clarke for what he did to you and your wife. We'd like for you to testify."

The words stopped Bobby cold. "He's already under a death sentence, isn't he?"

"We want to send a message to the rest of Dodds Prison that we will hold people accountable for their actions. More politically, there is some rising dissatisfaction on the island with executions, which makes it more palatable to execute a man who is under multiple death sentences. It destroys the argument that one murder doesn't make a man a murderer, that he can still be rehabilitated. A man like Clarke is hopeless. A trial and a conviction puts him back in the spotlight as a multiple murderer and satisfies the bleeding heart element that we've given him enough opportunity to reform and that he hasn't complied."

"When do you need me?"

"We would like to schedule a preliminary hearing in Magistrates' Court as soon as possible. How soon can you come to Bridgetown?"

Bobby looked at his calendar. "I can fly in Wednesday night and be ready to testify Thursday."

"That would be brilliant."

*****

Debbie had her face buried in her computer when Bobby sat in a chair across from her desk.

"Want to go to Barbados?" he asked.

She regarded him skeptically. "I thought you said you'd never go back."

"They've captured Clarke They want me to testify against him. They're going to prosecute him for . . ."

His voice trailed off and he lowered his head. Debbie reached across the table and placed her hand over his.

269

"You okay?"

He nodded. "Yeah." His voice was barely a whisper. When he raised his head, tears glistened in his eyes.

"You sure?" She gripped his hand tighter.

"Yeah. Anyway, they want me to testify against him in some kind of preliminary hearing on Thursday. I'm not sure I'm up to it by myself."

"Why don't you ask your brother to go with you? Or Andy?"

Bobby shook his head. "I want you."

She locked eyes with him and searched for any signs that might tell her what he was really thinking. "Why me?"

"Because I want another chance."

"How's that gonna look?" she asked.

"Does it matter?"

"You tell me. I'm just a lowly associate. You're the partner."

"Well, does it matter to you what people might say?"

She looked away. Bobby knew that going with him was a big risk for her. Was he worth the rumors that would spring up as soon as people learned she'd made a personal trip with a partner? He had already hurt her once. Would he do it again, to add insult to injury?

"Think about it and let me know," Bobby said. He stood and turned to leave.

"Bobby?"

He turned back around and looked at her.

"When do we leave?"

CHAPTER FORTY ONE

Bobby picked up Debbie at her apartment and drove to the airport. She was nervous, walking a fine line between casual conversation that distracts and inane chatter that irritates. Bobby tolerated her talking though, in truth, he wished she would shut up. At the same time, he was glad for her company even though he preferred silent company. She didn't have to come, but she did, and for that, he was grateful. He knew she wasn't sure about his feelings, which probably made her uncomfortable. He also realized that he wasn't sending any signals to let her know what was going on in his head, so that wasn't her fault.

But it wasn't his fault either, because he wasn't sure of his own feelings. It seemed strange to be returning to Barbados, almost one year to the day from his last trip, with someone other than Karla. It scared him to go back to the place where his life had fallen apart – literally returning to the scene of the crime. He wondered how he would react when he got there and saw the familiar sights. He knew it would call up memories. Good ones or bad ones?

He also wondered what his reaction would be when he saw Oliver Clarke in the courtroom. Would he be able to keep his emotions in check, to say and do the right things? Or would he fall apart? After all, this was the man who had stolen his happiness and almost stole his life. Bobby didn't look forward to the confrontation.

In San Juan, they changed planes for the final leg of their flight to Barbados's Grantley Adams Airport. Debbie finally exhausted what seemed to be an endless supply of trivia and small talk. As the plane left the runway, she turned to Bobby. He sat solemnly by the window and stared out – just as he did on that flight a year ago.

"Penny for your thoughts," Debbie said.

"Huh?"

"What are you thinking?"

"Nothing."

"You seem like you're a million miles away," she said. "You have been ever since I said I'd go."

Bobby fought back a wave of irritation. "I don't know. Just – I don't know. Everything's kinda hazy right now."

"I know this is hard on you, but it's hard on me, too. I don't know how to act or what to say. I don't want to get in your way or step on your feelings, but I need a little guidance here."

"I don't want to talk about it," he said.

"You have to sooner or later."

Bobby's temper flared. "No, I don't. I don't have to talk about it at all. Ever."

"So what am I supposed to do?"

"You do whatever you want to do."

"But that's just it," she said, her lip quivering. "I don't know what I want to do. Or what I should do. Or what you want me to do. How do you think that makes me feel?"

"This is not about you."

"I never said it was. But I'm starting to wonder why you asked me to come."

"That makes two of us."

As soon as he said the words, Bobby knew he might as well have slapped her in the face. But he couldn't bring himself to apologize. The only emotion he felt was anger. His problem was that he didn't know where to direct it, so he aimed it at the only person close by.

He turned and stared out the window. Debbie opened a magazine. A tear streaked down her cheek.

*****

The plane landed in the darkness at Grantley Adams Airport, then taxied to a stop near the terminal. Bobby led Debbie off the plane, walking silently a few paces ahead of her down the steps to the runway, then to the customs checkpoint inside the terminal. Wallace Walker met them after they cleared customs. He and Bobby shook hands crisply.

"Mr. Reavis, so good of you to help us."

"I'll do what I can." He turned to Debbie.

"Sergeant, this is Debbie Grant, a lawyer in my firm."

Walker clicked his heels and took Debbie's extended hand. "Wallace Walker. Ms. Grant, a pleasure."

"Thank you."

"Sergeant Walker's been working this case since day one," Bobby said. "He's the one who called to let me know they've got Clarke."

Debbie listened to Bobby then nodded at Walker. She didn't seem to know what to say, so she said nothing.

"Let's collect your luggage," Wallace said. "I have a car waiting to take you to your hotel."

Within a few minutes, they left the terminal. Aided by Walker, they avoided the second line of customs officials who checked luggage. Soon, they were speeding down the ABC Highway toward the turnoff to Sam Lord's Castle. Bobby sat in the front with Walker while Debbie rode in the back. Walker quickly filled them in on the details of Clarke's capture then lapsed into silence. It was as if he sensed the tension between the two Americans and decided to cease talking for his own protection.

As the small car maneuvered its way around curves and turns onto narrower roads, all the time nearing the Castle, year-old memories overwhelmed Bobby. He recalled traveling these same roads while Karla laughed, teasing him about his driving problems. Glancing in the backseat at Debbie, he envisioned Karla, her dark hair blowing in the soft breezes flowing through the open windows, green eyes flashing and sparkling over her ivory-toothed smile as she tossed her head back and laughed. He heard her chattering in his ear, filling him with facts about chattel houses and flying fish and other Barbados trivia. The ache in his heart, the one that he had finally been able to cover up after a year of trying, jabbed again at his soul. He quickly turned his head and gazed out the window.

At the Castle, Walker dropped them off at the front desk with a promise to pick them up again in the morning at nine o'clock. The hearing was scheduled for eleven, but the prosecuting attorney wanted to spend some time with Bobby going over his testimony. After Walker left, they got keys to their adjacent rooms on the ground floor of Building 1, the Ixora, on the bluff overlooking North Beach. The bell captain threw their luggage into the back of his cart and they rode to their rooms without speaking.

Debbie unlocked her door and stepped inside. Bobby followed, carrying her suitcase. He placed it on the bed, then turned toward her. She stood with her back to him, staring out the sliding glass doors into the dark. He debated whether to say anything, then turned and left without speaking.

In an adjacent room, Bobby tossed his own suitcase on the bed then opened the sliding glass door, stepped outside, and took a seat in the padded patio chair. A full moon and bright stars blazed in stark contrast to the blackness of the cloudless sky. The surf roared below. Though he couldn't see it, his mind called up images of six-foot waves crashing on the white sands of Long Bay. He pictured lounge chairs spread about on the beach and under the palm trees, the Rastafarian craftsmen hawking their crafts. He almost felt the hot sun warming his body. Hard to believe a place this beautiful had produced an evil as ugly as Oliver Clarke.

"Bobby?"

He barely heard Debbie's voice over the pounding waves. In his imagination, it was Karla's voice, but he knew he would never hear Karla's voice again. Turning in the direction of the sound, he realized Debbie's patio was just on the other side of the wall his chair leaned against.

"Yeah," he said.

"Can I join you?"

Bobby got up and rounded the corner. Debbie sat in a similar chair, her back to Bobby's, listening to the surf.

"I wasn't sure you were over there," she said. "You were so quiet."

"Just thinking."

He picked up his chair and carried it to Debbie's patio where he set it down facing her.

"Is it as pretty here as it feels?" she asked.

"Prettier. You'll see in the morning."

Debbie closed her eyes and took a deep breath. "I love the sound of the ocean." She opened her eyes and gestured into the darkness with her outstretched hand. "Is there a beach right there?"

"We're on a bluff that overlooks it."

"It sounds rough."

"It is."

"I like it that way. Untamed. Or untamable."

They lapsed into silence for a while, both staring into the blackness. Debbie studied Bobby's face. His strong profile contrasted with his kind and, for a while now, sad eyes. His features registered the hurt he had felt during the past year.

Bobby sensed Debbie watching him. He turned to her.

"I'm sorry," he said.

"That's okay. I understand."

"I know you do. And that makes me feel worse."

"Don't worry about it," she said.

"I really am glad you're here."

"Yeah. Me, too."

He stood and reached out his hand. "Let's walk."

They meandered through the hotel grounds, breathing the salt air, allowing the breeze to wash over them. At first they walked silently, but this was a different kind of silence. This one was comfortable, even pleasant. The magic words "I'm sorry" had wrought their miracle.

At last Bobby broke the silence. "I was thinking about what it will mean when this is over."

Debbie looked at him.

"Earlier," he said. "On the plane. That's what I was thinking about."

"You mean after you testify?"

"It'll be like the final chapter with Karla will be over. Then it'll be time to get on with my new life."

"You have to sooner or later," she said.

"I know. But sometimes I don't want to. It's like if I just hang on to yesterday, then she'll still be here."

"That's what memories are for."

"And it came to pass."

She cocked her head and looked at him. "What?"

"I heard a preacher once say that was his favorite verse in The Bible. 'And it came to pass.' He said he was glad the bad things in life don't come to stay – they come to pass."

They stopped on the edge of the bluff and gazed out to sea.

"I think I'm about ready for them to pass."

CHAPTER FORTY TWO

Breakfast at the open-air Wanderer restaurant might have been pleasant had not Bobby's stomach been tied in knots over the upcoming hearing. As he did a year ago, he filled his plate with an omelet, fruit, bacon, and biscuits. But, unlike a year earlier, he left half of it on his plate. Debbie was more sensible in filling her plate, but was also as unable to eat.

Sergeant Walker picked them up at the appointed time and drove them into Bridgetown. After they arrived at the court building, Walker escorted them to the office of prosecuting attorney Giles Leacock, a small, wiry man with thinning white hair neatly framing his ebony face. Constable Glenroy Wood was also waiting. After introductions were made, Leacock explained the procedure they would follow that morning.

"This hearing is only to establish probable cause. I believe we can do that quickly, without putting Mr. Reavis through too much on the witness stand." He directed his attention solely to Bobby. "I understand you are an attorney."

"Yes."

"Are you what the English call a barrister or a solicitor?"

"I'm a litigator. A trial lawyer."

Leacock nodded. "A barrister. Then you know that Clarke's attorney has the opportunity to cross-examine."

"I expected that."

"And you know that I can't protect you once he starts questioning you."

Bobby nodded. He wasn't familiar with the rules of evidence in Barbados, but he assumed there were some limits to cross-examination. Still, he understood Leacock's point. Once he started testifying on the stand, he was fair game for Clarke's lawyer to take potshots at his credibility and to try to poke holes in his story.

"I will be brief with you on direct," Leacock continued. "All I have to do is establish probable cause that a crime was committed and that Clarke committed it. I don't have to prove my whole case today."

"What's the scope of cross-examination?" Bobby asked. "Is he limited to matters covered on direct, or is the door wide open to anything?"

"Wide open. Provided the questioning is relevant, of course."

Bobby nodded again.

"All I want from you is what happened," Leacock said. "As briefly and precisely as possible."

"Who is Clarke's lawyer?"

"Sylvan Ward."

"He any good?"

"He's an old war-horse. He's represented criminals for decades. He represented Clarke at his last trial."

"The one where Clarke got the death penalty?" Debbie asked.

"Don't let that fool you," Leacock said. "Good lawyers can lose if they've got bad cases."

"Believe me, he's got a bad case," Bobby said.

*****

The hearing took place in District "A," Criminal Court "B," Magistrate Dennis Mantooth presiding. The courtroom was small and congested, its floor space crammed with the magistrate's bench, the lawyers' tables, benches for spectators, and a long bench next to windows that looked out to the congested Tudor Street/Baxters Road area. This was the prisoners' bench, where criminal defendants were stationed while their cases were heard. Leacock told them that Court "B" had become a popular escape route. Crowded onto the bench beside the unbarred windows, in the past year nine prisoners managed to jump through the half-closed windows, covering the ten feet to the ground and then disappearing down Tudor Street.

After nine escapes and a year of unhindered access to freedom, according to Leacock, bars were finally placed on the windows. Other security measures were also undertaken, including the use of restraints such as handcuffs and foot-shackles for prisoners brought into the courtroom. The latter measure provoked an uproar from some lawyers who argued that mechanical restraints should be used only for violent prisoners, but their outcry went unheeded. Another security move was to shift the prisoners' bench farther from the wall, filling the gap with benches reserved for the public. Now the only unsecured exit from the Court was the unbarred window located near the magistrate's bench.

At the appointed time, Leacock and Walker seated themselves at the prosecutor's table. Bobby, Debbie, and Constable

Wood sat on a bench immediately behind. A bent, wizened old man, whom Bobby assumed was Sylvan Ward, sat alone at the defendant's table. He shook Leacock's hand, nodded at Walker, then studied a notepad he produced from his briefcase. He never glanced Bobby's way.

At five minutes past eleven, Magistrate Dennis Mantooth entered the courtroom. He was a stern-faced Bajan, roughly forty years old, standing six feet tall and weighing a rail-thin one-hundred-thirty pounds. In his robe, with round wire-rim glasses perched on the end of his nose, he fit the picture of Caribbean justice. He seated himself at the magistrate's bench, then turned to the uniformed officer standing at the side door.

"Bring in the prisoners," he commanded in a shrill voice.

The officer opened the door. Almost immediately, the sounds of shuffling feet, mixed with the jangling of chains, floated through the opening. The first of four prisoners appeared, hands cuffed in front of him and feet shackled by thick metal. He led the way to the prisoners' bench with his head down. Three more followed, assuming the same posture and gait as the leader. Bobby watched as they sat stiffly, their backs rigid, but still with their heads down.

Then his attention was diverted back to the door by the sound of more jangling. He swiveled his head just in time to see the same scar-faced, dreadlocked man who had shot him in the canefields. Even shackled, Ocee strutted. Unlike the other four prisoners, he held his head high. He looked around the courtroom at the spectators and participants as if he were surveying his subjects. With dreadlocked hair flowing behind him like a mane, he looked for all the world like a lion prowling the jungle. King of all he surveyed.

Debbie put a hand on Bobby's knee. "Is that him?" she whispered.

"That's him."

A guard finally dragged Ocee to his place on the bench, ending his one-man parade. Magistrate Mantooth banged his gavel and called the court to order. The first case he called was that of the government of Barbados against Oliver Clarke. Leacock announced his appearance on behalf of the government, while Ward announced his on behalf of the defendant, Oliver Clarke. After the charges were read, Ward entered his client's not guilty plea.

"Mr. Leacock," the Magistrate said, "please call your first witness."

Bobby walked to the stand when Leacock called his name. Silence hushed the courtroom. All eyes focused on the tall, handsome American, neatly dressed in a navy pinstripe suit, blue button-down, and red power tie. He put on a facade of confidence as he sat and looked to Leacock to begin his questioning.

"Please state your name, sir."

"Robert Reavis," Bobby answered in a strong, clear voice.

"And where is your residence, sir?"

"In the United States. I live in a suburb of Dallas, Texas."

"Do you live there alone?"

"Yes, I do."

"So you're not married?"

"I'm a widower." Bobby glanced at Debbie after he answered. She smiled and nodded.

"How did your wife die?"

"I don't know exactly."

"When and where did she die?"

"In April of last year. I'm not sure exactly where. Her body was found on the island of St. Lucia. The last time I saw her was here in Barbados."

Bobby's voice quivered on the last answer. He looked again to Debbie for support. This time, Ocee followed Bobby's gaze to see where he looked. He saw Debbie smile at Bobby.

"Please tell the court what happened the last time you saw your wife," Leacock said.

"Karla and I had just been married in Dallas and were on our honeymoon here. Staying at Sam Lord's Castle. One afternoon we visited the Flower Forest and were going back to the hotel through St. Joseph Parish. A car was tailgating me on a road through a canefield, so I pulled over to let him pass. When I did, he cut in front of me and forced me to stop. Then the driver got out, pointed a gun at me, and fired. That's the last time I saw Karla."

"Would you recognize the driver of the car if you saw him again?" Leacock asked.

"I have seen him again, and I do recognize him."

"Is he present in the courtroom?"

Bobby turned his attention to Ocee. Ocee stared at Bobby, like a boxer staring down his opponent in the ring. Bobby met his gaze, unflinching. He leveled his finger in Ocee's direction.

"He's sitting on the end of the bench, there."

Ocee continued to stare at Bobby, waiting for him to wilt or look away. But Bobby refused to be intimidated by his stare.

"For the record, Mr. Reavis has identified the defendant,

Oliver Clarke," Leacock said.

"So noted," Magistrate Mantooth said.

"That's all the questions I have of Mr. Reavis," Leacock said, then returned to his seat.

"Mr. Ward," the magistrate said.

Ward gave a slight bow, then gathered his notes in front of him on the table. Staring down his nose through his glasses, he studied the top page of his notes. Then he looked up at Bobby.

"Mr. Reavis, had you ever seen my client before that day in the canefield?"

Bobby and Ocee were still engaged in their battle of wills, eyes locked, as Bobby answered. "No. But I saw his picture in the newspaper."

"What paper was that?"

"A Barbados paper. *The Nation*. I saw his picture and read his description."

"How can you be sure the man you saw in the canefield was the same man as in the newspaper?"

"He looked like his picture and he fit the description. When he got out of his car, he was no more than ten or fifteen feet from me. I recognized him from the scar on his cheek and the missing fingers on his hand."

"But it all happened fast, did it not?"

"Yes."

"And you were frightened, were you not?"

"Yes."

"As you sit here today, only having seen the gunman a year

ago, how can you be sure of his identity?"

"The scar is still there. And the fingers are still gone."

A few snickers rippled through the courtroom.

"And I saw him in Dallas only a couple of months ago," Bobby added.

Ward drew back in surprise. This seemed to be news to him.

"He was even in my house."

Bobby and his antagonist, Ocee, still stared at each other. Bobby found his willpower increasing as he pounded each nail into Clarke's coffin.

"And I shot him."

As he said the last words, Bobby narrowed his eyes. His lips curled into a slight smile, noticeable by no one other than Oliver Clarke.

Ocee averted his eyes. Game over.

Bobby knew Ward must have staked his whole case on Bobby being unable to identify his client, but the revelation of events in Dallas seemed to have stunned him. His whole train of thought derailed. Bobby was surprised that he didn't try to pin down the details of the shooting in Dallas. If he had, he could have established that Bobby was shooting blind. But Ward was probably operating under the assumption that if Bobby shot a man, he must have seen him. And he probably wasn't anxious to drag Ocee's transgressions in the United States before the magistrate. Better to do some investigation before trial than to flail about on that one now.

With a slight stammer, Ward passed the witness.

"Very well, Mr. Reavis, you may step down," the magistrate said. "Mr. Leacock, do you have any other witnesses?"

Leacock stood. "Crown rests, Your Honor."

"Mr. Ward, I understand you are not calling any witnesses."

Ward remained seated, visibly shaken. "That's correct."

"A wise decision," Mantooth said. "It is clear to the court that probable cause exists to bind the defendant over for trial on charges of murder, kidnapping, and attempted murder. The defendant will be detained in HMP Dodds Prison until such time as he may be tried. This hearing is adjourned."

CHAPTER FORTY THREE

After the prosecution team and its witnesses had left the courtroom, a police guard motioned for Ocee to get to his feet. Ocee rose sullenly and shuffled across the front of the courtroom. He paused in front of Sylvan Ward at the defense counsel's table. Ward was packing his briefcase, but he sensed that Ocee was staring at him. He straightened and made eye contact with his client.

Ocee smiled. A cold chill coursed down Ward's spine.

"Sam Lord's, eh?" Ocee said. He cackled at his own hilarious joke.

Ward studied Ocee, fearful of what he meant. He strained his memory to recall whether he had told Ocee where Robert Reavis was staying. The prosecutors told him that Reavis was flying in from Texas and would be staying at the Castle. He remembered telling Ocee, when they talked in Dodds Prison yesterday evening, that Reavis was in Bridgetown to testify. He just couldn't remember whether he mentioned the hotel or not. Even though Ocee was in custody, he had friends on the outside.

"No," Ward said.

"Yah, mon," Ocee said. He smiled, flashing his white teeth.

"Sam Lord's. Coo-coo never done till de pot turn down. If greedy wait, hot will cool. Mind you mout'."

In the years he had been representing Clarke, Ward learned that Ocee loved to talk in riddles, spouting proverbs and colloquialisms. He also learned to translate the cryptic expressions. "Coo-coo never done till de pot turn down" meant that an issue is never settled until there is a definite sign of finality. "If greedy wait, hot will cool" meant that if one waits patiently, one will get what one wants. "Mind you mout'" meant keep your mouth shut.

The message was clear – a promise and a threat. Ocee had business to take care of at Sam Lord's. He was going to kill Reavis and he would kill Ward if he talked.

Ward finished packing his briefcase and quickly left the courtroom.

*****

A guard ushered Ocee to the ground floor and down a long hallway to a back door where a car waited to return him to Dodds Prison. The guard pushed Ocee into the back seat, then moved to the passenger side and slid in beside the driver. The car pulled onto the street and toward the prison on the outskirts of town.

Her Majesty's Prison Dodds, or simply Dodds Prison, had been open in St. Philip Parish since late 2007, as a replacement for Glendairy Prison, which had been nearly destroyed by fire in a prison uprising. Glendairy, which more resembled a run-down, inner-city high school than a prison, had been located just off a busy street in the Station Hill area of Bridgetown and was surrounded by a residential neighborhood, no more than fifty feet from the prison walls. The second floor had unbarred windows, and Ocee had made one of his previous escapes by making the fifteen-foot drop to the ground and gaining unobstructed access to the nearby neighborhood. Escaping from Dodds was more problematic, although he had been successful once. He was now ready for his second.

As the police car made its way up to Dodds, a battered Suzuki fell in behind it. A gaunt-faced Rastafarian sat behind the wheel of the Suzuki. A stocky man sat beside him in the passenger seat. Both men carried pistols. The driver held the car close to the bumper of the police car, like a typical Barbadian tailgater ready to pass.

Ocee glanced over his shoulder. He had seen them at the last intersection. Now he checked to ensure that they pulled out and followed as planned. Seeing his friends in place, he relaxed. He turned back around, holding his hands in front of him. He stretched the chain on the handcuffs until it was taut.

The two-car parade drew closer to the turn-off to the prison. Suddenly, the rear car pulled out to pass. Its driver accelerated around the police car and pulled hard to the left, ramming the vehicle hard into a parked car on the side of the road.

Ocee whipped his hands over the head of the guard seated in front of him and pulled back sharply. The suddenness of the car's stop and the jerk of the amazingly strong Ocee was all it took to crush the man's windpipe. He blew out his last breath with a gasp.

The driver, his seatbelt unbuckled, flopped face forward into the steering wheel. Nose cartilage crunched. Blood splattered onto the wheel. His head spun.

The passenger in the escape car jumped out and rushed

to the police driver's window. The stunned driver moaned. He grabbed clumsily for his holster as the assailant put the muzzle of a gun to his temple. Cold steel touched the driver's skin. His eyes widened.

The gunman pulled the trigger twice in rapid succession, the sound of the shots exploding into the air. The driver slumped over, toppling into the lap of his broken-necked partner.

Ocee leaned over the front seat and fumbled with the guard's key-ring. After securing it, he unbuckled the man's holster and stripped it of its weapon. He gripped the gun in his hand-cuffed hands, aimed it at the back of the guard's head, and fired. Then he scrambled from the police car and hopped into the back seat of the getaway car as it sped off.

The whole affair had taken no more than thirty seconds.

*****

"You hungry?" Bobby asked Debbie after the cabdriver dropped them off at Sam Lord's Castle.

"Not really," Debbie answered. "The hearing got to my nerves."

"You want to go down to the beach? Or do you want to rent a car and drive around?"

"We can rent a car tomorrow. I'd like to spend today on the beach."

Bobby smiled. "You'll like it just fine."

Fifteen minutes later they were suited in their swimwear and ready for the beach. Bobby stopped off to pick up beach towels and then they were on their way. Just past The Wanderer restaurant, they turned left toward the beach access. As they neared the steps, Debbie pointed to the arched gate Bobby and Karla had passed through a year earlier.

"What's through there?"

"That's kinda like a lover's lane. It goes out to the ocean."

They veered away from the steps to the beach and continued along the sidewalk to the gate. On their left, a short retaining wall, lined with hedges, separated them from the sand below. In the distance, the beautiful waters of the Atlantic sparkled. They strolled hand-in-hand to the arch that led to the elevated walkway beyond, then followed it to the end.

"Looks like the maintenance man is falling down on the job," Debbie said as she stepped over a loose board that hung by one nail from the bottom rail of the wooden fence.

Bobby grabbed the board and gingerly put it back in place by fitting the extended nails in the too-loose holes in the post. "Maybe that'll hold for a while. At least it'll keep someone from tripping over it."

"I know how your mind works. What you're really saying is it'll prevent a lawsuit."

He laughed. "Boy, you've really got me pegged, don't you?"

They leaned on the rail at the end, fifteen feet above the jagged rocks that broke the surf with a vengeance. To their left, a stone stairwell led down from the walkway, ending with the last step six or seven feet above the rocks. Spray from the waves lightly bathed their faces.

Debbie stretched and then hugged herself. "It feels so good to get this testifying over with. I can just imagine how it must feel for you."

Bobby smiled, put his arm around her, and drew her closer. "Ever since this happened, I've felt this need for – I don't know, revenge or vengeance or something. But I've never felt right about it. Even when I shot Clarke in my house, it didn't feel right. But this feels right. Testifying felt right. It's the best revenge because now the law can do what it has to do. Maybe now I really can get on with my life."

Debbie looked up into his face and met his eyes. "I'd like to be part of it."

Bobby kissed her on the forehead and whispered softly, "You will be."

CHAPTER FORTY FOUR

The battered Suzuki sped away, leaving behind the wreckage of the police car with its two hapless victims inside. As the gaunt-faced Rastafarian pushed his foot to the accelerator, Ocee slumped in the back seat, out of sight to the passing world. He extended his hands over the front seat. The stocky passenger in the front twisted his body around and fumbled with the key-ring Ocee had lifted from his captors. He tried the various keys in the lock on the handcuffs. Finally, with a faint click, the cuffs snapped open. Ocee tossed them out the window and rubbed his red, raw wrists.

He took the key-ring from his friend and tried keys on his leg shackles. The fourth one worked and he tossed the shackles out the window. He tossed the keys out after them, then rubbed his swollen ankles.

"Gimme dat rum," he said to the stocky man.

His friend passed back a half-empty bottle of rum. Ocee threw his head back and guzzled the warm brew. The brownish liquid splattered out from the corners of his mouth and ran down his neck as he greedily emptied the bottle in one chug-a-lug. He tossed it aside and brushed his arm across his face.

"De white mon and de pretty leddie goes to Sam Lord's. All two of dem sees Ocee again."

The gaunt-faced driver glanced at Ocee in the rearview mirror. "Ocee takes care at Sam Lord's. De las' calf kill the cow." Translation: Taking the same risk too often can have disastrous consequences.

"De calf don' kill Ocee," Ocee snarled. He threw his head back and laughed maniacally.

The driver focused back on the road. "Evah pig got a Satuhday," he muttered under his breath.

Ocee slapped him hard on the back of the head. Rage contorted his features. He leaned forward and whispered in the driver's ear, "Today ent my Satuhday. Today is de white mon's Satuhday."

*****

The same Bajan craftsman who, a year earlier, had hawked his wares on the landing of the stairs leading to the beach was still there. Bobby recognized him from the monotone, sing-song pitching of his goods.

"Will you be wan-tin' a bargain today?" the man asked. He gestured to his beads, necklaces, and cloth bags.

"Not today," Bobby laughed. He grabbed Debbie by the elbow and steered her quickly down the stairs. "Not today."

"All right then. You have a good day," the Bajan called after them. "When it's a bargain you be wan-tin', you know where to come."

Bobby and Debbie maneuvered the last few steps, reached the sand, and headed toward the ocean. Bobby was still chuckling at the craftsman, shaking his head as he walked.

"What?" Debbie asked. She looked at him with a quizzical expression on her face.

"That guy was there every day last year. He always had the same thing to say, over and over again. Like he's the only guy in the world with a bargain to offer."

"I was going to stop if you hadn't grabbed my arm."

"That's exactly why I did it. Otherwise he'd never let you go. Those guys are worse than used-car salesmen."

"Well," Debbie said, glancing back over her shoulder. "I'm going to look at that stuff a little bit closer before we leave. You mark my words."

Bobby laughed. He motioned to a teenaged Bajan who was already unstacking two lounge chairs.

"Sun or shade?" the teenager asked.

"Sun."

Bobby went to where the sand crested and dropped off to the ocean. The Bajan followed and positioned the chairs facing the sun as Bobby directed. Then he returned to his resting spot under the tall palm tree to wait for his next customer.

Bobby quickly slapped on sunblock, then passed the bottle to Debbie, who had just removed her beach cover-up. Bobby had never seen her in a bathing suit, and he admired her lithe, curvaceous form as she stuffed her cover-up in the beach bag and applied lotion to her arms and legs. Like Karla, Debbie had an athletic figure, graceful and muscular, though she was not as tall as Karla, so she didn't have that same glamorous, leggy look.

Bobby was suddenly aware that Debbie was watching him. Their eyes met; he blushed and grinned sheepishly. She smiled back, but didn't say anything. Shaking her head, she spread her towel over the lounge chair and lay down facing the sun. Bobby followed her example, hoping to avoid comment.

Debbie reached across the small gap between the chairs and took Bobby's hand. He gladly gave it to her, then laid his head back and closed his eyes. With the sounds of the waves crashing along the shoreline, the steady breeze on their faces, and the warm sun heating their bodies, they soon dozed into a light sleep.

*****

Ocee leaned his chair back in the small, one-room rum shop. He braced himself with one foot on the floor and put his other foot on the scarred table. A half-dozen empty bottles cluttered the top of the table. He held a seventh tightly in his hands, which rested against his stomach. He and his friends had made a clean getaway from Dodds Prison to the relative safety of St. Joseph Parish. By now, he was sure the carnage near the prison had been discovered. It had probably been discovered within minutes of their exit. He was also sure that, as happened before, the alarm had already sounded island-wide about yet another Oliver Clarke escape.

A faint smile crept across his lips. For law enforcement to keep him in check was an exercise in futility. He chalked up another victim in his colorful life's history. His senses dulled by drink, he reveled in the feel of the policeman's wind-pipe crushing beneath his grip in the car. His only regret was that his friend had killed the driver and not given him the opportunity.

But there were further victims to come. Once the sun went down, he would go to Sam Lord's Castle. To exact his revenge from the American who shot him.

And to enjoy the forbidden pleasures of the American's new woman.

•

CHAPTER FORTY FIVE

"What's this place like?" Debbie asked as they walked past the driveway entrance to the Castle grounds. The security guard in the sentry station waved to them.

"You'll like it."

"I don't remember seeing anything that looked like a restaurant when we were coming or going."

Bobby laughed. "It's easy to miss. It sort of looks like a house. But it does have the sign out front."

"And what's it called again?"

"The Lantern. So named, I guess, because of the Sam Lord legend."

"I just hope it's not a disaster reminiscent of that legend."

She locked arms with him as they walked side-by-side down the dusty road. The sun was not all the way down, but the sky darkened on the horizon into a beautiful orange-pink. They walked the last hundred yards in silence, both continually glancing westward to soak in the sunset. A few minutes later they were comfortably seated at a small table by an open window, studying the menu. Again, a sense of nostalgia overwhelmed Bobby. He remembered the dinner he and Karla had shared the previous year. He closed the menu and placed it on the table in front of him.

"No point in looking at the menu," Bobby said. "You've gotta have flying fish."

"Flying fish?"

"It's the national food. Trust me."

Debbie folded her menu and put it on top of Bobby's. "Flying fish it is."

*****

Darkness settled over the island and Ocee began to prowl. Alone, he drove the battered Suzuki through the canefields of St. John Parish, crossed back into St. Philip Parish just past Moncreiffe, then headed for Long Bay and Sam Lord's Castle. In his pocket, he carried the Smith & Wesson he had taken from his police captors. On the seat beside him lay an 8-inch, double-edged knife. His erection throbbed with thoughts of revenge and murder.

He carefully thought through his plan. He had been to the Castle before and knew he could access the beach just this side of the hotel proper. From the beach he could make his way up to the lookout point and, from there, would have unrestricted access to the hotel grounds, unless the gate to the archway was locked. If that was the case, he could descend from the lookout point to the other side and from there climb up the fifteen-foot cliff to the back side of the property. He knew that the beach was closed to guests after dark and that he should be able to move around unhindered.

Although he knew the Americans were staying at Sam Lord's, he didn't know in which room. But he believed that, at some point during the evening, they'd walk about the hotel grounds.

The key was to position himself for the best view of the busiest stretch of sidewalk between the pool and the front office. If he waited patiently, surely he'd see them.

He passed The Lantern restaurant. At the entrance to the hotel, he turned right into a small parking area outside a bank. No one lurked in the lot as he parked the car and quietly slipped out. He skirted past the front of the bank and around the corner. A narrow pathway penetrated the dense growth that separated the bank from the beach, lined on one side by the hotel's fence and by dense tropical vegetation on the other. At the end of the path, a wooden stairway led down to the beach.

Ocee paused at the head of the stairs. He glanced over the rail to see if anybody was on the beach below.

No one.

He quickly descended the steps two at a time and disappeared into the shadowy trees in the sand below.

*****

After paying the check, Bobby returned his credit card to his wallet and placed it back in his pocket. The waitress refilled their coffee cups and bid them good evening. Bobby knew that was the signal for them to leave. A waitress who had said her good-byes was not likely to return.

Debbie sipped her coffee, then placed the cup back in the saucer. "It fooled me."

"What did?"

"The flying fish. It was great."

"Did you think I'd steer you wrong?" Bobby smiled. "I didn't think I'd like it the first time I had it. I'm not much of a seafood eater, but I'd rank that right up there with grilled ahi."

"What's ahi?"

"It's a Hawaiian yellow-finned tuna that I discovered in Kauai. There's a little place in Hanalei, on the north shore, that serves the world's best ahi."

"I've never been to Kauai."

Debbie sipped her coffee and stared big-eyed at Bobby. Bobby read the message in her eyes.

"Let's talk about it sometime."

*****

Ocee stood at the base of the steps that led up from South Beach to the lookout point and listened intently in the darkness. Nothing but silence. He moved swiftly and quietly up the stairs, then crouched momentarily at the head. No one in sight.

He moved out to the walkway.

*****

Walking arm-in-arm, Bobby and Debbie meandered along the driveway that ran alongside the Castle where the front office was located and circled to the lawn behind it. They cleared the structure and faced toward the ocean where the strong sea-breeze met them head on. They continued silently, around the windmill and then over to a sidewalk that curved along the perimeter overlooking the beach. The metal gate to the lookout point stood open.

*****

Ocee crouched in the shadows on the landing of the stairwell where the bargain-selling Bajan accosted hotel guests on a daily basis. The sounds of voices approached above. He shrank back into the darkness.

Two heads suddenly came into view. Ocee pulled back farther and pressed his back against the small shed on the landing. He couldn't believe his good fortune. There, oblivious to his presence, strolled the two Americans. Carelessly walking toward the lookout point that Ocee used to access the hotel grounds. The same point he would use to make his getaway.

He watched in disbelief as the two Americans did what, for them, was the worst thing possible. For him, it was the best. They walked onto the point – right into the spider's web.

His mouth twisted into a grin as he hurried up the steps.

*****

A strong wind brushed against their faces. The Atlantic pounded its percussion on the beaches and rocks of Long Bay and rustling leaves of palm trees hummed harmoniously. They strolled down the walkway to its farthest reach where they stood silently and stared seaward. The cloudless sky painted a black backdrop, punctuated by a spangle of stars. A full moon passed its light earthward, its reflection shimmering on the ever-moving water.

"Looks like your carpentry didn't hold," Debbie said. She pointed to the loose railing that lay, nails up, next to the fence.

"Good thing I went to law school. I'd starve as a carpenter. Just don't step on the nails."

They skirted the board and walked to the end of the way. Bobby put his arm around Debbie's shoulder and turned her to face him. First their eyes met.

Then their lips met.

And Ocee sprang across the circular garden toward them. In one smooth motion, he landed on his feet and brought his knife-wielding hand upward. Its blade caught Bobby just below the rib cage, cutting deep into his side. Air left Bobby's lungs with a groan as Ocee forced the knife upward, then twisted it with a flick of his wrist.

With one hand, Bobby stiff-armed Debbie away. "Run!" he gasped.

Debbie staggered backwards from the force of the thrust and banged against the wooden rail that protected her from the fifteen-foot drop to the beach below.

Ocee pulled downward to extract the knife, struggling to release it from the solid layer of muscle that girded Bobby's trunk. Warm blood oozed from the wound and poured across his hand. Bobby was still twisted from his initial defensive movement, his arm thrown across his chest, exposing his rib cage. With a reflexive movement, he brought his arm back hard, his elbow crooked, turning it into a battering ram. It landed squarely across the bridge of Ocee's nose. Bones crunched under the blow.

Ocee fell. As he did, he jerked the knife out, swinging his arm to the side. Bobby dropped to one knee, weak from pain. He saw Debbie standing against the fence, her eyes wide with fear, her mouth open in a silent scream.

"Run!" he yelled. But his voice came out in a hoarse whisper.

Debbie's eyes told him she understood the command, but her terrified limbs refused to respond. At least that was what Bobby thought. He turned his attention back to the fallen Ocee, who sprawled at her feet. He took a step toward them and tried to place himself between the murderer and Debbie, but Ocee scrambled to his feet before he could get there and turned toward Debbie. His eyes widened in surprise as two nails in a board approached his face. He jerked away, but not in time. Debbie's well-aimed swing caught the side of his face; the nails ripped a jagged chunk from his cheek.

Debbie pulled the board back to swing again. Ocee jumped back and extended his knife toward her. But instead of aiming for his head again, she brought the board at a downward angle and plunged the nails into his knife hand. His fingers uncurled and the knife fell to the ground. He dropped to his knees and grabbed at it, but it skittered off the edge to the rocks below.

Bobby made eye contact with Debbie over Ocee's shoulder. "Go! Get help!"

Instead, Debbie raised the board over her head, nails aimed for the back of Ocee's skull. As the wood swung down, Ocee rolled away. The end of the board smashed against the ground and broke in half.

Bobby looped his arm around Ocee's neck and yanked upward, pulling him to his feet. "Run," he said to Debbie.

She dropped the board at Ocee's feet and turned to go for help. Ocee swung his left leg out; his foot connected with the board and sent it skittering toward Debbie before she could move. The jagged end slammed into her heels. With a cry, she stumbled for a step, nearly regained her balance, then hit the ground on her face. Ocee bent his arm and turned his elbow into a battering ram that he drove into Bobby's wounded side. Already weak from pain and dizzy from loss of blood, Bobby's grip loosened on Ocee's throat. Another thrust from Ocee's elbow and Bobby released him as he fell backward.

Ocee pulled a gun from his pocket and, in two quick steps, had Debbie back on her feet with the muzzle pressed to her temple. Bobby stood and started a charge.

"Back, mon," Ocee barked.

Bobby stopped in his tracks. Once again, a flood of memories overtook him. Memories of how he had once failed to protect somebody he loved. Tears formed in Debbie's eyes and trickled down her cheeks. He understood her terror. She looked at him pleadingly and formed the word "Help" with her lips, but no sound came out.

Bobby heaved his shoulders and straightened up. He tried to take in a deep breath, but the mere act of breathing pained him. The wound in his side continued to gush. He placed his right hand over it and tried to stop the flow of blood as his mind worked desperately to form a plan.

He locked eyes with Ocee just as he had done in the courtroom. He honestly believed he had intimidated Ocee that time and hoped he could do it again. The question was whether he could do it quickly, before Ocee pulled the trigger. Ocee stared back.

"Dis leddie, she pretty, pretty, pretty," Ocee said. "Just like de las' time. Wha' happened to that leddie? Huh, mon? Wha' happen to you woman?"

He ground the muzzle of the gun into Debbie's temple. Blood trickled down her cheek, mixed with her tears. Ocee's smile transformed into an ugly grimace. Bobby knew he faced a stone-cold killer who would take both of their lives with no more thought than stepping on a bug. Silently, he prayed and called on his same God that he once believed had abandoned him on this very island.

*****

Ocee watched the white man's face give way to fear. He may have won in the courtroom, but out here, Ocee was king.

Ocee's finger tightened on the trigger. He would watch the white man's face as he blew his woman's brains all over him. Then he would kill the man and be gone. But instead of fear, the man's face turned to calm, maybe even relief. As if some inner strength had kicked in. And that was when Ocee saw it.

The duppy of the dead woman, floating in the air above the white man.

"Come, Ocee," the duppy said. "It's your Saturday."

*****

Ocee suddenly looked away. Cut his eyes to the left and above Bobby. Then he narrowed his eyes and squinted, as if focusing on something over Bobby's left shoulder. His eyes widened, his eyebrows raised high. His mouth dropped open with a look of disbelief. He relaxed his grip around Debbie's throat and dropped his arm to his side, pulling the gun away from her temple. He began waving it wildly about, then pointed it in the air.

Bobby glanced over his shoulder, but saw nothing. Debbie stood in her spot, rooted with fear, as if unaware that she had been released.

Ocee took a step backward. Then another, until he pushed against the wooden fence. Bobby grabbed Debbie's arm and yanked her toward him with a violent heave. She snapped out of her trance and immediately complied as he positioned himself between her and Ocee.

Ocee continued to stare into the air. His hand trembled and the gun shook. "Get back! Get back!" he yelled.

Bobby and Debbie moved back a few steps.

Ocee fired the gun twice in rapid succession into the air. The sound of the gunshots exploded the stillness of the night.

Bobby and Debbie cringed, then dropped to the ground. Bobby put his arms around Debbie and pulled her close.

"Duppy!" Ocee exclaimed, still in a hoarse whisper. He leaned harder against the fence rail. His upper body angled out over the drop to the beach. "Away, duppy! Away!"

His voice sounded frantic now, rising to an hysterical scream. "You don' see she?" Ocee asked. "You leddie? You pretty leddie?"

But Bobby saw nothing.

Ocee grabbed the gold earring dangling from his ear. With a yank, he tore it away, leaving ragged flesh for an earlobe.

"Take it, duppy. Take it!" he screamed as he threw the earring over Bobby's head.

Bobby chose that moment to charge. He delivered a blow with his head and shoulder, like a linebacker, into Ocee's mid-section. He heard the unmistakable sound of cracking wood, then felt Ocee sag as the fence gave way. Digging in his heels, Bobby struggled to regain his balance. He grabbed at a post and held on as Ocee, already leaning awkwardly across the fence, tumbled over and down to the beach below. Bobby watched as Ocee fell headfirst in a dive. The snap of his neck resounded even over the roar of the waves. Then Ocee crumpled into a heap on the beach.

Debbie rushed to Bobby, who leaned on her for support. He was starting to weaken from the loss of blood. They looked down to where Oliver Clarke sprawled on the beach below, his twisted head mute testimony to his broken neck.

"What was he saying? Duppy?" Debbie asked.

"That's the spirit of the dead."

"The dead?"

Bobby nodded. Tears formed in his eyes as he leaned on Debbie, his arm around her shoulder. She led him away from the point. Back to Sam Lord's Castle.

THE END

MIKE FARRIS

MIKE FARRIS is a 1983 *cum laude* graduate of Texas Tech University School of Law, where he was an associate editor on the Texas Tech Law Review and was inducted into the Order of the Coif. Now retired, Mike's practice as an attorney in Dallas included commercial litigation as well as entertainment law, focusing on the movie and publishing industries.

Mike was lead counsel for the plaintiff in what has become known as the *Fifty Shades of Grey* lawsuit (*Jennifer Lynn Pedroza v. Amanda M. Hayward and TWCS Operations Pty. Ltd.* in the 153rd District Court in Tarrant County, Texas), which resulted in a plaintiff's judgment, following a jury trial, in excess of $13.2 million (including pre-judgment interest and attorney's fees). Mike has also represented various university presses and has successfully placed subsidiary rights to their published books with film producers and Hollywood studios, such as *The Free State of Jones*, published by University of North Carolina Press.

Mike was three-time Chair of the Dallas Bar Association's Sports and Entertainment Law Section and is currently the Chair-Elect for the State Bar of Texas Entertainment and Sports Law Section. He has been an adjunct professor at the University of Dallas in its Sports & Entertainment Management MBA program, where he served on the Sports & Entertainment Advisory Board.

A multi-time published author, Mike's most recent book is *A Death in the Islands: The Unwritten Law and the Last Trial of Clarence Darrow*. Mike previously collaborated with former ABC-TV anchorman Murphy Martin to write Martin's memoir of his years in journalism, entitled *Front Row Seat: A Veteran Reporter Relives the Four Decades That Reshaped America*, and also collaborated with rodeo cowboy-turned-actor/producer/director Robert Hinkle on Hinkle's memoir of his years in show business, *Call Me Lucky: A Texan in Hollywood*, for University of Oklahoma Press. On the fiction side, he is the author of six published novels in addition to *Every Pig Got a Saturday: Isle of Broken Dreams, The Bequest, Wrongful Termination, Kanaka Blues, Manifest Intent,* and *Rules of Privilege*.

CPSIA information can be obtained
at www.ICGtesting.com
Printed in the USA
LVOW13s0756040617

536872LV00002B/3/P